Jamaica
Blue

St. Martin's Minotaur ✣ New York

Jamaica Blue

DON BRUNS

2-10-15
23

NIC
12/18

2-10-2015
NIC 23

This is a work of fiction. All of the characters and events portrayed in this book are either fictitious or are used fictitiously.

www.minotaurbooks.com

Design by Susan Yang

Title page photo © Yukimasa Hirota/Photonica

ISBN 0-312-30490-0

First Edition: October 2002

10 9 8 7 6 5 4 3 2 1

To my road companions,
Mike Duling and Mike Trump

Acknowledgments

This book would not have been possible without the friendship, support, and generosity of Sue Grafton. I love you, Sue.

Thanks to my friends Lee Child and William Kent Krueger, whom I admire greatly. Thank you, Jay Waggoner, Mike McNamera, and Don Witter, for your encouragement. Thanks, Clay from *Last Flight Out*, for all your stories. Thanks to Mike Trump, my best friend and a constant source of inspiration. Thank you, Charlie and Joshua from St. Martin's, for your enthusiasm and for helping me through the process, and thank you, Jane. Finally, thanks to my wife, Linda, the English teacher who proofs and proofs and proofs again.

Jamaica Blue

PROLOGUE

The boatman had come and gone, peddling his drugs to the adventurous tourists in the midday sun. He'd paddled his mud brown canoe up to the sugar-sand beach, bellowing to the sun worshipers, "Who wants to buy some?" He motioned to the curious newcomers and to those who had visited before. His dark brown skin contrasted with the pale women, their white breasts with rosy pink nipples taking on a blush from too much sun too soon. He smiled, watching their hips lightly sway as they walked to the water's edge, eager to partake of his goods. Some wanted more. He touched the top of his head for luck, his hair in dreads, knotted on top with a leather thong. From the shade of a palm tree, a tightly muscled midnight black security guard gazed at the men and women as they paraded down to the boat. Speed, ganja, crack; very special, Jamaican blend. "Who wants to buy some?"

She was native, a student from Kingston, her dark, coffee brown skin glistening in the bright sunlight with the sweet coconut oil the portly American had poured on her. She'd stayed back from the shore, lying on a padded lounge chair as he made the short trek to the boatman and his wares. For fifty American dollars and a bag of ganja, she'd devoured the small circumcised penis that swung freely between his legs as he swaggered back to her. American men were so predictable, and so easily entertained.

A shimmering gold river of sun cut across the water as the ball of fire sunk slowly in the Jamaican blue sky. The boatman had come and gone, and the American slept soundly in his air-conditioned room, the rum and ganja like a heavy cloud inside his head. The student studied the soft light by the pool, then dove into the water, surfacing as the beads of water cascaded from her nubile body. Tomorrow was Sunday, a day of rest. There would be no mind-numbing classes, no aging American tourist with a need for oral relief. Sunday was her special day. A day to sleep, to read, to walk the water's edge and dream. A day to listen to her music and dream of her music man. His promise of escape seemed closer than ever.

She stretched out on a brightly colored towel, splashes of melon pink and turquoise blue, mint green and frangipane orange, caressing her deep brown skin. Late shadows lingered on the beach as the sun descended behind the stucco-covered guest suites lining the far side of the pool. She pulled a CD player from her woven bag, put on the headphones, and pushed the play button. His rhythmic guitar played for her alone, and his soft voice whispered in her ears. "Somewhere, sometime, my moonlight lady, we sail away on an ocean breeze. Find a place, my moonlight lady, we make love under tall palm trees."

The tourists had vanished to their rooms for some late afternoon delight, or to the dining rooms for the evening buffet. She was alone with her music man. "Dream with me, my moonlight lady. Whatever you dream it might come true. Dream of me, my moonlight lady. Dream of me, I dream of you."

She felt the knee press into her back, pushing her into the towel, and the sharp steel blade of a knife slide under her throat. Struggling to turn over, gasping as the knife sliced through her skin, she watched in horror as her crimson blood added yet another bright color to the beach towel. She lifted her head and could feel the gaping hole where her windpipe had separated. She tried to breathe but no breath would come. Bright white lights exploded in her eyes and still she struggled. Thrashing on the ground, she rolled her lithe body and landed on her side. For a brief moment her vision cleared and she viewed her assassin. Her brown eyes grew wide and she fought to speak, but no sound would come. Her lips formed the word as she pulled back, seeking refuge in the towel. "You?"

The final explosion felt like a firecracker in her head and she heard her music man one last time. "Dream of me, I dream of you."

Chapter One

.

I'm tellin' ya, Mick, this kid is like the second coming of Bob Marley." Bobby Vane waggled his fat index finger at a waitress as he stuffed another shrimp in his mouth. "We got him comin' over here to tour with Brandy this summer, but hell, if it goes good, we might just bolt the Brandy thing and take off on our own." He smiled at the waitress as she walked to the table. "Another Scotch, honey, the Glenlivit or whatever you got, okay?" He waved her away.

A smile played on Mick Sever's face. Bobby Vane always had a new artist, a new recording contract, a new tour to promote. And each one was guaranteed to be bigger than the one before.

"Were you a Marley fan, Mick? Huh? Were ya? Ya know, the kids today, they all got Marley in their CD collections, and hell, the guy died like in 1981, before most of 'em were even a gleam in their old man's eye. So I figure that this guy's gonna just be the hottest thing." He wiped his greasy fingers on the green linen napkin in his lap and scanned the table for any last bites of food he may have missed. "Ya want anything else, Mick? Just name it."

"No, I'm fine."

"Ya know, ya eat like a bird. Like a fuckin' bird. So, watcha think? You get a chance to see Jamaica, the sun, the sand, the honeys, and you get to see his concert."

"What's the name again?"

"Derrick Lyman." Vane put his meaty hand on Sever's and patted it. "Mick, if this isn't the biggest thing since grunge . . ."

"Bobby, I was never a real big fan of grunge."

Vane looked at him. "It's reggae and hip-hop. It's like dance hall, rock steady, and ska all wrapped up in one sound and it's just plain hot. I've got a rough mix right here." He reached down to a scuffed brown leather bag and pawed through the contents until he found the jewel case. "Here, this'll give you a little taste of what this guy does. Derrick Lyman and the Laments."

"Laments?"

"Well, we're still working with that. Marley had the Wailing Wailers, and they changed it to just the Wailers. We'll get it right before we go big-time. Right now I want you to see how electrifying this boy is with a crowd. He brings 'em to their feet and never lets 'em sit down, Mick. I'm tellin' ya, you're gonna want to do a story on him. And I'm willing to give you first crack."

"How many writers have turned you down?"

"You hurt me, Mr. Sever. I want you to follow this career. You're a powerful man. People believe what you say. Give me . . . give my boy a break. If I'm wrong, you still get a vacation in a tropical paradise."

"I get to spend three days in a Third World country where the white man is not only in the minority, but in many cases not too well liked."

"Come on. *Rolling Stone* already said they'd pick up the tab. I just gotta get you to do the article." He looked at Sever with his big brown eyes, much like a dog Sever had had in the sixth grade. The dog, Waddles, or something like that, had run away from home and was never seen again.

"All right, Vane, I'll go. We'll see what this Derrick and the Laments is all about. So what do we call this music? Reggae rap?"

"Well, you're the word man. Rasta rap, reggae rap . . ."

"So he's Rastafarian?"

"Hell, isn't everyone in Jamaica? He sprinkles the songs with some of that philosophy mumbo jumbo. Worked for Marley. It'll work for Derrick." Vane grabbed the Scotch as the waitress set it down and he took a gulp, pounding the glass back onto the table. "Here's to a new superstar. Here's to reggae rap." He raised the glass.

Sever picked up his water glass, glanced around at the other tables to be sure no one was staring, then softly clinked his glass with Vane's. "Bobby, no promises. If I don't like the kid or his music, that's the way the story will read."

"I know, I know. I'm not worried. The kid will bowl you over. We got a hit here, Mick, and you're gonna thank me for steering you in his direction." He finished his Scotch, pushed his corpulent body back from the table, and gave Sever a huge grin. "Damn, life is good! Life is good!"

Chapter Two

Mountains of moss green disappeared beneath them as the plane skirted the heights by what seemed only several hundred feet. Forests of palm trees dotted the hills, and the lush green valleys, deep and wide, spread out in all directions.

"Fucking beautiful country, eh?" Bobby Vane spread his thick arms out, almost touching both sides of the Cessna. Sever nodded. The view *was* breathtaking. He wasn't a fan of flying in jumbo jets, much less of the private two- and three-seaters, but the scenery was beyond description at this low altitude. The entire view would have been lost in a commercial jet.

Five days had raced by as Sever canceled several meetings, obligations, and two book signings. The latest book on the murder of rock star Job Jobiah was topping the charts, and his publisher wasn't happy about the lost opportunities. His book was front-page news and Mick Sever was the hottest literary property in the country. Still, there were new worlds to conquer, and Jamaica was one of them.

The small plane swooped down into the valley, then climbed

the hillside, almost brushing the thick foliage of green and orange.

"Derrick?" Sever said the word as if to question its authenticity.

"Derrick," Bobby Vane repeated.

"Derek and the Dominoes was Eric Clapton's group, and Clapton made a hit out of Bob Marley's 'I Shot the Sheriff.' Any coincidence?"

"Far as I know, Derrick Lyman is his real name. If it has a little of Mr. Marley's mystique to it, then so be it. Ya gotta go with the story, Mick. Once you hear this guy and his band, well, they'll knock you out. The product is what it's all about. You said that yourself in that article you did for *Spin* a couple of years ago. Shit, who cares if they make up a name or a background? If the product is good, then it's solid."

As the plane reached the top of the hill, it leveled out, then started its descent to Montego Bay. Sever reviewed his notes. Jamaica, population 2.5 million, "discovered" in the late fifteenth century by Christopher Columbus and now populated primarily by people of African descent.

"The venue ain't exactly Madison Square Garden. I mean, this is a poor country, and they haven't got all the amenities, if ya know what I mean." Vane handed Sever a small poster advertising the concert for that evening. A dark, blurred picture of six people standing shoulder to shoulder appeared on the white card. It would have been impossible to identify any of them. Faded red lettering announced the band, appearing oceanside at the Round Hill Beach. "Should be a sellout by the time we land. Derrick will be waitin' for us about now. We'll get a car to take us there and you can do the interview before the concert. Gotta tell him. Reggae rap! He'll love it."

"But there's no recording contract yet?"

"You heard the rough mix? You tell me if they won't be beatin' down the doors. Shit, Island Records will be movin' in on this kid so fast. They'll be there tonight."

Sever closed his eyes for a moment as the small aircraft banked and the sharp turn over the crystal blue water put them directly above Montego Bay. The plane descended rapidly, and the wheels hit the ground with a bounce.

Bright sunlight glared off the tarmac and Sever put his sunglasses on. Everything looked hot, waves of shimmering heat causing distortions of distant views. They walked from the small Cessna to a waiting car. Sever looked over his shoulder to see an attendant struggling with their four bags, his soiled white short-sleeved shirt clinging damply to his glistening black skin. Sever dropped back and took his travel bag and laptop from the young man. The luggage handler smiled, teeth gleaming.

"Thank you, mon. This load be mighty heavy."

Vane stood impatiently by the small Toyota, glancing at his watch. Sever swung the smooth leather bag into the open trunk. The bag was a miracle: attractive, functional, and loaded with room. He carried his sport coat, trousers, a couple of shirts, underwear, his toiletries, and everything else he needed in the main compartment. The outside pockets were for passport, airline tickets, notebooks, pens, calculators, and an assortment of books that he was reading. Traveling was a way of life, and the bag was an important part of that life.

Vane waited until the attendant forced his three bags into the trunk, then he climbed in the passenger seat of the white car. Sever sat in the back, his long legs cramped from the tight quarters. He felt the familiar twinge in his left knee and massaged it as the car gathered speed.

"Like I told you, we're goin' to the Round Hill Hotel and Villas. We rented a little villa there for Derrick and the boys. And Marna."

"Marna?"

"She sings sometimes, plays tambourine, and washes their shirts. Kinda like a housemother to the Laments. Anyway, this place has an outdoor arena, and that's where the concert is. This is a nice place, Mick. Paul McCartney, he stays here, and the Kennedys. Lots of high rollers."

Sever wiped the perspiration from his forehead. His deep blue cotton shirt was damp, and his khakis were in danger of losing any crease they might have once had. The car swung around partially paved roads, throwing loose stones into the dirt ditches on either side, and the town fell behind them. As they approached the Villas, he could see the gleaming white homes, all trimmed with forest green, and nestled with hibiscus and bougainvillea. The scene was straight out of a Cary Grant movie.

Derrick and the Laments were housed in the seventh villa and were gathered in the back, around the crystal clear swimming pool. Barefoot and shirtless, they casually lay back in chaise lounge chairs, all five of them dressed in cutoffs. Sever breathed deeply, the smell of tropical flowers and ganja thick in the air.

"Mick, this is the band." Two of them nodded in acknowledgment. Vane pointed to the nearest chair. "This is James, our drummer." James took a drag on a joint and gave Sever a faint smile. He held the smoke in for a moment then slowly let it escape into the pungent air. "James is the newest member of our little group, and over here is Ricky. Rick is our very talented keyboard player." Rick stood up, flashing Sever a bright smile and offering him his hand. "It's good to meet you, mon."

They shook hands and the young man walked to the small service bar and poured himself a glass of what appeared to be orange juice. "Sudahd, over there," Vane pointed to a short young man, a Zapata-style mustache covering his lips, "he plays guitar. Man, does he play guitar. And here we have Flame. Flame plays a mean bass."

Flame smiled. "Hey, man. Whassup?" A light cocoa shade of skin, and from just three words Sever had the feeling the kid would feel right at home in the United States' hip-hop community.

"And finally, Mick Sever, meet Derrick. Derrick, this is Mick Sever."

The black singer glanced up with heavy green eyes, slowly stood up from his lounge chair, and waited for Sever to make the first move. Sever took two steps toward him and shook his hand. The musician was tall, maybe 6'3", and thin as a rail. His hair hung shoulder-length in dreadlocks. The hint of a mustache colored his lip and his stoic, level gaze surprised Sever. He'd expected a more animated response. Musicians were usually only too glad to meet him, and until he had either praised or panned their work, they wanted to be his best friend. After Vane's buildup, Sever had expected a friendlier tone.

"So, Bobby thinks you're going to be the next Bob Marley." Sever brushed his damp hair from his forehead.

"There be nobody gonna be Bob Marley. Not Ziggy, his kid, not nobody. I be the next Derrick. Marley was who he was. I'm now." His thick Jamaican accent seemed punctuated with icy tones. Derrick glanced over his shoulder at the four young, bare-chested men gathered behind him. James and Sudahd were both sucking on a reefer, but all four were watching intently. He returned his gaze to Sever. The deep green eyes were hypnotizing, like emeralds in a pool of white.

"I listened to the CD." Sever found himself avoiding the gaze, glancing around for his bag and his notebook. "I like most of it. It's got some traditional themes, but it's fresh. And you've got some very powerful lyrics. I would say they were powerful . . . and somewhat disturbing." He sat down on a padded lawn chair and waited for the singer to sit too. Instead, Derrick walked to a small service bar and poured himself a glass of water. He returned and sat down, squeezing a lime into the drink and glaring at Sever.

Vane watched nervously, approaching Sever as he started writing. "How about a drink, Mick? We've got it all right here."

Sever ignored him. "Derrick, did we get off on the wrong foot here? I made a change in my plans so I could come over here and see your show. Bobby's gone to great lengths to make this thing a success, and you act like you wish we'd just go away."

Derrick was silent. He studied Sever, holding his eyes. He took another sip of water and spoke. "Bobby done okay by us. But let me tell you one thing, mon. White man is no friend of Rasta. The white man is sometimes a necessary evil, and that is all he will ever be. To throw off his oppression, to break free of his tyranny; that's what I am about."

Sever smiled. "I don't mean to be rude, but isn't this kind of old?"

"It may be old for you, but nothing changes. It is new to every black baby born. It's truth I speak. My song is for the black man and woman. Yet I need a white man to open my doors? This is not the Rasta way."

Vane poured himself a whiskey and Coke and walked over to the young singer. He put his big hand on the man's shoulder. "Derrick, we talked about this. Mick here is a friend. He's here to write a story, hopefully a good story. If he likes what he sees, hell, we'll be as big in the States as, well, as big as Marley. Now if you're gonna sit here and try to piss him off—"

"Write about the music. The mon means nothing. My words

and my songs are what you must concern yourself with."

"Okay, let's talk about the music. The lyrics. 'Living in the Real World'—is that a song about your faith?"

"The black man lives in a different world than you. He knows the world he lives in, and he only sees a glimpse of yours. Neither is his world. He must live in a real world, with hope and opportunity, a world that for him does not yet exist."

Sever looked down at his notes where he'd jotted down some lyrics. "Okay, let's talk about the lyrics. Your lyrics. 'Push away *his* real world, and leave your world behind, living in the real world is more than state of mind. We'll crush his world, we'll stand up, we'll conquer and he'll fall, you'll find living in your real world is not so hard at all.' Is that metaphorical? Or are you trying to start a fight?"

He'd hoped for a smile, but once again the green eyes bore into Sever's. "The white man keeps all blacks beneath his boots. If I lift your boot off to find my real world, then so be it. And I *will* lift your boot, Mr. Sever."

"Jesus, Mick, I'm sorry. Derrick and his boys are just edgy, the concert and everything. Look, you guys probably should be goin' out to do the sound check now, right?" Vane guzzled his whiskey and Coke and went back for a refill.

Derrick locked his gaze on Vane, stood up, and motioned to the four. They followed him into the villa, Flame trailing behind. He caught Sever's gaze and shrugged his shoulders as if to say, "That's our Derrick. What can we do?"

"He can be kind of a pissant at times, Mick. Even the guys in the band get a little tired of his attitude, but I never saw him go off like that," Vane said.

"Don't worry about it. I've had stranger interviews. Try talking to Keith Richards when he's stoned."

Vane attempted a laugh. "We're staying at the hotel just up

the road. Maybe you'd like to freshen up a little before we see the show. It's supposed to start in about an hour, but hell, we're on island time now. Could be two or three hours before things start to happen." He downed his second drink and headed toward the house. "Let me just wish the boys good luck. I'll only be a second." He entered the house, and Sever could hear the familiar strains of "Jammin," one of Bob Marley's many anthems, floating from inside the house onto the tropical breeze.

He flipped through his legal pad, briefly reading his notes. Derrick; the newest member, James; Rick; Sudahd; and Flame, with his "Whassup" attitude. And the tambourine-playing, shirt-washing Marna. Well, why not? The world was waiting for the next discovery. From hip-hop to grunge, to Latin, and now reggae rap. Sever leaned back in the chair and soaked up the warm Jamaican sunshine.

He'd grown up listening to his parents' music from the forties, the sophisticated swing of Benny Goodman, the whorehouse blues of Louis Armstrong, then the vocal groups like the Mills Brothers, the Four Freshmen, and the Four Lads that spilled into the fifties. He'd been a fan of folk music from the early sixties, and when the Beach Boys started making waves with three guitars and drums, he'd been hooked on rock and roll. He'd envisioned oceans of young, nubile, bleached-blond surfer girls swaying to the music—maybe his music—and he took every penny he'd saved and purchased a Sears and Roebuck electric guitar.

The biggest disappointment of his teenage years was that he couldn't play the guitar worth a damn and worse yet, his singing voice sounded like an out-of-tune musical saw. Still, he loved the music and he loved the girls, so in order to stay in the loop he started to write about music.

He began working as a press agent for local bands, then started writing a record review column for a local newspaper in

Elgin, Illinois. Later he became a stringer for the *Chicago Tribune*, reviewing rock concerts in the Chicago area. Before he was out of school, he was syndicated by the *Florida Sun Coast*, and his column was printed in 120 newspapers around the country. He made more money in a week than any high school rock-and-roll band made in a year.

Unlike the exaggerated accomplishments of most showbiz types, Sever's bio was for real. He'd been a columnist for the biggest rock newspapers in the country. He'd been a featured reporter on *Entertainment Tonight* and MTV and two of his four books had been made into movies. In some ways, Mick Sever was bigger than some of the acts he wrote about. He liked the money, he liked the fame, he liked the girls, but he still liked the anonymity of being an author instead of a musician.

His work had run the gamut of the rock-and-roll business, with its many transformations. The music had grown from the raw, unpolished, raucous sound of the early fifties, with Little Richard, Chuck Berry, and Dion and the Belmonts, to the polished, sophisticated sounds of the Beatles, the Moody Blues, and Crosby, Stills, and Nash. Then he'd seen the genre do a complete turnaround with the Seattle grunge sound. Now there was reggae rap, a combination of past and future styles.

There were times when he wanted it to stop, or maybe he wanted to stop. He'd been defining new styles and generations of music for too many generations. Maybe it was time to turn it over to someone a lot younger . . . with a lot more energy. Still, the money and the perks were attractive.

The soft voice startled him.

"I said, are you the famous Mick Sever?"

He struggled from his reclining position, sitting straight up and fighting the daydreamed cobwebs in his mind. He glanced up at the soft brown eyes, the long eyelashes, the high cheekbones, and the gorgeous smile. Dark black hair cascaded around her bare caramel shoulders, and the colorful silk that wrapped her upper body did little to hide her perfect breasts and the protruding nipples.

"Uh, yeah. I'm Mick Sever. You must be the tambourine player? Marna?"

"I am, among other things." She pulled up a pool chair and sat down. Tight white jean shorts highlighted dark-skinned legs. Sever had always been a leg man. Except for the dark skin and the color of her hair, she reminded him of the first love of his life, maybe the only love of his life, a younger Ginny . . . his ex-wife.

"Bobby refers to you as the housemother. I met one of your charges."

"I heard you talked to Derrick. You must understand, Mr. Sever, he's a passionate man. I find that attractive in men. True passion in any form is hard to find."

He watched her, her figure so firmly defined, and felt somewhat like a pervert. A female friend of his, another writer, had called his constant fascination with sex very juvenile. At his age, he supposed that was some form of a compliment. "Passion?" He frowned. "He sounded very political."

"Oh, believe me, Mr. Sever, his passion is very real. Derrick believes he can lead the black man out of bondage, and tonight you will see what his passion and fervor are capable of. The poor people love him. He is their shepherd."

"And you? Are you a follower, or just someone along for the ride?"

"I believe I am an independent thinker. I make up my own mind. However, Derrick has some very good thoughts, not unlike my own. What about you, Mr. Sever? What are you about?"

"I'm along for the ride. I'm simply a scribe."

"And a poet too, I see." Her warm smile was inviting and he felt a moment of weakness. "Bobby says you can prepare the world for Derrick. You must be a very well-respected scribe." She gazed over the pool to a gathering of palm trees, their wide leaves moving hypnotically in the soft ocean breeze. She seemed spell-bound for the moment.

"Is Derrick as dedicated to his cause as he seems, or is some of it for show?" Sever pushed the sleeves up on his shirt, and stood up. He walked to the service bar and poured himself a cola.

Her eyes returned to him. "Derrick believes he is chosen. He believes in his message. Derrick is Derrick." This time her smile was wistful, somewhat sad and melancholy.

"You're in love with Derrick?" It seemed a logical progression.

"I love his passion. His work is his love. Do you have passion in your work, Mr. Sever? I would think that to be such an important scribe you must know passion. Look at the sky. Only in Jamaica is the sky so blue, every day." She stood, the breeze caressing her hair and the silk top. He'd seldom seen anything as perfect. She turned and walked into the house as Bobby Vane walked out, brushing lightly against her.

"Give a guy a woody gettin' that close to her, huh, Mick? Isn't she a prize? Doesn't do much on stage but look good, but she does that so damn well." He wiped his palm through his thick, shiny hair, and motioned to Sever with his hand. "Well, let's go. We'll get somethin' to eat," he patted his ample stomach, "and then get back here for the show. Gonna be a kick-ass show, Mick. A kick-ass show."

Chapter Three

Blankets, folding lawn chairs, burlap bags, and black bodies littered the white sand. Sever estimated that about twelve hundred people had paid five dollars a head to see the band. Just in front of the stage, a roped-off area reserved eight folding chairs. Bobby Vane pushed his way through the standing crowd, leading Sever and a contingent of four men and a woman from Island Records to their seats, waiting until one of the burly black security guards removed the rope. A second security guard stood by silently, arms folded.

"Mick Sever, this is Randy and Roland Jamison. Randy and his brother work security for Derrick. Anybody wants to get to Derrick, they go through these guys first."

Randy stuck out his arm, the muscles firmly defined all the way up to the shoulder. He gave Sever a wide grin. Even with his foreboding shaved head, his broad flat nose, his large torso, and thick legs, he seemed amiable. "I read some of your books. You have a way with words. It's good to meet you."

"Randy used to work for the Negril police force. Roland

here," Vane paused as if he was searching for the right words, ". . . he's had some . . . security work before. Randy and Roland are gonna be travelin' to the States to work security on the Brandy tour, right Randy?"

"Lookin' forward to it, Mr. Vane."

"Are you friends with the singer, or is this just a job?" Sever asked.

Roland Jamison stood silent. Shorter and stockier than his brother, he shared the shaved head and facial features. Obviously conversation was not his strong suit.

"We've known him for some time," Randy said. "I suppose we're friends," he glanced at his brother, "though I'm not sure that anyone is close to Derrick. He keeps to himself much of the time, which makes my job much easier, mon."

Roland glanced at Vane, then at Sever. "I think," he hesitated as if the words were difficult, "I think it is better not to be friends with this band." He nodded his head for emphasis, then looked at Vane again as if hoping for approval.

"Why is that?"

"Oh, hell, Mick, he's just sayin' that it's not a good idea to get too involved with the guys you're working for. Right, Roland?" Vane gave the man a stern look.

"I am happy for the job, Mr. Vane. I did not mean to speak out of turn."

"These guys respect Derrick. He's the reason they're here."

"I met him today. Very opinionated."

Randy gave him a broad smile. "Oh, that he is. That he is. His philosophy and his music go hand in hand. Still, it's a good job. And the women that we meet are not too bad either." He laughed loudly.

"He's in a mood tonight, Randy. Very deep, very philosophical, our Derrick." Vane eased his bulk into a chair, and let out a deep sigh. "It ain't easy runnin' these young bucks. If they could all get fame at about our age, eh, Mick? A little seasoning on 'em."

"There wouldn't be much passion, Bobby. And apparently passion is what it's all about."

"Well, forget this afternoon. Concentrate on the music. And let's see what kind of effect he has on these people tonight."

Randy Jamison walked back toward the makeshift stage, his brother hanging back. Roland reached out his hand and touched Sever on the sleeve.

"Mr. Sever, maybe it's not a good idea to get too involved with the people you write about. There are things that are better left unsaid." He smiled, nodded, and walked off, mumbling to himself.

"Don't pay any attention to 'em, Mick. They're all just a little high-strung tonight."

Reggae music blared from a CD player onstage, a synthesized shuffle beat with an infectious rhythm. Bodies in the sand swayed to the sound. Sever let his eyes wander. Young men and women ambled aimlessly about, conversing with friends and strangers. Many of the assembled men wore their hair in dreads, some with wool caps pulled low, and the women with patterned long skirts and their hair high. Others dressed in shorts and T-shirts, the crowd on the ground spreading out on their multicolored blankets and woven burlap bags, smoking marijuana and drinking from fruit jars. A large yellow, green, and red sign announcing Derrick and the Laments hung limply between two posts. A white banner below claimed THE LOST TRIBE OF ISRAEL.

"Mick, meet Donny Ambrose. Donny's the A-and-R guy from Island Records. Used to work with Marley."

The two shook hands. "Mr. Sever, it's a real pleasure to see you. I met you a number of years ago when you did an article on the Wailers. You were one of the first writers to give us a positive review. It was a turning point. I'm very interested in your take on this band."

"I like what I heard on the CD. I think some of it is a little extreme, but extreme sells."

The voices quieted. A large, bare-chested man stood on the stage and held his hand up. "Ladies and gentlemen. Tonight we are very, very excited. The Music Mon has come to Montego Bay. The mon with so much to say. If you have heard the music and the message, you know what I'm talkin' 'bout. If you are new to his sound, you are truly in for a thrill. I introduce to you, *Derrick and the Laments.*"

The applause was polite, the cheering was restrained. Sever glanced at Vane, whose hands were clenched in his lap. The man had a lot riding on tonight.

The band came straggling out, no urgency in their manner. James stepped behind the drums and with some sleight of hand, did some quick rolls with his sticks, going smoothly from snare to toms, cymbal to cymbal. Rick ran his fingers over a Roland keyboard, set to sound like an old Fender Rhoades electric piano, an organ effect with a mournful wail. There was a bluesy feeling on the warm night air. Sudahd strapped on his guitar, Flame the bass guitar, and they started a chunky reggae rhythm, reminiscent of an old Jimmy Cliff song. James caught the beat, familiar and comfortable like a groove in a vinyl record that repeats itself over and over again. Rick punched the two-chord fill on the keyboard as the band settled in.

A light scattering of applause and catcalls greeted Marna as she wandered out onstage, still dressed in her silk top and white shorts. She slapped the tambourine against her perfect thigh. Sever was jealous of the percussive instrument. She was radiant, and her generous smile seemed directed at him alone. He returned the smile as she melted into the background.

Now the applause quickened, the calls became louder, shouting for the *Music Mon.*

"Music Mon! Music Mon!" The cry became rhythmic, the crowd chanting for Derrick Lyman. He walked onto the stage, long and lean, his pale green shirt unbuttoned and his black skin glistening. Blue jeans and a pair of red sneakers completed his outfit. Taking little notice of the crowd or their adulation, he grabbed a microphone from a stand and posed with his back to the audience, his legs spread wide. Swaying gently with the soft rhythm, shaking his head, and throwing the dreadlocks around, he presented a sensual, sexual energy that surprised Sever. Marna walked to the front and placed a kiss on his cheek as the audience quieted down.

The Music Mon spun around, kneeled on the floor, and like a caged animal started hissing into the microphone. He prowled, looking this way and that, his eyes darting from the crowd to the band and back again. Suddenly he leaped to his feet, pointing at the revelers, and talking to them slowly, with the beat, rhythmically weaving his words into a hypnotic incantation.

"You, you got the power. Jah, he give to you. You, no one can take it. You, I tell you true." As he pointed to the people, they yelled back to him, "YOU!" He pointed again. Again the crowd answered, "YOU."

Once more he spoke, in a singsong voice, bobbing and weaving his body along with his lyrics. "You, the second coming, You, as Jah has said, You, the chosen people, You the white man dread." He pointed again and the sound was deafening. "YOU!" And again, "YOU!" Twelve hundred people were on their feet, pointing back at the stage, screaming to be part of the mantra.

Sever looked back at the swaying mass of Jamaicans and then

glanced at Bobby Vane, his smile a mile wide. Two lines into the
first number and Derrick Lyman had the crowd in the palm of
his hand. It was truly an amazing feat.

Randy, Roland, and two barrel-chested bald security men
stood their ground in front of the stage, each armed with what
looked like a wooden baseball bat. It didn't appear to Sever that
the crowd was going to rush the stage, but the men seemed ready
just in case.

The hypnotic effect of the words and the sexual energy of
the singer seemed to send a magical spell into the night, envel-
oping everyone in the audience. After the powerful "You," the
band segued into a romantic tune from the CD called "Moonlight
Lady." The lovely Marna strolled stage center as Derrick walked
around her, whispering the lyric like a warm tropical breeze.
"Someday, sometime, my moonlight lady, we sail away on a summer breeze. Sometime, somewhere, my moonlight lady, we make
love under tall palm trees."

Lovers around them clutched each other's hands and women
laid their heads on the shoulders of their partners. No one sat,
and they swayed together, an infectious island rhythm floating
out to sea.

Fourteen songs in all, half from the CD and half Sever had
never heard before. Derrick manipulated the disciples, weaving a
strange spell with the music and lyrics. Some of the tunes were
lustful and romantic and others, like "Take Back the Street," reminded him of gangsta rap. The lyrics were brutal, about a Jamaican girl who prostituted herself and was killed by her own
family so they could save her soul. Derrick had climbed up on
one of the stage speakers, screaming with rage the profane re-
frain: "Damn the woman, be his sister, damn the woman, gut the
child. Fuck the creature he has made her, take her spirit from the

wild!" He leaped off the speaker back onto the stage, "Take back the street! Take back the street!"

The people screamed and women cried. Bobby Vane leaned over to Donny Ambrose, shouting above the din. "Donny, if half of this excitement translates to his CD, you boys could have a hell of a winner here!" Ambrose nodded.

The last song of the evening was a reprise of "Moonlight Lady," and despite thunderous applause and vocal encouragement, the band walked off the stage and disappeared in the darkness. Randy, Roland, and the two security guards stayed in front, stopping the occasional observer who wanted a look behind the stage. The crowd slowly dispersed, walking up the beach, riding brightly colored balloon-tire bicycles, or starting up rusted automobiles with bald tires and chugging down the road to their homes in Montego Bay.

Vane stood up and stretched, let out a satisfied belch, and pulled a Partagas cigar from the pocket of the white knit shirt that stretched over his large frame.

"Boys, now tell me if we don't have a genuine star here. Just tell me. This shit is gonna blow the Brandy tour away. Just blow it away." He grunted and lit the cigar, filling his mouth with the rich smoke and letting it drift from his mouth in a slow, easy stream.

"Mick, did I tell you? I just knew this kid was good." He reached into his pocket and pulled out another cigar. "Rude of me. Terribly rude of me." He offered it to Sever, who took it and bit off the end.

"Bobby, you act like the manager of a prizefighter who just won the heavyweight title." He accepted a light from the pudgy man.

"Mick, I feel like a fucking manager of a prizefighter. Man, this just feels so right. Tell me, are we gonna get a good story out of this or what?"

"I'm impressed. The band did what you said they would do. And you're right, the product is what's important. Your boy puts out good product."

Donny Ambrose walked up with two young men, one black, one white, swaggering behind him. Sever knew the junior executive types from the recording companies. They wore Parrot Head shirts made of multicolored cotton, unbuttoned so their gold chains shone brightly against their naked chests, and trendy khaki cargo shorts with pockets everywhere. The apparel appeared to be a uniform. They were the type that had no talent themselves, but assumed the magic and allure of the artists that rubbed off on them. They threw the parties, gave out the passes, arranged for the women, and wanted the world to know just how cool they were.

"Mick, this is Stevie Binder and Scott Parton. Guys, this is Mick Sever."

They shook hands all around.

"Mick," Stevie Binder thrust his hands in his pockets and looked up at Sever, "do you think the States are ready for another Bob Marely?"

Sever took a puff on his Cuban cigar, savoring the sweet smoke. "Do you think Derrick is another Bob Marley? Derrick takes great offense at that. He says he's his own man."

"The political stuff, the black versus white," he glanced at his counterpart. Scott Parton smiled. "The class envy, and especially the song about killing a woman?"

"We've got much worse at home," Sever said.

"Oh, I know. My point was, are the people in the States ready for more of the same? Is it old hat? I think maybe it's been done to death, and speaking of death . . ." He trailed off, glancing at Vane, a thin smile playing on his lips.

Bobby Vane cut in. "Oh, shit. You gonna bring that up? I'll tell you what he's gonna say, Mick." He pointed his cigar at Binder. "In the last three months, two girls have been murdered after a Derrick concert. Both the girls were Jamaican, and both had been to a concert. There's nothing at all that ties Derrick, the band, or anybody else to the killings."

"Nothing except they were both known to be a little loose in the morals department, and it kind of hit home when Derrick sang 'Take Back the Street.' People talk. And they figure somebody took Derrick's song to heart. Maybe the Music Mon himself." Binder smirked, nodding at Vane.

"Mick," Vane looked pleadingly at him with those puppy dog eyes, "this isn't the kind of thing you want to write about. Jeeze, it's got nothing to do with the product. It *was* good product, wasn't it? No deaths, no murders; just great music and a great show. Am I right?"

"I'm writing about the music and the show, Bobby. You're right."

Vane shot Stevie Binder a hateful look, grabbed hold of Sever's shoulder, and steered him toward the stage. "Fuck 'em. I'll get a record company that wants 'em bad. 'Cause we've got a winner here, Mick. Honest to Christ, a real winner!"

Chapter Four

The images of the concert ran through his mind. He closed his eyes and saw the colorful assortment of characters that wandered the beach. He isolated an old man, bare-chested with a shark tooth hanging from a lanyard around his neck, and when the white-haired man smiled, he was toothless himself. He picked out a young girl barely in her teens who never stopped moving, shaking in a frenzy, almost as if possessed. The music seemed to feed her demon. Sever needed to see it all again in his mind. The writing process was lonely, isolated, unlike the event he was writing about. He had to make it come alive again, to re-create it so he could capture the moment in words.

The plane trip back had been uneventful except for Vane complaining about the reaction from Island Records. "Shit, Mick, when we get on this tour, they'll be lined up with contracts. You know I've got almost every group I've ever handled signed and this band is better than most. Sons of bitches act like they're just not sure if this is gonna fly. Like a fuckin' witch on a broom, this is gonna fly. Up their noses!"

Sever sat back in his chair and stared at the computer screen. The motel in Miami was not his first choice of accommodations, but the Brandy tour was breaking there in two days, and he wanted to follow the story a little further. He closed his eyes once more, and could almost smell the thick odor of ganja, the herbal choice for Rasta.

"It's in the Bible, mon," someone with Marley had told him. "Genesis. *Thou shalt eat the herb of the field.*" He remembered the first time he'd smoked a joint. It was 1962. He was fourteen years old and Johnny and the Hurricanes and Eddie Cochran were performing at the local armory. He'd asked Ginny to the show and her mom had to drive. The little minx had introduced him to grass behind the armory. *Herb of the field.* That had been some show. Virginia had been some date . . . some wife. Now, "Summertime Blues" was just a sweet memory.

The hum of his computer blended with the hum of the motel air conditioner. He heard the music, and could see Randy, Roland, and the other two security guards, their legs wide apart in a stance, daring anyone to approach the stage. He focused on Marna, the dark goddess of the tambourine. He'd have to spend some serious time describing her. After the show she'd talked to him again, thanking him for coming and hoping the review would be kind. She'd been on a personal high, and had kissed him lightly on the cheek when they parted. She seemed to be a very affectionate woman. As much as he enjoyed replaying the show in his mind, he had to start writing.

The Rastafarian faith has a new champion, and the music of Jamaica has a new Music Mon. If the Montego Bay crowd reaction to **Derrick and the Laments** is any indication of the response the band will get in the United States, then the Jamaican music makers will explode across this country on a whirlwind summer schedule that will have other tour headliners taking a backseat. Pretty good for a group that doesn't even have a label.

He studied the opening. Bobby Vane would love it.

What Vane wouldn't like was that Sever had decided to look into the murders. The article for *Rolling Stone* was strictly a review of the concert and the band. But the main reason for staying in Miami was to see what happened opening night. The last story he'd worked on involved an onstage murder in front of twelve thousand fans, and his journalistic endeavors had earned him the number-one book in the country. Murder had never entered into his writing before, but the story of Job Jobiah and the Faith had been too good to pass up. And as the tale unfolded, it contained all the essential ingredients. Sex, drugs, rock and roll. Now, with faint rumblings that murder might be following the Laments' tour, he had decided to stick with the band for another couple of days.

He stood up from the writing desk, wincing at the twinge in his knee. Straightening out the leg and gingerly walking to the window, he pulled back the curtains and looked out on the Miami night. From five stories up, a full moon over the city silhouetted a skyline of shadowy buildings. In the parking lot of the motel, strategically planted palm trees formed a linear pattern. Southern Florida had a special look: concrete and palm trees. Sever limped back to the computer and punched the keys, determined to finish the story tonight so he could concentrate on the U.S. opening.

Chapter Five

"This be the pass, mon." Roland handed him the laminated badge, the smiling face of Brandy on one side and a series of numbers and letters on the other. "You can go where you want." He stood in Sever's motel room doorway, his muscular, six-foot-three frame filling the space, his shaved head gleaming.

"Roland, come on in for a minute."

"I got places to be."

"This will only take a minute. You worked security with your brother the nights that the girls were killed." Sever motioned to a chair, but the dark man stood still. "How long after the concerts were they attacked?"

Roland gazed past Sever to the bright sunlight pouring through the window. "The sky is not so blue as in Jamaica."

"Look, I just want a little background. I heard that one was killed at a resort. The other was found in a parking lot outside a bar where they were playing." Sever brushed the hair from his forehead and tried to disarm the big man with a smile.

"I didn't work for the Music Mon at that time. I worked for that resort, Crystal Beach. I found her."

"The one on the beach?"

"Yeah, mon."

"You worked there?"

"Security. I found the girl, early evening. She been workin' a white man."

"Working a white man?"

"Yeah, mon."

"What does that mean?"

"She worked him. For money, for ganja."

"Ah. Worked him. Did you know her?"

"We knew who she was. She liked the band."

"Derrick?"

"No, mon, I'm not goin' there. We knew who she was. That's all I got to say." He shifted, uncrossed his arms, and turned to leave.

"Roland, was she friendly with Derrick?"

"Ah, Mr. Sever. I told you it was best not to get close to the people you write about. I tell you for your own good and for my good. I need the job. Please. Leave the story be."

"You make it sound like there's a lot more to learn."

Roland closed his eyes. He gently pressed his index finger and thumb to the closed eyelids, then slowly opened them. In a brief transformation, Sever could see the sorrow of the world in those eyes. If eyes were windows to the soul, this soul was tortured.

"Mr. Sever. Have you ever learned that a good friend has betrayed you?"

"As a matter of fact, yes."

"For some people, it can seem like the end of the world. Like nothing will ever be right again." Roland turned around and walked down the hallway shaking his bald head back and forth and muttering to himself.

Sever watched him until he reached the elevators. An older woman with a straw hat and a beach bag stepped out as the big Jamaican brushed past, never even seeing her. She jumped back in surprise. "Well, I never," she said, shooting an evil look at the closing elevator doors.

Sever remembered the punch line. "Well, maybe you should." He turned back to his room and closed the door.

Chapter Six

The hum of voices surrounded them like angry bees buzzing over a disturbed hive. The News Café was the breakfast restaurant of choice on South Beach, and Bobby Vane was trying out the cuisine, two and three dishes at a time.

"Damn fine French toast here, Mick. And the cheese omelet with these little things," he picked at the sun-dried tomatoes and pimentos, "very tasty. You, with your coffee and bagel? Shit, you miss the finer things in life, my friend."

"I got the pass yesterday from Roland." Sever's eyes wandered to a couple of blondes who strolled by in halter tops and brief shorts. As they passed the table, he noticed they were holding hands. "Roland and Randy. They seem like good choices for security. Big guys, nobody's going to mess with them."

"I'm a little concerned with him over here. He's not on his own turf anymore. You know, none of those boys has ever been off the island. They're kind of edgy. Randy and Roland help keep 'em settled." He stabbed a forkful of greasy sausage and bit off half a link. Chewing fast and swallowing, he washed the food down with a swig of orange juice. "Roland says you wanted to talk about the girls who were killed."

"It's not in the story."

"I know, and I appreciate that. But there's nothin' to those girls. They were at a concert and later they died. That's pretty much all there is."

"He seemed to get a little defensive when I asked him about it." Sever watched Vane's brown eyes shift, then stare at the plate half full of toast, sticky syrup, and eggs.

"I told you, they watch out for Derrick." He lifted his eyes and looked past Sever.

"I didn't mention Derrick."

"Not to me you didn't, but you asked Roland if Derrick was friendly with the girl. Hell, Roland found her. Her throat was slit and she's layin' there buck naked with blood all over. Of course he's being a little defensive. Cops had him up half the night, and they're thinkin' he might have killed her. Crystal Beach should have given the boy a medal, and instead they laid him off. Now you tell me why he wouldn't want to talk about it. He's a decent kid and they treated him like crap!"

"But she'd been to the concert. He said the band knew her." A busboy dropped a tray and the dishes crashed to the floor, the din of voices fading for several seconds.

"It's a small island, Mick. People know people. She hung around a lot of bands. Truth be known, she probably was a groupie, but it doesn't mean the band had anything to do with her."

"Did they?" Sever reached for his coffee. Vane put his hand firmly on Sever's wrist and stopped him.

"Mick, there've been rumors. These boys are a big deal back there. Derrick is like a prophet, a preacher, a holy man. He's clean. He doesn't drink, eats I-tal . . . all-natural foods. Hell, he doesn't even have a Coke or cup of coffee. He believes in people being pure. It's part of the Rasta thing, and it's in the music that he writes and sings. So there are always people who want to find fault, who want to prove that he's not the perfect Music Mon. And there are a lot of whites in Jamaica who feel threatened by what he says and writes. So when there's even a hint of scandal, everyone wants to pile on. No different than it is here." He removed his hand and Sever took a sip of coffee.

"Okay, it's the reporter in me. I told you the product is good. You've got a hit on your hands. You've had hits before, but this one goes a little deeper. The boy bands, the one-hit wonders, the little fourteen-year-old schoolgirls who sing about bedding their boyfriends; there's no substance there. This band has legs, Bobby. But the story is in Derrick and the effect he has on people . . . the way he takes total control of the audience. You know I can't just stop here."

"Hell, Mick, we haven't even got started over here yet. At least let us get a chance to make a name for ourselves before you start crucifying us." He grabbed a fork with his thick fingers and scooped up a forkful of hash browns from his second plate. He shoveled them into his wide-open mouth.

Sever reached down to the floor and picked up a copy of the *Miami Herald*, folded in half and already turned to the entertainment section. He laid the paper in front of Vane and studied the hefty man as he started to silently read the front-page story.

"In an article to be published in next month's *Rolling Stone*, journalist Mick Sever says that the Jamaican band Derrick and the Laments just might be the hottest ticket on the concert tour this summer. 'And the band doesn't even have a label,' says Sever. Watch for record companies to be out in force tonight at the

Miami Brandy concert, as Derrick and the Laments appear as the warm-up act. Sever says they may eclipse the headliner. Expect the show to be a sellout."

"Shit, how can I be mad at you?" He mumbled through the food. "I knew gettin' you to Jamaica was the best thing that could happen to this band." Vane grinned, the mouthful of potatoes now mashed into paste spilling out as he wiped the corners of his mouth with a cloth napkin.

"Let's hope the story doesn't follow them over here. And, let's hope he's got the same karma that he had the last time I saw him."

"He's worried about that. The whole fuckin' band is worried about that. But as much as he protests the comparison to Marley, he knows it's good for business. Strictly off the record, that boy has a pretty good business head. He knows what sells."

"And tonight, we'll see who's buying." Sever finished his coffee and looked out over the beach, watching the early morning volleyball game already in progress. The cute waitress with the short black skirt and white apron filled his cup, caught his eyes, and smiled.

"I know you from somewhere. Are you a regular?" she asked.

"No," Sever gave her the white teeth, a smile set off by his deep tan that seemed to last all summer, "but I may become one if you work here every morning."

She gave him a quizzical look. "That wasn't a pick-up line. I really do know you from somewhere. It'll come to me." She cocked her head, studied him for a second, then walked off with a flip of her hair. He watched her until she turned a corner. He should have tried just a little harder.

Vane tapped his finger on the table. "Can't have every woman you see, Mick. I know you love the women, but there are some that don't necessarily love you."

"And you can't have a hit with every group you find, Bobby. Because not every band is going to measure up." He took a sip of the fresh coffee.

Vane smiled. "By the way, Frankie Romano is having a little party tonight after the concert in honor of the boys. He's invited some people you probably know, so why don't you come along?"

"Romano? I haven't seen him in two, three years. It seems to me those were some pretty wild parties."

"Seems to me you wrote some pretty wild stories for him. The *Florida Sun Coast* got you some pretty good exposure." Vane speared the last piece of French toast, dragged it through the smeared yellow yolk, and shoved it into his mouth.

"On the boat?"

"Jesus, don't call it a boat in front of Frankie. It's a million-dollar yacht. He gets his feelings hurt when people call it a boat. It's the *Christy Lee*, okay?"

"I'll be there. Do you think Derrick will approve, with the alcohol, the drugs, and the women?"

"I told you Derrick knows what sells. And how do you know that Frankie hasn't mellowed in the last three years?"

"Frankie?" Sever frowned. "Frankie would never mellow." He sensed the stranger moving up behind him, then looked up at the tall pale-faced man standing over the table. Hands folded in front of him, he seemed to be patiently waiting for the conversation to pause.

"Gentlemen, excuse me." New York, or New Jersey. With just three words, Sever had him pegged. The stranger continued, "Which one of you is Bobby Vane?"

Vane wiped his mouth, swallowing the last of the egg and toast. He rubbed his hands together and stood up, blocking the light from the window. "I'm Vane. What can I do for you?"

The man offered his hand, and Vane shook it. "I'm Ron Gillian with Mega Records. We're going to be at the concert tonight, and I want you to know that we're very interested in talking to you about Derrick and the Laments."

"I knew you guys were comin', but I didn't know you'd heard the band."

"Haven't heard a note, but I've heard a lot about them. And obviously if you're working with them, we'd like to talk to you."

"You come tonight. If you're half as excited as I think you're going to be, I'm sure we'll be talking." Vane tugged at his yellow Italian knit shirt, pulling it down over his ample stomach. He scratched at a brown syrup stain, then smiled at Gillian. "You won't be disappointed."

"The only way we'll be disappointed is if we don't get the chance to sign them." He dropped a business card on the table and strolled off.

"Mega is a big player. It's gonna be a feeding frenzy. Fucking frenzy. I told you, record companies are gonna be lined up!"

Sever saw her headed their way. Her eyes were bright, determined. He admired her tan, athletic legs, and the black apron that did little to hide her ample bosom.

"MTV. You're on MTV. You do music news. And June says you've got a book out too. I told you I knew who you were. You're big-time." She beamed. "Can I have your autograph?"

He signed the paper she offered.

"I'm here Tuesday through Saturday, six 'til ten, if you want to stop by again." She grinned, looked at the signature, studied him for a second, then waltzed away.

"Maybe we were both wrong," Sever said.

"What's that?" Vane asked.

"Maybe they all *do* love me, and maybe everyone you handle *is* a hit."

Chapter Seven

The name *Frankie Romano was* a buzzword in publishing circles nationwide. He was born in New York City and had dropped out of school in the seventh grade to start a neighborhood newspaper. Gathering juicy gossip from the women in his Bronx apartment building and steamy stories from the streets, he'd talked area retailers into sponsoring his little venture. The mixture of crazy neighborhood stories and business hype had been a success, and the paper expanded until he'd sold it at the tender age of fifteen. At sixteen, Romano moved to Florida, lived in Miami with an uncle, and started a shopper, using the same basic formula. By the time he was twenty-one, he had seventeen newspapers spread throughout southern Florida and a net worth of four million dollars, and he was living the life of Riley.

Romano was forty years old when he bought the *Florida Sun Coast*, a run-down rag with a dwindling subscriber base that was sold to retirees in the Miami area. He'd changed the focus, given the paper a hip modern look, and paid double what other publications were paying to attract a handful of very young, very current writers who had fresh views and weren't afraid to speak their minds. The former rag lost all of its subscriber base—the retirees and advertisers deciding the plug had been pulled—then hit the newsstands with an explosion. The look, the hype, and the writing caught a young generation's attention and the *Sun Coast* sold out every copy every day. Within two weeks, advertisers stood in line, and the *Florida Sun Coast* stories were fodder for every drinking fountain conversation in southern Florida. Mick Sever was a regular contributor, covering the music scene, reviewing records, and candidly discussing SDRR—sex, drugs, and rock and roll.

Romano had become the patron saint of struggling young journalists and struggling young rock acts. A writer or musician with talent and an introduction could get an audience with the saint, and if he was blessed, he not only got the introduction, but he got a shot at celebrity and stardom. And he was invited to the best parties, sampled the best dope, drank the best booze, ate the best food, and was guaranteed the best sex anyone had ever experienced. Frankie Romano was the south Florida Hugh Hefner, and the *Christy Lee* was his Playboy Mansion.

Sever had some fond memories of Romano, and not-so-fond memories of Romano's parties. It had been one of those blowout affairs that had ended his marriage. Ginny hadn't understood why a coked-up Sever had two nude platinum blond models lying next to him on a queen-sized bed in the forward stateroom when he was supposed to be finding her purse and taking her home. This was the straw that broke the camel's back. She filed for divorce the next day.

Still, a party on Romano's boat had sounded tempting. Sever genuinely liked the little man, and it had been too many years since their last meeting.

The concert had been a huge success, with three encores for

Derrick and a great response for Brandy. The brooding Jamaican singer had strutted, preened, and grasped the audience from the moment he walked onto the stage. He whipped the crowd into a feverish frenzy and Vane had beamed like a proud father. The band was pumped, and Sever felt obligated to follow the story just a little further. He hated that inbred feature. There was no satisfaction in the present. It was always the future that intrigued him—what would happen next.

Now, reggae music blared from the *Christy Lee*'s oiled teak deck, "Stir It Up" the song of choice. About forty people lined the deck and crowded the bar in the main cabin. Gone were the shiny aluminum bowls of white powder, the razor blades and straws that years ago had been strategically placed on coffee tables, end tables, and the bar. The casually dressed group tonight ate from heaping plates of steaming jerk chicken and fish and drank from short stout bottles of Red Stripe beer and mineral water. The occasional doobie was passed around, and Sever knew that select members of the invited were in the head, snorting their drug of choice, but keeping a lower profile than he'd ever witnessed before. Maybe Frankie Romano had mellowed, or maybe his crowd had matured.

Someone turned down the stereo's volume, and Romano's voice blasted over the speaker system. The short, squat man stood on deck wearing tailored shorts and a golf shirt, tufts of white hair peeking from behind his small ears and from the neck of his shirt, like stuffing escaping a torn mattress. "On behalf of the *Florida Sun Coast*, I want to thank all of you for coming out tonight. I'm sure the free food and booze didn't have anything to do with your attending. . . ." There was polite laughter. Romano held the mike with one hand and shoved the other deep into his pocket. "Most of you saw the show tonight, and as usual, we think Bobby Vane has picked a winner." Reserved applause. "This little get-together is to introduce all of you to Derrick and the La-ments, soon to be one of the new super groups in the recording industry." More applause, and then the band was there, behind Vane, waiting for the introduction. "Let me introduce you to ·Bobby Vane, the man behind the Music Mon." He handed off the microphone to Vane, who was tearing off a piece of the spicy chicken with his teeth. He belched uncomfortably close to the mike.

"I'm sorry. This chicken is just too much." He washed the jerk meat down with a swig of Red Stripe, wiped his chin with the back of his hand, and checked behind him to make sure the band was all there. "Well, we've got James on drums, Rick on keyboard, Flame on bass, Sudahd on guitar, and Derrick himself on lead vocals and guitar." The crowd applauded politely. "If you saw 'em tonight, you know what they're capable of. This is one kick-ass band, my friends." Introductions over, the band drifted through the assembled guests.

Several women engaged the young band members, brushing up against them and speaking in hushed tones. Sever watched the unveiled attempts to make arrangements for later tonight. One of the women was married, her husband sitting on a deck chair, staring vacantly out at the water, a joint hanging from his fin-gertips. She steered Rick further out on the deck, and clasped his hand. The keyboard player put his free arm around her and played her back down to her cute rear end, like the keys on a baby grand piano.

Sever searched the gathering for Marna. She hadn't been in-troduced with the band, yet he'd seen her on deck not more than twenty minutes ago. For a brief time she'd been in an animated conversation with Derrick, pointing her finger and raising her voice. Now she was nowhere to be seen. He turned his attention to Romano, as the publisher walked up and grabbed him by his shoulders.

"Mick, it's good to see you," he beamed. "Ya look the same as the first day we met. Ya never change."

"Frankie, I wish I could say that about you, but you had hair when we first met."

Romano laughed. "And it was dark brown and wavy. And I had about thirty less pounds. And hell, I think I've lost of couple of inches in the height department. But all things considered, I'm doin' all right. And by all accounts, you are too."

Sever looked down at the balding little man and noticed the twinkle in his left ear lobe. "What's this? At your age? Where's the tattoo, Frankie, the one that says KORN, or something inane?"

Romano chuckled. "Gotta do somethin' to let 'em know I'm still alive." He caressed the diamond stud. "You know the worst thing about gettin' old? It's not the aches and the pains. It's not even gettin' a little soft around the middle, or maybe losin' a little in the sex department. It's losing the respect of the youngsters."

"You haven't lost any respect. What are you talking about? You're still on top, the kingmaker."

"Naw, you don't see it yet. You will. It's in their eyes. I've got the money, I've got the power, but I'm gettin' old and they know it. They smile, they joke, and they don't think I get it anymore. And no amount of trying to be hip is going to convince them that I'm still twenty-five at heart."

The yacht shifted with a slight roll from the wake of a loud cigarette boat as it faded down the shoreline. Sever rested his arm on the polished brass railing and watched the running lights disappear in the distance. Romano had been like a father to him. He'd taught him about the finer things in life. And as wild and woolly as the older man had been, Sever had always had immense respect for him. His own father had been a miserable beer-guzzling, wife-beating, whiskey-swilling, skirt-chasing old man his entire adult life, and for the most part, he'd ignored his kids as if they simply didn't exist. Sever had no respect and no love for his old man. Romano, on the other hand, showed interest in him. They'd talk for hours about life in general, about music and women, and Sever never felt that Romano was in it for the money. The older man seemed to relish the relationships he so carefully cultivated. Monetary concerns came after the relationships.

"Vane's got himself a hot band, but I don't think he knows what to do with it," Romano said.

"It depends on what the band, or Derrick, wants to do with it. He starts off telling me that the message is what's important. He wants nothing to do with the publicity machine, nothing to do with the white kingmakers, then he shows up at one of your parties. I think Derrick wants it both ways."

"He's young, and he's poor. He'll get a taste of the big time from this point on, and he'll change his tune."

"I hope not. His *tune* is what makes him hot, a rebel. Dreads are going to be all the rage next year."

As if on cue a young black girl with tightly braided hair walked up to Romano, holding a tray of champagne flutes filled to the brim with the golden liquid. Romano took two and handed one to Sever. "I heard you gave up drugs. I assume you still imbibe?"

Sever smiled. "I'll always have a drink with you." They clinked glasses and silently sipped the sparkling nectar, gazing into the darkness where the trail of a silver sliver of moon weaved a wavy pattern across the black water.

"Hell, Mick, I'm gettin' too old for this shit. I can feel it around me. Maybe I don't get it anymore. It's a business for twenty-year-olds."

"It always was, Frankie. And as long as we still feel twenty years old, we've got a future."

"And you, my boy? You're still young enough to handle it?"

"I don't know, Frankie," Sever drained the champagne. "This last year, it just seems I'm disconnected. Maybe I don't care anymore."

"You still care about the money, the ladies, the finer things in life."

"Do you keep doing something just because of the rewards?"

"Mick, come on. Ninety percent of the working stiffs in this country hate their fucking jobs, and they make a fraction of what we do. And they're lookin' at us, sayin', 'I want to be like them.' You're a role model, son! You can't quit now."

Sever looked out over the water. A fine yacht, expensive champagne, good friends—maybe this was what it was all about. "I don't know, Frankie. You? Money, women, power."

"I suppose there's still something there. There's a young lady . . . well, it's not important. I've only gotten to know her for a short time. On the yacht here, she—"

"See? If you think young, and date twenty-year-old girls, you'll never grow old, Frankie!"

From down below they heard the wailing. Above the din of voices, and the pulsing sound of Bob Marley and the Wailers singing "No Woman, No Cry," above the sound of glasses clinking and high-pitched laughter, they heard the desperate wail, cutting through the sound like the cigarette boat had cut through the water. It was a woman, and the wail became a shriek, and a cry for help. Romano turned and bounded down the stairs to the staterooms, Sever right behind him.

The sound came from behind the closed door on the left. Romano twisted the knob, shoved, and the door shot open. Sever stood behind, staring over the short man's shoulder at the mulatto girl's body lying on the bed. Blood covered her chest, soaking through the white cotton blouse and matting the bedspread. Roland Jamison stood over her, frozen in profile, a white, bone-handled knife clutched firmly in his hand. In the corner of the room, Marna cowered, softly sobbing. She looked at Sever, then Romano, with pleading eyes.

"Please, somebody do something."

The burly security guard turned and gazed at Romano and Sever. His eyes looked down at the bloody knife in his hand and his eyes widened as the dawn of awareness washed over him.

"I did not do this." He looked pleadingly at Sever and dropped the knife. "You must believe me. I did not do this."

Romano glanced back at Sever. "There's a cell phone at the bar. I think somebody needs to call the cops. And Mick, on your way up you might give notice to those folks who've been hittin' the head on a regular basis. They may have somethin' they want to throw overboard before the authorities arrive."

Sever nodded. The old Frankie Romano would have moved the body off the boat, cleaned the room, and then dealt with the authorities, making sure that his guests were taken care of first. Maybe Romano was getting older. And wiser. He glanced back at Romano then limped up the stairs, the sharp pain in his knee more pronounced. Marna had collapsed in Frank Romano's arms, sobbing uncontrollably. Romano looked back at him and shook his head. Mick felt old too. Too old for this.

Chapter Eight

*T*hree *hours later, the last* of the revelers was interviewed. The young woman's body, violated by twelve visible stab wounds, had been covered and sent to the coroner. She apparently had come alone, spent some time on deck with Derrick, and no one had seen her for at least half an hour before her death. Two detectives and a handful of uniformed policemen had gone over the scene repeatedly. They'd all left, but for one.

"She wasn't on the guest list, but then that list was pretty loose." Romano sipped a cup of strong black coffee as he talked to the lead homicide officer, Harry Kohls. "Might have been a guest of Derrick's."

"Except Derrick isn't here. Seems he conveniently disappeared." The detective sucked the smoke from his unfiltered cigarette and glanced up at Sever. "Are you always around when we find dead bodies?"

"Only once before, Harry. It's not my favorite thing to do."

"The Job Jobiah murder was pretty damned lucrative for you, wasn't it? With your book and everything?" Kohls turned his attention back to Romano. "So the security guy stands over the body with the knife in his hand, and says, 'I didn't do it'?"

"That's exactly the way we saw it. The girl tells us she walked in and there he was."

"I don't want to jump to conclusions, but this seems like an open-and-shut case. Not often you catch the murderer in the act. We get a time of death from the coroner that matches and we might wrap this one up by morning."

Sever eased himself off the rattan chair and poured himself a cup of coffee from the Bunn warmer on the bar. "What's the motive?"

"I don't know the players. Maybe you can give us some ideas. Could be this Derrick was boinking her and the security guy got upset. Maybe there was an argument. Maybe it was a drug thing. Oh, I know there were no drugs here tonight. . . ." he smiled at Romano. "Mr. Romano is too important a person here in our fair city to ever accuse of having drugs at one of his *affairs*."

"It's just that it seems too simple."

"Hey, we're entitled once in a while. And from what Bobby Vane said, this guy was the first one on the scene at the beach in Negril. Now that seems to be a coincidence, doesn't it? Sever, sometimes we get lucky and we get our man right away. I just hope that's the case this time." Kohls loosened his tie, exposing the frayed collar on his off-white shirt. He stood up, looking around the room. "We need to talk to this Derrick. The boys didn't find him at the hotel, and we can wait until tomorrow, but by noon I'll put out an all-points bulletin on his ass if somebody doesn't produce him."

"Tell Vane. Derrick is his charge, not mine."

Kohls tucked his shirt into his wrinkled slacks. "I've told him. You remind him. Hell, Sever, you may as well do some work for the next million dollars you'll get out of writing *this* story." He put his cigarette out in a stale cup of coffee, grunted, and stalked off. Turning back, he shot Sever an angry glance. "And another thing. I don't like the way I came off in that book. I think I'm much more charming than you gave me credit for. I ooze charm, Sever. You just didn't pick up on that." He continued his walk off the deck, up the walkway, onto the dock to the parking lot.

"I think he's very charming," said Romano. "There's a certain elegance in his manner."

"Yeah. And he loves the entertainment industry, in case you didn't catch that. Where's Marna?"

"I've got a lady who works for me, Denise. She took Marna to her condo. She can stay overnight, get some rest, and stay out of the limelight. She got pretty hysterical."

Sever sipped his coffee from the china cup, thinking he should have put some liquor in it. "It all seems too perfect."

"Jesus, to walk in on the guy actually stabbing the girl. What do you figure got into him?"

"I don't know. I originally took him for muscle. But the few times I've talked to him, it seems to be more than that. He's hinted at some mystery involving the group. It's like he wants to say something but knows he can't. It's very strange. I think he's a good kid who's in over his head. On the other hand, his brother Randy seems like a pretty sharp guy. Like Kohls said, nobody really knows the players."

"I'd like to know Marna." He gave Sever a strange look, wide-eyed, innocent. The old Frank Romano always played the innocent when he was on the make. "When she calms down, you bring her around."

"I don't think she's going to want to see this boat for a long time."

"Boat? Now the *Christy Lee* is a boat? One little murder and we downgrade from a yacht to a boat?"

"Frankie, we've had some times on this *boat*. I think I may have ended my marriage on the *Christy Lee*."

"I was here, my boy, I was here."

"I promised Vane I'd see him back at the motel. He wants to talk about Derrick. Says there's something more I should know. Cloak-and-dagger-sounding stuff. I'll call you in the morning and we can compare notes." Sever poured the remainder of his coffee over the side of the boat thinking maybe the caffeine would keep the fish awake, and walked off the yacht, picturing the scene in his mind. Something bothered him, and he was pretty sure it was the look in Roland's eyes. A look of total surprise.

Chapter Nine

Vane sat on the edge of the bed blowing smoke rings from his cigar and generally fogging up the room. Sever's room.

"Bobby, this is getting to be routine."

Vane held a mouthful of smoke, then slowly released it, watching the trail head toward the ceiling. "It's funny, Mick. How the range of human emotions can go from the highest level to the lowest level in a matter of seconds. I wonder if animals work like that."

"I don't think animals have emotions." Sever straddled the desk chair and looked Vane in the eyes. "You never had a clue that Roland was the killer?"

"Never. I've known those boys for two years now. Randy and Roland. They pick up girls every once in a while. Randy more than Roland. I mean, the boys in the band seem to do pretty good for themselves and like any other rock group, the rest of the staff gets the leftovers. So, I figure that maybe Roland is trying to get into these girls' pants and they say no. So he's got a little buzz goin' on with the ganja and whatever, and he says,

'Fuck it. You won't put out, so . . .' Oh, hell. This sure as hell puts a damper on the first night, doesn't it?"

"This business gets pretty crazy. It's like, if you're with the band, you get anything you want. Money, drugs, sex, and you get as much as you want, anytime you want. Maybe you're right. Maybe he was just trying to claim what he thought was his."

Vane tapped the ash from his cigar in the glass ashtray beside him and lay back on the bed. "And why do the cops want Derrick? He was long gone before she bought it."

"I think it's just to clear up some loose ends. She was hanging with him earlier."

"Hanging hell, she went downstairs and gave him a hummer. He comes up with a big grin on his face and says, 'She gives good head.' I mean, this guy doesn't beat around the bush . . . or maybe I should say he *does* beat around the bush."

"What happened to all this purist Rasta bullshit?"

"Hey, he lives it and breathes it, but when some little chicky is pushing the pussy, Derrick is only human."

Sever stood up, picking up his tablet from the desk. He turned the chair around and sat at the desk, making notes.

"Oh, hell. Now don't be takin' notes on everything I say. This shit is strictly off-the-record. He's a good kid, Sever."

"He gets a blow job from this girl half an hour before his security guard kills her. What if he set it up? What if he doesn't want anyone to know that he's screwing the fans?"

"Hell, he told *me*, didn't he?"

"Yeah, but there's no one who was there to verify it. Was he intimate with the other girls? The ones who were killed?"

"I honestly don't know. I don't want to know. What the boys do is their business. Hell, I know I'm not gettin' any."

Sever checked his watch and reached for the television remote. He flipped it on, and the soft light of the screen welcomed him to greater Miami. The young woman on the screen told him that Miami was still the "fun-and-sun capital" of the world, and proceeded to go into detail, describing the nightlife, the restaurants, the entertainment. After a minute Sever flipped through the channels until he caught a local news segment. The funny little man with the big glasses and zigzag patterned tie was wrapping up the weather. He turned it over to the anchor, a typical hair-sprayed, tan thirty-year-old with capped teeth, who teased the next segment.

"And in other news, newspaper mogul Frankie Romano throws the last party for a Miami girl. No more parties for Sabrena Petrata. That story when we return."

Vane stubbed the cigar in the ashtray and stood, fists clenched by his side. "Well, I wanted the fucking publicity, and I suppose we'll get it."

Sever spun the chair around and straddled it once again, watching the commercial featuring a grizzly bear and a can of beer. He was remembering the other side of Miami, embodied in a T-shirt he'd seen only yesterday. The picture on the front was the barrel of a gun, pointed right at the viewer. Under the picture was the slogan SEE MIAMI LIKE A NATIVE.

Chapter Ten

When the sun was straight up in the sky, and the ocean breeze was blowing just right—just enough to drift through the smell of rotting seaweed, iodine, boiled shellfish, and fried foods—and the sky was a pale blue, not a Jamaican blue but a southern Florida blue, then Sever could almost buy into the life-style. And there were the stucco homes and the enclaves of gated communities, the red tile roofs so different from the wood and shingles of his native Chicago. Here, as in any area of the country, smell identified much of the city. Miami was the pungent odor of orange blossoms mixed with spicy Cuban fried pork, fresh fish, and chlorine. He drove the deep blue rental Chrysler with the top down, wondering if he could live in Miami. Maybe. But he preferred the lifestyle further down the Keys where things were a little more relaxed. A place he could go fishing and kick back. It played in the back of his mind that there was no one to kick back with.

The neighborhood was middle-class, Chevys and Chryslers sitting in the concrete driveways. The Hispanic girl's home was

one in a circle of homes, little turquoise pools dotting the back-
yards of the small cookie-cutter stucco houses. He knocked on
the door and waited patiently, listening to the frantic barking
from inside that announced his presence.

Slowly a woman opened the door, blinking into the bright
light from the noonday sun. The small dog growled behind her.
Her eyes were black and piercing and she appeared to have been
crying.

"Yes? What do you want?"

"I am very sorry to bother you, ma'am, but I'm a reporter,
and I was on the boat last night. I—"

"I've talked until I can't talk anymore." Her voice bore no
trace of emotion. She seemed to be drained of all feeling.

"I want to help find out why someone did this and—"

"Someone? The police told me they had the man in custody."

"They do. I know this is a terrible time for you, but was there
anyone else at the concert with her?"

"I told them." She pointed to a house on the circle. "Vicky
Morrow. They went to all the shows together. Wanted to see
Brandy, watched her TV show every week. They were hoping to
get backstage, and then she calls on the car phone and says they're
goin' to somebody's yacht, and me I'm sayin', 'You go, girl.' Can
you believe that? I felt good about it. Like my baby was hangin'
with the players. 'You go, girl.' " She looked pleadingly into his
face, her expressive eyes imploring him to bring her girl back
home.

He thanked her, expressed his condolences once again, and
left, wondering how a parent ever moves on after the death of a
child. His father would probably have done very well. He slowly
drove down the street, around the circle, pulling in behind an
older Chevy Blazer. Vicky Morrow's mother led him to the back-
yard, where her daughter sat in a lawn chair, watching a plastic

duck float in the in-ground pool. She smoked a cigarette and merely glanced up when he appeared, returning her gaze to the pool. She was a small girl, dark skinned with shoulder-length coal black hair. Her nose was just long enough to take her out of the model category, but she was an attractive young lady dressed in shorts and a T-shirt.

"You were with Sabrena last night. I'm trying to find out what happened. How did you get invited to the yacht?"

"The guy who killed her. He was working the crowd. He'd stop and talk to some girls and ask them if they wanted to go backstage and meet the band. Some said no, most of them said yes."

"You go to a lot of concerts?"

"With Sabrena. Yeah."

"And that happens a lot?"

"Sure. Sometimes we're not what they're looking for. But I think most of the time, if someone's got tits and an ass, they'll try to get them to come back."

"Is it always about sex?"

"They always ask."

"So you know what's expected?"

"I didn't say it was expected. I said they ask. I didn't say I *did* anything." She glanced at the house, squinting her eyes, then took a puff on the cigarette. She flicked the ash on the deck and looked back at the pool. "Sabrena thought the Jamaican guy was pretty hot."

"The guy who worked the crowd?"

"No. The lead singer, Derrick. She said he's got a dark side that she'd like to explore. So I guess she explored it."

"How old are you?" Sever watched her as she hesitated. She kept her eyes trained on the concrete pool deck, never looking up.

"We're both sixteen. I just got my driver's license about five months ago. Sabrena doesn't have hers yet. . . . Oh, God, she'll never have it, will she?" Her face crumbled and she quietly sobbed. Sever was quiet for a moment, as the girl tried to compose herself.

"I was on the boat for just a couple of minutes. It didn't feel right, the kind of people there, you know? So I told her we should split. But this Derrick guy, he'd already told her he'd like to get to know her a little better and he'd see she got back, so I drove home. I wish I'd never. If I'd stayed there, she'd be here and we'd be laughing about the stoned black dude who tried to get her into bed. Jeeze, I wish I'd stayed. God, why didn't I stay? She was my best friend."

"Vicky, you're sure the guy who picked you up was Roland Jamison, the guy accused of her murder?"

"Yeah. If it's the same guy whose picture's in the paper this morning. That's him. Jeeze, I wish I'd stayed." She paused, studied the burning tip of her cigarette, then looked at him with a teary wide-eyed stare. "You know what I just thought? Sabrena, she'll always be sixteen. Always." She broke down again, and Sever quietly made his way to the car.

Chapter Eleven

Kohls was adamant. "Fingerprints all over the place, Sever; blood holds fingerprints very well. This guy is all over the knife. We've got our killer. Hell, you walked in on him, what more do you want?" The squad room was warm and humid, the stale smell of old cigarettes permeating the walls, curtains, and furniture of the cramped quarters. Gunmetal gray desks were lined up three in a row, four rows deep, half of them occupied by detectives. Several were on the phone, some worked on laptops, and two of them sat, feet propped on a desk, reading the paper. On the wall was a white erasable board covered with black marker scrawls. One corner of the board seemed to be a crude map of a Miami suburb, another section listed last names, and in the far corner was an outline: 1) Perp says no one was home 2) Perp's wife says she was home 3) Victim is found in basement (a) storage closet . . .

"Harry, I *was* there and I saw his face. The guy was very confused, surprised. I don't think he understood what had happened."

"Look, Sever, I shouldn't tell you anything. This case is still open, but it's about to be closed. I got the same information you did. Roland is pimping for this Derrick guy. It's not much of a stretch to figure out why our suspect killed the girl. He picks 'em up, Derrick gets the blow job, and Roland wants some of the action. He did the work and he figures she owes him. When she refuses, he kills her. I think the murders in Jamaica are the same story."

"What do you know about the murders in Jamaica?"

"Not much, but we're looking into them." Stretching his large frame and scratching the back of his neck, Kohls stood up. "I appreciate your interest in the case, and I know you think I owe you. You may have helped solve the Job Jobiah case, but you also got in the way and fucked up a lot of good detective work. I've been asked to keep you at a distance on this one. We've got our boy, so back off."

"What about Derrick? Do you know where he is?"

"Oh, we'll interview him. The guy disappeared for twenty-four hours. That's not a lifetime. He'll show up."

"And what did Randy have to say?"

"The other bald brother? He's upset to say the least. His brother is looking at murder one, so of course he's not happy. If we hadn't caught the other one red-handed, I'd consider bringing him in, but we did catch the killer . . . and I'm convinced we've got enough to put him away for life. Do you know how often we never catch the killer? And do you know how many times we lose the suspect we have because we can't make a case? Come on, Sever! We've got this asshole dead to rights."

"Harry, you didn't see this guy when we walked in. He was frozen, like he'd just found the body. Just for the sake of argument, let's say he walks in, sees the girl already dead, picks up the knife, and Marna walks in on him. He panics, decides he's got to protect whoever killed Sabrena, slams the door shut as Marna starts screaming, and we walk in. Isn't that possible?"

"And Jesus walked on water. Hell, yes, it's possible, but it didn't happen that way."

"Why was the door shut?"

"The way I figure it, he was going to kill this Marna too. He slams it shut and it's a good thing you guys got down there when you did." Kohls grabbed Sever's elbow, steering him toward the door. "Now, you leave it to your Miami PD, Sever. We'll take care of this little mess. You can write about it, you can tell your friends about it, you can go on television and tell the world about it, but I don't want you interfering in the investigation. If you do, then you might become a part of it. Understood?"

"I think he was protecting somebody. Maybe one of the band members. I saw these guys on Romano's yacht. A lot of women were making some serious plays for them. And I think you've got to look at Randy and Derrick. Hell, you're not going to get a time on this killing. It all happened within two hours, the murder and the finding of the body. With a two-hour window, it could have been anybody on that boat."

"Could have been you! Now, get out of here, I've got work to do."

Sever took a deep breath, wishing he had a cigarette. "Harry, I hope you're right, but if you're not, I'll be around to say I told you so." He walked out of the police station, blinking his eyes in the harsh Miami sun, thinking that he'd love to walk away and leave the investigation to the friendly, charming Miami PD, but he couldn't. Once an idea got into his head, it wouldn't leave and this idea was just getting a full head of steam.

Chapter Twelve

When Denise let him in, Marna was sitting up on the couch, looking fresh and very pretty. She'd applied some makeup and her high cheekbones, dark eyes and lips were striking. The television was on in the corner of the small living room and she was gazing intently at Rosie O'Donnell as the talk-show hostess talked to a hand puppet from some children's show. She glanced up and gave him a wide smile.

"Mr. Sever, my favorite scribe."

He returned the smile. "Bobby suggested I bring you back."

"First, I should thank you for saving my life."

"I don't know if I'd go that far. I do know you've got a very loud voice."

Just for a second she closed her eyes, composing herself. "I have never seen a dead person before. I don't really remember much after I walked in." She tossed off the white afghan that covered her and he noticed the bright, patchwork, multicolored blouse, open at the throat, and her tight black pants, hugging her hips and legs. Again, Sever wished for twenty-five years.

"You seem to be doing much better. Ready to head back to the hotel?"

"Yeah. That would be nice. Bobby said he'd send Randy, but under the circumstances . . ."

"Have you heard from Derrick?"

"No, but he'll show up. He goes away like that. He meditates."

"He gets stoned."

"You don't understand. He meditates. It's his inspiration for writing."

"You two were having a major argument last night, half an hour before . . ."

"Oh, yes. We have those from time to time. He wanted to leave even before the introduction. I told him he had to stay, to mingle with the crowd. As you have already seen, Mr. Sever, Derrick is not a social person."

"Can you call me Mick?"

"Mick? No. Not now. Maybe later." Brushing a strand of fine black hair from her face, she looked back at the screen. Rosie was droning on about her next guest, hopefully a human being this time.

"I don't know you yet, Mr. Sever. And you don't know me."

"Did you see Roland stab the girl?"

"No. I don't think so. They asked me that this morning. I opened the door and he was standing there, the knife in his hand. I didn't see him move. I remember screaming. I think I was afraid he would kill me next."

Denise appeared in the doorway, an overnight bag in her hand. "Marna, it was so nice to have you stay for a night."

"And you, what a wonderful hostess. Thank you so much for putting up with me." They briefly hugged, then Marna took the bag and walked to the door.

And those black pants seemed just a little tighter than necessary. Sever opened the door and they walked to the car, Marna easing herself into the convertible.

"I did hear from him," she said meekly.

"Oh?"

"He told me to keep it to myself, but he got the phone number from Bobby . . . so they know he's okay."

"And?"

"And he was meditating. He read about the girl in the paper this morning. He was very surprised."

Sever drove slowly around the circular drive and pulled out onto the main road. The hotel was fifteen minutes away if the traffic was light, and the traffic didn't appear to be light at all. "Surprised she was killed, or surprised at the killer?" He kept his eyes on the road, aware that she was fidgeting with her fingers, clasping and unclasping them as she talked about the singer.

"I don't think he knew the girl. But Roland and Randy have been friends of his for years. He was concerned about what would happen to Roland."

Sever took a right and passed an upscale shopping area with a street mall to their left. He noticed the Gap, and a Starbucks coffee as they drove by. He wondered if Marna had ever tasted Starbucks, and if it even came close to Jamaican coffee.

"Marna, do Roland and Randy pick up girls for the band on a regular basis?" He was fishing.

She folded her hands together and bit her lip. Silent for a moment, she seemed not to have heard him. Finally she spoke. "I don't know you, Mr. Sever, and so I should not share my thoughts with you. Derrick is a strong person, and as I have mentioned to you, he is filled with purpose and passion. His beliefs are strong, yet I believe that he and the other musicians succumb to temptation like all mortals."

Sever turned his head and studied her face. Her bright eyes narrowed, and her brow creased. "It's not what I asked you, but apparently you are aware that Derrick spent some time with the young lady."

She said nothing.

"You know the guys in the band. Isn't it possible that someone else was with that girl? Maybe she decided she didn't want any more . . . attention, and she refused them? Maybe James? He seems to have a darker side."

She raised her eyes. "James is new to the band. I don't know much about him. He and Derrick tend to quarrel . . . about music style . . . and his moment in the sun."

The odor of boiled cabbage was in the air as they passed through a Puerto Rican neighborhood with small restaurants and food shops on both sides of the narrow street. The cabbage odor was mingled with a sweet smell, like shrimp boiled in beer. The late afternoon sun still cooked the pavement and bounced off the hood of his car, glaring onto the windshield.

"His moment?"

"Mr. Sever, Derrick is very . . ." she paused, searching for the right word, "charismatic. Some of the band members feel he overshadows them. That doesn't mean that they are killers."

He tried again. "Do you think Roland was drunk? On drugs?"

"Ganja. Nothing more. Derrick would not stand for anything stronger. They would be off the tour."

He pushed the sleeves back on his shirt, the breeze from the moving car providing only a small relief from the humid heat. "As of last night, he's off the tour anyway."

Again she was silent. Then in a small voice that was almost a whisper she said, "Yes. And maybe now we can lay these killings to rest."

Chapter Thirteen

Dreadlocks represent the roots of the Rastafarian faith. When a white man wears dreads, when a nonbeliever wears them, it angers me. But when a Rastafarian shaves his head, I believe he has forsaken his faith. Roland shaved his head. He has forsaken Ras Tafari and Jah." Derrick sat by the pool, his deep green eyes focusing on the interviewer from Channel Seven. His white T-shirt sported a yellow banner touting Shabba Ranks, a Jamaican singer. The young reporter leaned in and held Derrick's gaze.

"Did you believe that Roland was capable of murder?"

"He has forsaken Jah. With no faith in a higher being, there be no laws to the lower land. Then I believe a man is capable of anything."

Sever watched intently. He glanced at Vane, who stood stoically, grasping a bottle of Red Stripe beer, his lips pressed tightly together.

"The police have interviewed you and your other security guard, Randy, the suspect's brother. Can you share with us anything that was said?"

For a moment Derrick seemed ready to speak, his mouth open and his expressive eyes looking beyond the reporter and camera technician. Then he closed his mouth and his eyes lost their fire. He shook his head and rose from the pool chair. It appeared the interview was over. He strolled to the hotel door and disappeared into the lobby.

"Well, it hasn't been a walk in the park." Vane slugged down the remainder of his drink and banged the bottle on a vacant table. Sunbathers who had gathered to watch the interview ambled back to their seats and towels, more interested in their week's worth of tan than any more news of a high society murder.

"Marna didn't see the murder." A little girl in a pink one-piece bathing suit jumped into the pool, splashing drops of water on Sever's deck shoes.

"Marna doesn't know what she saw. She was in shock."

"She's pretty sure about the fact that she didn't see the murder take place."

Vane shook a cigarette from his pack and lit it with a gold lighter. "And what does that prove? What's your point?"

"We didn't see Roland kill that girl either."

"Come on, Mick, where is this going?"

"I don't think Roland killed her. I think he walked in on a dead body."

"So who the . . . oh, no! You don't think that Derrick—"

"I don't know. I think somebody else killed her, and it could have been anyone on that boat. And there are several members of the band that come to mind. James seems to have a sinister side to him, and I get strange vibrations from Flame. And then there's your moneymaker, Derrick."

"Derrick? He couldn't have done it. Peace and Love. Couldn't do it." He sucked in a lungful of smoke and slowly exhaled, shaking his head rapidly.

"Bobby, I know it's just a thought and you're the last person I should share it with, but what if he has a real problem with these women being as free and easy as they are? And after he has his little fling, he becomes God's hit man."

"Jesus! Mick, what the hell? 'God's hit man'? What the fuck have you been smoking?"

Someone's cell phone rang and Vane started patting his pockets. He found the small black fold-up phone in his back pocket and snapped it open. "Vane here. . . . Yeah, he's clean. They just wanted to clear up some details. . . . Well, yeah, of course we talked last night but in light of everything that's happened . . ." He tapped the ashes onto the concrete deck, his breath coming in short gasps. "Well, I can only tell you that I agree. Gotta strike while the iron's hot. . . . I told you, I represent them. If I say it's a go, then it's a go. . . . Well, I say it's a go. We can talk tonight over drinks. . . . Before dinner then. And to you." He snapped the phone shut and stared off into space, the cigarette almost burning his fingers. He dropped it, stubbed it out with his toe, and turned to Sever. "Derrick and the Laments, Mick. Fuckin' Mega recording artists. They wanta' sign 'em on our terms. They figure the national exposure of the murder will do nothing but help sales. How about that, huh?"

Sever wiped perspiration from his brow. "Well, at least the girl didn't die in vain."

"Hey, Mick, we take what we can get. Turnin' lemons into lemonade or some such shit. Be happy for us, Mick. We've got a record deal."

Chapter Fourteen

Sever lay back on the bed, working the pillow under his neck until it felt just right, the phone cocked between his shoulder and ear and a tablet resting on his upraised knees. One ring. He hadn't talked to her in maybe three months. Two rings. It was always awkward at first, they'd been so close, then the dam would open up and they'd talk for hours about all kinds of . . . three rings.

"Hello? Mick!"

"How did you do that?"

"Caller ID. I heard you were in Florida. Now who calls me this late at night from a motel in Miami?"

"I hope nobody."

"Protecting me, or just jealous?"

"Probably a little of both. Always has been a little of both."

"So you're back in the thick of it."

"Well . . ." He sketched a cartoon face on the tablet, a little man's face with big eyes and teardrops rolling down his cheeks.

"A lot of things happen on Frankie's boat, don't they?"

"At least we're both alive, Ginny. The young girl last night didn't get off so easily."

"No show tonight?" She kept on moving, the reporter's instinct still in her blood.

"No. They canceled the show in Tampa. Police spent the day questioning the group and 'suggested' that we all stay in town for twenty-four hours. It was a pretty strong suggestion."

"Lots of refunds and a pissed-off promoter."

"Yeah, I suppose. You've got to admit a murder is a pretty good reason to cancel."

"Mick, you called just to shoot the crap?"

He glanced at the television screen. A black-and-white Jackie Gleason and Art Carney were yelling at each other, but the sound was turned down and their animated antics were even funnier without words. *The Honeymooners.* One of the sound stages had been somewhere in Miami. He remembered his dad, sitting in his easy chair, beer in hand, laughing out loud at Gleason and Carney and Audrey Meadows. And Gleason always closing that show saying something like "And as always, Miami Beach has the greatest audiences in the world." Something like that. He'd turn up the volume at the end of the show and listen to the exact words.

"Mick?"

"Remember when I did the piece about Marley?" He poised his pencil over the tablet.

"Sure. I edited that piece for you. I think I may have done some of the research. I was doing a lot of that while you were out doing your own research."

He ignored the jab. "So give me your best abbreviated version of Rastafarians."

"Jeeze, Mick, it's not easy to abbreviate."

"Give it a shot. I need some background here and I need some help refreshing my memory."

"Well, it has to do with millions of Africans kidnapped by European and Arab slave traders. This goes back, I don't know, centuries ago. Now I'm probably not going to get all this right, but there was also an exiling of supporters of Solomon and Sheba. So all these people are sold off to the Europeans and Arabs."

"To become slaves?"

"And, of course, as all good people of the white race, the Europeans used Christianity to justify the slavery. They captured them, sold them, and tortured them to teach them the Christian way of life."

"We're an outstanding group of people. So far I remember all of this." Sever wrote down key words. *One hundred million? Europeans and Arab slave traders. Solomon and Sheba. Christianity.*

"But it backfired. When the slaves learned to read, they read the Bible. And they figured out that in the Book of Genesis there is reference to a river flowing from the Garden of Eden. It separated into four parts, and one of those parts flowed over Ethiopia. Wow! This is coming back to me."

"Yeah. And then, the slaves started wondering . . . if Ethiopia was part of the Garden of Eden, cradle of mankind, how could the Ethiopians be inferior to whites when man originated in *their* native country. So it really is a race thing." Sever wrote faster now.

"So you remember some of this too?" she asked. "Here they are, slaves all over Europe, and all the people in Africa are under the domination of white people, except, except for Ethiopia. Ethiopia is still the bastion of African independence and pride."

There was a knock at the motel room door. "Ginny, hold on for just a second. I've got someone at the door." He stood up and opened the door. The uniformed bellman held a tray draped with a large cloth.

"Mr. Sever? Your dinner, sir."

Sever set it on the table by the window, tipped the man five dollars, and brought the phone and tablet to the table.

"I'm sorry."

"So what are you having?"

"You tell me," Sever said.

"A small steak, cooked rare, a house salad with a side of ranch, maybe a potato and a bottle of red wine. Cabernet?"

He lifted the cloth. The steak was still steaming, the dressing looked a little runny, the lettuce was firm, and the cabernet was a deep red. "Damn."

"Anyway, coming to the end of my recollection, Ras Tafari is crowned king of Ethiopia somewhere around 1930. He changed his name to Haile Selassie. He's emperor of a throne that's over three thousand years old. Oldest empire in the world. So African Christians all over the world start looking at the scriptures and prophesies."

"Mumbo jumbo."

"Not to them, Mick. God told his people that because they sinned, he would scatter them to the four corners of the earth. They would be ruled by a foreign power and be servants of other nations. When, and if, they finally returned to him, he promised to reunite the family of David and Solomon and he would set up his promised kingdom on earth and as soon as they got their act together, they were all invited."

"And Haile Selassie was the sign that all this was about to happen?"

"Ras Tafari, alias Haile Selassie, had an attitude. Dignity, discipline of character, purpose, mission, and by all accounts a great leader. But I don't think he ever bought into the fact that people started worshiping him. He was emperor of Ethiopia. That was it."

"But it's a Christian religion. Right?" He cut off a piece of the hotel steak, a little tough, a little overcooked for his taste.

"Mick, I can hear you chewing. Now I'm going to have to get out of this warm bed and make myself a cold ham sandwich or something. You made me hungry."

"Hungry? Any other passions I've stirred?"

Ginny ignored him. "They believe in Jesus. They believe that Jesus was the savior and that he was dark skinned."

"Yeah, and I remember . . . they reject with a vengeance Michelangelo's painting representing Jesus and Mary with blond hair and blue eyes. The biggest part of the race issue is that they feel the white man is inferior; that *we're* second-class citizens, yet *we* continue to run things."

"Sure. They feel that to this day—that their dignity has been taken away because of the world's belief that Jesus was a white man."

"They believe in Christianity and they believe that Haile Selassie was the sign that they could go home again." Sever chewed another bite of steak.

"They believe that Ethiopia will be God's kingdom on earth. A true Rastafarian leads a very pure life and is very dedicated to the cause. Now that's as much as I can remember."

He finished his notes. "So they use biblical references to prove whatever point they want to make. I remember they have numerous references to herbs, so they figured God wants them to smoke grass."

"Mick, if people really believe in something, they find ways to make it work."

Sever was quiet. A barely audible hiss came through the receiver, mingled with her breathing from several thousand miles away.

"Mick?"

"And I didn't believe in us enough to find a way, right?"

"I wasn't even going there. We both made mistakes." Now she was quiet. They both waited, letting the moments pass uncomfortably as the three years had passed before. "Sometimes I wonder what you do believe in."

"It's funny you'd bring that up right now," Sever said. "I'm starting to wonder the same thing. I'm just going through the motions anymore. It's like this vicious cycle. Maybe it's just old age. I'm tired of what I'm doing, but I can't stop. I mean, I can't."

"Maybe you just need a little R and R."

"Got something in mind?" He smiled, thinking about the last time they'd seen each other. The marriage might have dissolved, but the chemistry was still alive.

"You know that can't be good for either of us. However, I just finished an assignment for the *Trib*, and if you need some help, well . . ."

"Let me call you tomorrow. I'll do an outline of what I've got so far and see if another great mind can help."

"They've got the killer, don't they?"

"They've got a suspect. I don't think it's the killer. I think what they've got is an innocent, confused young man."

"Mick, be careful."

"Yeah. I'll call tomorrow. G'night."

He hung up the phone, poured a glass of the deep red wine, and pushed the rest of the meal aside. Stretching his stiff knee, he eased out of the chair and hobbled to the window. Sometimes the pain was severe, sometimes it was barely noticeable, but it was always there. From thousands of miles away the moon poured light onto the parking lot, flooding the blacktop with a late-night iridescence. At a distance he could see the colored mist of neon lights as they reflected off the atmospheric haze. He thought of Ginny, sitting in the apartment in Chicago eating her cold ham sandwich. He needed some distance, some room for reflection. There was nothing keeping him here, nothing at all. Nothing except he needed to get the final story. That and the fact that Miami Beach had the greatest audiences in the world. *Shit!* He glanced back at the television. *The Honeymooners* was over. He never had heard Gleason's last line.

Chapter Fifteen

The studio was cramped, with a small control room behind the glass wall, out in front of which four musicians gathered around a keyboard. With headphones on, they listened to the playback. Bass, keyboards, and drums. The rhythm track matched the click track, an electronic metronome that kept the rhythm in perfect time. From the control room Sever watched James, Rick, Flame, and Sudahd bobbing and weaving with the beat.

"Mega needs two more cuts for the CD, and we've got two more days off. Timing works for me." Bobby Vane sat on a high stool with casters, his enormous bulk spilling over the seat. He slurped at a glass of ginger ale and rocked back and forth on the fragile-looking stool.

"Who wrote the song?" Sever asked.

"Derrick. Who else?"

"Have you heard the lyrics?" Sever stood by the glass wall, a sheet of paper in his hand.

"What? Can they be any worse than the ones about killing his sister?"

"Maybe more of the same. Listen to this." He read from the paper. " 'The one woman lonely who gives up her soul and takes others with her to hell in her hole/The time and the race, the time and the place, the longer it takes to look God in the face.' Pretty heavy stuff."

"And what the hell does it all mean, Mick? It means they knock out one more and we've got our record deal. I did tell him to do somethin' a little more soft, like that 'Moonlight Lady.' That's the kind of song that's gonna break out right away."

Sever lay the paper on the control board, an eight-foot-long panel with slides and switches and multicolored lights that bounced with the music. The engineer, a twenty-something black man with rough stubble on his face, adjusted the slides, tweaking the bass and sweetening the mix in the control room.

"Derrick doesn't like women. I think there's a real issue here."

"Oh, shit, Mick, give it a rest. Roland killed the girls. Snoop Dog advocated killing cops. He hasn't been implicated in any cop killings. Eminem did numbers about whacking his wife and mother, and last I heard they were alive and kicking. Shit, Johnny Cash sang about shooting a man in Reno, just to watch him die. Have they arrested him yet? What's the drama here? I told you, Derrick has a strong sense of what sells. He's not the fanatic that you want to make him. It's an image thing. We get this record out, we'll see how it plays. Hell, he'll probably be doing *Hollywood Squares* in another six months. Let's get this thing behind us."

The engineer faded the rhythm track, marking the time on a computer screen. He flipped on his microphone. "Okay guys, let's lay a guitar track down. Uh . . . Sudahd, right? Got a feel for this? What kind of sound we want? I hear something that lays in the background and gives it an edge. Don't want something that overwhelms. When Derrick lays the vocals down, I don't want to fight it with the guitar. Do we agree?"

Sudahd picked up his Les Paul Gibson with the bright flame burst pattern in the wood and strapped it on. Once again the engineer played the rhythm track back as the guitarist ran through the piece. Sever had sat in on hundreds of sessions. One track could be done in three minutes, or it might take all night. He sipped from a cold Styrofoam cup of coffee and watched for several seconds. Then he folded the lyric sheet, stuffed it in his shirt pocket, and nodded to Vane.

"I'll see you later. I've got to call an old friend."

Vane was again rocking on his seat, keeping time with the music. The stool was in grave danger of breaking down. Sever walked out into the sweltering Miami heat.

A bank of dark clouds threatened the skyline as he looked to the west. A little rain might help cool things down just a bit. Sever started the convertible and pulled into traffic, letting the top down with the push of a button. The four lanes were busy with rush hour traffic, rush hour being almost any time between 7:00 A.M. and 7:00 P.M. in this overcrowded city. The bright red Firebird in the next lane pulled close and Sever slowed down, easing off the gas.

The Firebird slowed and stayed inches from his side, matching the speed. The driver behind Sever laid on the horn and Sever checked his rearview mirror, watching as the car edged up, and an agitated driver nearly locked bumpers with his convertible. He glanced to the right through the passenger window and saw his reflection in the mirrored window of the Firebird.

Now the red car eased closer, bumping his rental unit. Shit!

What was this all about? The car pulled away, then swung back and hit him harder. The rental car shuddered. Sever gripped the wheel, for safety, for fear, feeling the strain in his arm and back muscles. Semis bore down on the traffic to his left with only a thin median strip between.

He grasped the wheel, his fingers aching from the force, as the driver behind the dark windows bumped him again. Another shudder. Forty miles an hour and it seemed like he was flying! No break in the flow of cars and trucks, the semis just across the concrete as the Firebird hit him again, the grating crunch of metal on metal causing a shiver to race down his spine.

Somebody was trying to kill him. He hung on, wishing he could push the pedal to the floor.

There was no room in the front, just a Land Rover about thirty feet tall hogging the view, and behind him was the same road-raged maniac now bumping him lightly to let him know he was not happy with the slow pace and erratic driving.

For a second the tension seemed to ease and for no apparent reason the crowded cars seemed to separate. Sever grabbed a breath, only then realizing he hadn't breathed in a long time.

Picking up the pace, the Firebird drifted to the right, still matching Sever's speed. Frantically, Sever searched for a break in the traffic, slowing down again to the total exasperation of the rear driver, who lay on his blaring horn with no rest. The temptation to give him the finger was strong, but the will to hold onto the steering wheel was even stronger.

He breathed in short spurts, his heart beating hard and fast.

The Firebird slowed with him, the reflecting windows mocking every move he made. Glancing in the rearview mirror again, he noticed the angry driver, one hand on the horn, the other extended from his window with his middle finger flying.

The driver had eased back just slightly, and Sever stomped

on the brakes, hearing the squeal of tires up to ten cars back as drivers fought to gain control of their vehicles. The Firebird missed the sudden decrease in acceleration and was slightly ahead. Sever spun the wheel, pressed the accelerator, and shot in behind the bright red car, aiming right for the exit thirty feet straight ahead. He raced up the slight bank, watching the rearview mirror as the Firebird tried to brake, missed the turn, and was rear-ended by a Toyota pickup. The audible crunch reverberated in his ears. He raced down to the light, ran it red, and pulled over into a strip mall parking lot.

He sat stunned for sixty seconds, his hands still wrapped tightly around the vinyl-coated steering wheel. Then he wearily climbed out to inspect the damage. The right side of his convertible was scraped and bruised, dented and dinged, with deep red scratches in the door. The credit card he'd used to rent the car would cover the insurance. He'd pissed someone off, either on the road or somewhere else, and he had no idea who or why. He started up again and swung into a gas station, asked for some side street directions to the motel, and pulled into the lot thirty minutes later. Sever was still shaking when he entered the motel.

Inside, the message light was flashing. He stripped off his sweat-stained shirt and sat on the edge of the bed, punching in the numbers for the voice-mail system.

"Hi, Mick. I'm coming to Miami whether you want to see me or not. I've got five days and I thought I'd go down to the Keys. Remember the Keys? Anyway, I'll be at the airport at ten A.M. tomorrow morning. If you're there, great. If you're not, I'll rent a car and head down by myself. Either way, Mick." Click. Ginny was on her way.

Sever stood up and walked by the closet mirror. For a second he stopped and looked at the reflection of his figure. Genetics. For all his boozing and carousing, his father had always appeared to be in pretty good shape. Mick still had a pretty good physique. Oh, he'd added several pounds over the last ten years but carried it well. Tight stomach, good pecs, and not much exercise. He had a punching bag and gloves at the apartment in Chicago, and he could go a round or two with Billy Dukes back at the Bayfront Gym, but he wasn't home often enough to do much more. He pulled off the slacks, socks, and underwear and ran a shower. The hot, steamy water pulled the ache and strain from his tired body and he stood still and let it beat relentlessly on his skin. He should call the cops, but the Miami cops weren't that friendly with him right now. He'd had some pretty unflattering things to say about them in the book. He decided to leave it alone. If the run-in was an isolated incident, then it was over. If it had some deeper significance, then he'd hear about it soon enough.

Ginny. Did he want to involve her, and would there be any . . . of course there would. Then again, there was this distant little dream that maybe Marna would get past the Mr. Sever shit and maybe there could be a little fling with the Jamaican girl young enough to be his . . . sister. He smiled, turned off the water, stepped out of the tub, and dried himself. Some maniac had tried to run him off the road today—tried to kill him—and he was trying to figure out which woman held the most immediate promise in his life. He wondered if all guys were as fucked up about women and sex as he was. He wasn't sure, but most of the ones he knew were. Maybe women were his passion—or his addiction. Or maybe passion and addiction were linked together. He pulled on a clean pair of khakis, opened his laptop, and started writing.

Chapter Sixteen

Miami International Airport was truly international. Every country in the world seemed to be represented, except possibly the United States. Spanish was being spoken almost everywhere, with some Italian over there, Chinese back there, Russian in the corner and the counter girl at the newsstand didn't seem to understand any of it. He paid for his *Florida Sun Coast* and walked down to gate C18. Scanning the front page, he found no mention of the murder, just over one day old and yesterday's news. Romano had been careful not to give it much space that first morning, worrying about his reputation, but he had run a small story on page one. With no new developments, the story had slipped into obscurity. He eased into a vinyl seat in the long back row facing the gate and perused the rest of the paper. Page three in the second section had a short article saying that the Brandy concert had been canceled and that the next stop would be in Fort Lauderdale in two days. The show was a sellout and there was speculation that it, too, might be called off. The final paragraph mentioned that Derrick and the Laments had been signed to Mega Records, with the release of their first CD expected in six weeks. The title was expected to be *Perfect Justice in an Imperfect World*.

Sever laid the paper down, clasped his hands behind his head, and closed his eyes. He pictured the moment that Romano shoved opened the door. He first saw the shaved head of Roland, moved down to his broad shoulders and powerful biceps bulging beneath the tight white T-shirt, on down the arms to his right hand, holding the bloody knife. Then he glanced at Marna, her mouth wide open, sobbing in terror. He turned off the sound in his head, just watching the action. He pictured her brightly flowered dress and hair hanging at her shoulders. His imaginary gaze switched back to Roland, turning slowly now, the look of confusion and surprise on his face. Something was not right. He concentrated on the face, then saw the upper body, the bone-handled knife clenched tightly in his fist. Thick red blood on the hand, on the handle, and a swipe of red on the shirt. That was it! The young girl had been stabbed multiple times, and there was only a streak of red on the shirt. Blood spattered all over the bedspread, soaking the covers, blanket, and sheet. He could see it. No blood spattered on the shirt. He knew Harry Kohls and the rest of the detectives had noticed it, but everything else pointed to the security guard, so Roland was the main suspect. It didn't seem right.

Sever opened his eyes. He walked to the cluster of phones by a newsstand and dropped in thirty-five cents, calling a number he'd committed to heart.

"Harry Kohls, homicide." The voice reeked of boredom.

"Kohls, this is Mick Sever."

"Oh, shit. Sever, I told you, leave it alone."

"Harry, I've got to ask you this. Your suspect had on a white T-shirt. Isn't it strange that there was no blood spattered on it?"

Kohls was silent. Sever could almost hear the wheels turning in his analytical mind. "All right, hotshot, I'll go this far. We're looking into that."

Sever took his turn at being silent. Sometimes an embarrassing silence caused the subject to blurt out information he normally wouldn't divulge. There was no more information forthcoming. "So there should have been more blood on the shirt?"

"I said we're looking into that. We feel we've got the killer. Minor details, Sever. Now, I've got some paperwork here that is demanding my attention. Maybe you can help me. Seven across. The same word for a music journalist and the rear end of a domestic animal. Got any ideas?"

"Harry, could it have been someone else?"

"Drop it, Sever." A click and the phone went dead.

As he dropped the phone in the cradle, the Puerto Rican attendant announced, in Spanish, the arrival of flight 3867 from Chicago. As an afterthought, she announced the arrival in English as well. At least it sounded like English.

She walked through the doorway, silken blond hair brushed back, a summer-tan glow on her face and bare arms. Her garment bag was slung over her shoulder and her simple white knit top and black slacks accented her perfect figure. Sever was aware of the eyes watching her arrival, picking her above all the others to gaze at. Men and women, wondering who the lady was, and wishing she was with them. He let her make the entrance, giving the voyeurs their cheap thrills, her eyes searching for him and making contact with dozens of wishful spectators. The anticipation grew by the second, waiting for her recognition.

"Mick!" She quickened her pace and he stepped forward to meet her. She smiled mischievously, as if she knew the game and knew she'd been part of it. Ginny dropped the bag and threw her arms around his neck, hugging him and planting a big kiss on his lips.

Slowly they separated, Sever picking up the bag and grabbing her hand with his free one. They walked down the aisle, past the newsstand, the yogurt shop, the luggage store, and the duty-free shop. There were no words exchanged, just a gentle squeeze of hands.

Chapter Seventeen

The breathy, sultry trumpet of Miles Davis left the stereo and filled the air, escaping into the atmosphere as she leaned back on the leather seat and let the wind blow through her hair.

"Got yourself back into the thick of it again? And you tell me you're tired and you want to go home. Hell, Mick, this *is* your home."

He glanced at her, marveling at the soft skin with just a hint of fine, featherlike lines around the eyes. Full lips, long eyelashes; she could have been a fashion model or the girl next door. Instead she was the ex-wife. It hurt sometimes. "I can't put it down. Somebody on that boat has killed three women, and I really believe they've got the wrong man."

"It's nice being just a writer. You don't have to deal with the facts, like a reporter or a cop. You can act on a hunch, and your hunches have been pretty good in the past."

"And when they're not, you've been there to straighten me out."

She grinned, looking like a playful tomboy. "Tell me all about it. And start looking for a restaurant that serves good steak. You owe me, buddy boy, you owe me."

Ten minutes later Sever pulled into a Lone Star Steak House. "You're going to eat steak at eleven in the morning?" he asked as they entered.

"It seems to me you were eating steak at eleven P.M. a couple of nights ago. Order me the rib eye sandwich, medium rare, and a house salad—"

"With ranch on the side."

"I'm going to freshen up." She walked to the restroom as the hostess took him to a booth.

"The girl, Marna?" She had pushed half the sandwich and the fries aside twenty minutes ago, her passion for beef satisfied. As always, she was caught up in the story and the intricacies of the plot.

"No. She was freaked. Somebody else. Somebody either takes the girl below—"

"Derrick."

"Well, I think there's a strong possibility, but *somebody* takes her below and kills her then leaves the boat, or Roland stabs her multiple times in the chest and never gets one ounce of blood on his white shirt."

"Except the streak."

"Except the streak. It looked like maybe he'd wiped his hand on the shirt but it wasn't the kind of spatter you'd expect."

"And now you're an expert on blood spatter?"

"Ginny, even Kohls admits it doesn't fit. But you know Harry Kohls. He wants to wrap this up, and since Roland was holding the murder weapon above the girl . . ."

"It looks like a pretty solid case."

Sever pushed his salad around with a fork, staring at the lettuce leaves and tomato like they were tea leaves and he was expecting to see the future among them.

"But it's not. It's not a solid case at all."

"All right, Mick, I see it through your eyes. If you're right, this Derrick is succumbing to the charms of the band's groupies, and afterwards feels remorse and guilt. He decides these evil women are responsible for delaying heaven on earth, so he kills them."

"That sounds dumber than hell."

"And your point is . . ."

"Why am I even worrying about this?"

"Because you can't let it go, remember?"

"You know, you have a way of breaking ideas down to their simplest form."

"I'm a damned fine editor. It's what I do."

"All right, and you do it well, but let's go back to our phone conversation a couple of nights ago." The waitress brought a pot of decaf and freshened both cups with the steamy watered-down beverage.

"When I gave you the Cliff's Notes on the Rastafarian religion?"

"Yeah." He sipped the hot coffee. "I don't understand the culture, but if what you said is true, Rastafarians believe that heaven on earth is a reality only when the chosen people get their act together. Women with loose morals don't have their act together."

"Oh! And the musicians who seduce these underage females do?"

"Don't go there. We've both been there and it's not good for the relationship."

Ginny gritted her teeth, took a deep breath, and was quiet.

"I'm not saying that Derrick is rational, I'm just suggesting that he—"

"Isn't rational. Okay, I can buy into that. Too much weed, he's a little whacked out, and ... and he's a guy. Guys tend to justify their own sexual cravings, but can't tolerate similar desires in their women."

"Yes! That's where I'm coming from."

"Surprise. You'll never change, will you? You actually sympathize with this guy."

Sever paused. He could use a drink, a cigarette, maybe some cocaine. She did this to him. She knew the deepest darkest part of him, and it was the part he wished didn't exist.

"I don't sympathize with him. I understand him."

"Mick, I'm sorry. Too much history. I'm really glad to be here, and I'm glad you're confiding in me. You know I want to help. It's just that, damn it, we've got way too much history."

"I know it every time you finish one of my sentences." Sever picked up the cup of coffee and took another sip. Weak.

"So Derrick is the perfect suspect."

He looked into her blue eyes. Like clear deep water. "Yeah, perfect. But it could have been any one of fifty people on that boat."

"But no one else had an intimate relationship with her."

"I don't know that. The band was being hustled by a lot of women. I watched Rick go after a married lady, and I have a gut feeling that something about Flame doesn't make sense, but I only know what supposedly happened to Derrick."

"Mick, you're doing a story on the band, yet you've only talked to Derrick. Why not interview everyone in the group ... not about the murder, but about the excitement of coming to the States. About the thrill of finally landing a recording contract. It seems to me that you need to talk to the entire group and get a feel for what they're thinking. Maybe someone else in the band suspects Derrick too, but no one's asked their opinion. Come on, you're a writer. Get to the heart of this story and write."

Sever flipped over the check. Without looking at it, he reached into his pocket, pulled out his wallet, and laid his American Express card on the table. Experience had taught him the waitress would pick it up in thirty minutes or less. She surprised him by showing up in less than thirty seconds, picking up the card, and returning in another minute, to await his signature. He added a twenty-five percent tip and leaned across the table.

"Ginny, I know why we broke up. After this conversation, I know the reason. We were totally wrong for each other." He paused, thinking about the statement. "And I have no idea why we broke up. After this conversation, I have no idea. We were perfect for each other."

"One reason, Mick, was that I never understood you; I still don't. But you're still a challenge. A real challenge." She reached across the table and grasped his hand. When she looked into his eyes, it was like the last three years had disappeared and they were on top of the world.

Chapter Eighteen

He left her in the room down the hall, close enough if they wanted to be close, but separate. She kissed him on the cheek, then went in to freshen up. He asked her to leave dinner open and she nodded. "Something light. That steak for lunch still feels a little heavy," she said.

Sever rang Vane's room, surprised to find him in. "Bobby, what are the chances of talking to Randy?"

"Is this more of that 'Derrick might be dirty' shit?"

"Randy is Roland's brother. He and Roland were apparently hustling honeys for the boys backstage. I'd like to get his thoughts on what might have happened, okay?"

"Look, Mick, the cops have talked to him and every one of the guys. You might be a hot-shit journalist, but don't let the last book go to your head. You're not gonna solve every crime that comes down the pike."

"Give me twenty minutes with him. And Bobby, I'd like to interview the band, one at a time. You said it yourself, Mega Records thinks the publicity will help sell more records. So let

me help the publicity machine." Sever fiddled with the lock on
the in-room refrigerator, jiggling the key until it opened. He
scanned the bottles, chocolate bars, and peanuts, then settled for
a green bottle of San Pellegrino sparkling water. Glancing at the
list taped to the outside, he noticed the price was five dollars.
"Besides, I need to sell another story. I've got to pay for this
damned hotel somehow."

"It's against my better judgment," Vane said. "Daddy always
said, 'Never get into bed with the press.'"

"Oh, hell, your daddy was a limo driver. He never dealt with
the press in his life." Sever swallowed fifty cents' worth of the
water. "I'm not trying to build a case here. It's just that I haven't
talked to the other guys, and . . ."

"The young guy at the front desk told me you came in with
a beautiful blonde. Virginia's in town, am I right? And during a
discussion with your lovely ex, she suggested that maybe you
should do a little more background on the band. Tell me I'm
wrong, Mr. Sever. Tell me I'm wrong." Vane sighed on the other
end of the line.

"You don't think I'm capable of making decisions on my own?"

"Mick, why don't we stick to the music. This murder thing
is gonna blow over and then we've got to get people realizing
what a motivator this boy is. Write about the record contract,
the controversial songs, how Rasta influences Derrick's writing,
but lay off the other stuff, huh?"

Sever sensed the frustration. Bobby Vane was as close to a
friend as he had in the business, but *his* daddy had taught *him*
not to be friends with anyone you did business with. It was the
only lesson he'd learned from dear old Dad, but he learned it.
And it was a good lesson. Journalists who got too close to the
subject lost their perspective and became nothing but whores for
the industry. Keeping a distance was the reason Sever had done

so well in his career. He was convinced of it. Dad had given him one good piece of advice in his whole life, but it had made a difference.

"Bobby, I want to interview Randy and the band. They're off tomorrow. . . ."

"Gonna practice tomorrow, Mick. Gotta work out the new songs for the show."

"Fine. Where's the practice? I'll stop by and chat with the guys while they do setups, tear-downs, or take a break."

Vane let out another deep sigh. Sever could picture the bloated stomach, rising, then lowering as he let out his breath. "Bobby, it's just going to be an interview. Short and sweet. You've got to chill out or you're going to get your blood pressure up, have a stroke, and never be able to tell your grandkids how you single-handedly saved popular music for the world."

For a moment there was silence. Dead silence. Then Vane spoke. "Okay, we'll be in the downstairs meeting room, the Waldheim or some dumb-ass name. You'll hear us. We start about eleven P.M., so if you want to talk, come a little early and plan on staying a little late." Vane paused, took a deep breath, and said, "Do you believe that? Eleven P.M.? Fucking musicians don't feel it's gonna be any good unless they're doin' it in the wee hours of the morning."

"Are we talking about making music?" He could hear Vane chuckle. "And by the way, how did the arraignment go today?"

"We got him out on bail. It wasn't easy but I promised I'd stick with him."

"They let him out?"

"It wasn't easy, Mick. Between the attorney and the bail money we've got a sizable chunk invested."

"Can I talk to him?"

"He'll be there . . . at the rehearsal. Hell, he'll be anywhere I am. I'm gonna watch this sucker like a hawk. My ass is on the line for this one."

"So you've got your doubts, too." Sever smiled.

"This kid is in a strange country for the first time. He's scared and he needs some friends. I'm just his security blanket. Doesn't mean I think he's guilty or innocent. If not him . . . then who? Somebody killed those three girls, and Roland had the knife."

"Well then, I'll see you tomorrow at eleven P.M."

"Sever, I feel really good about this band. This could click, really come together. If you fuck with it, it could fall apart, so don't fuck with it. Okay?"

"I'll see you at eleven tomorrow if not before."

"I won't lie and tell you I'm looking forward to it."

"Bobby, before you go, who drives a bright red Firebird?"

"Is this a riddle?"

"No. Somebody tried to run me off the road this afternoon. I thought maybe you know somebody who . . ."

"Jesus, Mick! Now you're telling me it's getting personal? Someone is trying to involve you? I think you're taking this just a little too far, buddy."

"Settle down, Bobby. It was probably somebody with a little road rage to spare. I just thought that maybe . . ."

"Maybe you'd better stop thinking. I'll check out the rental cars for the band, but I don't think anybody is driving a red anything. Derrick rented a car, and maybe Randy. Yeah, Randy rented something. He drove over to see about Roland. Picked him up after the arraignment. I'll check into it. In the meantime, leave my band alone, okay?"

The restaurant featured stone crabs with drawn butter and extra lemons. Casual dress was suggested due to the spattering of butter and juice, and Sever and Ginny worked up an appetite by wrestling the meat from the crustaceans.

Ginny wiped her lips with a sheet of paper towels and studied the claw in her hand. "I never know where to start," she said. "If I pull back here," she said, prying the small part of the claw back, "then I won't need the crab cracker. Like this." The claw snapped and the white meat spilled out. She dipped it in the hot butter and sucked it into her mouth. Sever watched with respect. There was something almost seductive about the way she ate. It was a guy thing, the old story that a good-looking woman can look sexy in a baggy sweat suit, but damn, Ginny was sexy, even when she ate crab. And she didn't have a baggy sweat suit. Wearing a pair of form-fitting jeans and a Western shirt with a bandanna at the neck, she looked like a million bucks.

"I talked to an old friend of yours today." She set the shell beside her plate. "Remember the Stones tour back in seventy-six?"

"There were a lot of Stones tours. And that was a long time ago. Yeah, maybe Stevie Wonder was doing some of the warm-ups . . ."

"And the Quick."

"Oh yeah, my good friend Buzz." He shot her a nasty look. "How is your ex-boyfriend?"

"Look, buddy boy, you were in the middle of a relationship with some bimbo and her mother if I remember correctly. I needed a little companionship."

"Water under the bridge. Why bring that up now?" Sever speared a piece of soft meat and swirled it in the butter.

"Buzz lived in Jamaica for five years. About two years ago he bought a little bar and six cottages down in the Keys."

"And?"

"And he knows Derrick. And Roland and Randy. He used to hire Derrick's band in a bar he ran in Negril. He said he'd like to talk to you."

"Buzz wants to talk to me? Maybe we could compare notes on technique."

Ginny frowned. "If you want my help, I'll give it to you. If you don't, just tell me. If you're going to be an asshole tonight, then let's call it a night, okay?"

"I'm sorry. I remember the situation a little differently than you do. So Buzz has information on Derrick?"

"He said if you're interested, give him a call or drive on down. It's in No Name Key, a place called Backwater, about a two-hour drive."

"And what about you?" He stared down at the brown-paper table cover, spattered with grease spots.

"I'm not going, Mick. If you want to talk to him, go." She reached into her purse by her feet and pulled out a small black fold-over cell phone. Pausing for a moment, Ginny looked him in the eye. "If you want to go, come back with a good story. If you don't, don't. However, I'd feel better if you took this." She handed him the phone.

"We should have stayed married," he smiled. "Hell, we still fight like a married couple." Sever took the offered phone. He flipped it open and admired the sleek, slim design. Long ago he'd made a decision not to own one of these. His time was his own. He was passionate about the few times he had any privacy. Hell, at least there was something he was passionate about. "I'll drive on down. It'll give me time to think."

"I don't think most married couples go through what we've been through, Mick. The drugs, the sex, the scandals . . ."

"But when it was good, it was very, very good."

"And when it was bad, it was horrid." They finished their meal in silence.

Chapter Nineteen

The two-lane highway that leads from Miami to Key West was built mostly on the remains of an old railroad. Even that train would have been preferable to driving. Sever hated the drive. Traffic was slow, drivers were impatient, and the trip seemed to take forever. Industrialist Henry Flagler had built the railroad in the early 1900s, hoping to lure tourists to his fancy hotel in Key West. The hotel is still there, but the railroad was blown away during a hurricane in the thirties. Sometimes Sever wished that the highway would blow away too.

The convertible seemed confining for the long drive and he could feel a cramping in his leg. He listened to a Latin music radio station and tapped his fingers on the steering wheel, partly to keep time with the music, partly due to his frustration. The view wasn't that great either. Tourist attractions were scattered on both sides of the highway like empty McDonald's sacks tossed out of car windows. Shell sellers, dive shops, towel outlet stores, and worn-out mom-and-pop resorts consisting of little more than a handful of run-down cottages and a minuscule strip of beach littered the edges of the narrow road.

The line of cars extended forever in front of him and behind him, and checking his rearview mirror, he could see other drivers, heads popping out of their windows, trying to see why the drive was so slow. The second time he checked he saw what looked like a red Firebird about seven cars back. He considered the possibility and immediately dismissed it. Florida had a lot of red Firebirds.

He checked his rearview mirror from time to time and noticed the red car. A road sign announced that patience would be rewarded. . . . A passing lane was coming up in just three minutes. When the lane materialized, Sever slowed down to a crawl, waiting for the Firebird to go around him. The driver seemed to purposely stay seven cars back.

The thought of food tantalized him, and he pulled into the Green Turtle, a restaurant whose sign claimed worldwide fame. He watched the Firebird cruise by, around a bend and lost from sight. His knee was throbbing, and he opened the car door and stretched his leg. The muggy atmosphere was oppressive and his skin was damp and sticky in seconds. Seeing no sign of the Pontiac, he finally walked into the restaurant.

The air was cool, almost cold, and the light was subdued, a relief from the harsh sunlight that had followed him for the last hour. For a minute he relaxed, soothed by the soft carpeting and the dark wood-paneled walls, then he picked up a menu filled with delicious-sounding seafood dishes and his thoughts drifted to Bobby Vane. He pictured the corpulent manager, his table loaded, trying some of everything. The crab legs, oysters on the half shell, the shrimp and Florida lobster, all with a big mug of beer to wash it down. He smiled. Sever settled on a bowl of conch chowder and a Corona. The waitress was personable and he left a generous tip and walked back to his car, half expecting to see the red Firebird.

Sever hadn't gone five miles when the traffic ground to a snail's pace, then stopped completely. A man walking by told him work on an accident at Seven Mile Bridge had backed traffic up for two hours.

He jotted down some questions for Buzz while he waited, occasionally checking his rearview mirror to see if there was any sign of the red car. It bothered him more than he thought it would. Frustrated travelers exited their cars and held mini-tailgate parties on the highway, blasting their music, munching on sandwiches, and drinking pop and beer, waiting for the flow of traffic to resume.

By the time he arrived in No Name Key, his patience was totally gone. Tired and thirsty, he hoped Backwater served ice cold beer.

A brown pelican rested at the end of the gray wooden dock and two small outboards were tied to the old structure, with weathered rope, fishing rods, and bait cans scattered on the bottom. The pelican stared out at the channel like a sentry guarding the fort.

The water was deep and as Buzz tossed a handful of tortilla chips into the clear blue water, a parrot fish slowly spiraled up and broke the surface, pulling one of the chips below, repeating the performance until all the chips were gone. Buzz turned back from the water and motioned with his hand to the sloping tin-roofed building. Backwater resort was nothing but a bar with five cottages next door.

"It's not much, but it keeps me busy when I want to be busy," he said. "We can sit up there on the deck." He led Sever to a rectangular slab of concrete about three feet above the ground.

A graying, weathered, wooden rail surrounded it on three sides. The far side was the wall to Backwater's Bar. They sat on cheap, faded vinyl-covered dinette chairs. The tables were bargain-basement plastic lawn furniture.

The peaceful quiet was broken by the shrill calls of a flock of seagulls circling a fisherman's boat that was trolling up the channel.

"Trip okay?"

"I had to sit for two hours while they cleared a wreck off Seven Mile Bridge."

"I hate it when that happens. Want a beer?"

Without waiting for an answer he stood up and entered Backwater through a rusty screen door. A moment later he reappeared with two iced mugs, a foamy golden brew in each one.

"Kalick," he said. "From the Bahamas. A friend of mine flies it in from Nassau."

Sever savored the icy beverage. The two were silent for a moment.

"So, you miss the road?"

"I miss the road, I don't miss the life."

Sever stared out at the channel, wanting to ask about Ginny, knowing it was the wrong thing to bring up. He rubbed his thumb over his smooth onyx ring and watched the pelican spread his wings, leaving his post and slowly sailing out to sea.

"Ginny said you're interested in Derrick," Buzz said.

Sever sipped his beer. The man in front of him barely resembled the former lead singer of the Quick. Famous for his waist-length hair, the Buzz seated across from him had hair that barely covered his ears. He wore a long-billed fishing cap, and his sun-burned face showed a three-day growth of blond and gray stubble. Buzz was now a beach bum from the Keys, no longer the acid-tripping rock idol who used to set his guitar on fire and ignite the passion in young girls and other men's wives.

"I've got a lot of questions for you. Some about Derrick, some not, but maybe you should tell me a little bit about what you know first."

Buzz leaned close and looked in his eyes. He wet his lips with the tip of his tongue then sat back. "What do you really want to know? Why Ginny came to me? She told me it eats at you. We can cover that ground, Mick, but it was a long time ago. Did you come to talk about Derrick, or your ex-wife? Which is it?" He pulled out a pencil-thin cigar from his shirt pocket and lit it with a pack of Backwater matches. He sucked on the brown cigar until the tip burned brightly.

"Tell me about Derrick. Everything else is in the past."

"You know, sometimes I don't know there was a past." Buzz watched the smoke from his cigar curl up and catch a gentle breeze. "There was some lady here a couple of weeks ago. She looked this place up just to see me. She says we spent this passionate weekend together after a show in Cincinnati. Says it was the highlight of her life. The fucking highlight of her life, Mick. Hell, I don't remember the lady or the show and it was the highlight of this lady's life, a weekend with a rock-and-roll man. The women, the shows . . . they were nothin' but a blur, man. Yet this was the highlight of some woman's life! Damn!"

Sever nodded. "You must get a lot of people down here who wonder what you're doing now."

"Some. Curiosity seekers, fishermen, tourists who are lost. I don't usually volunteer the information, but they find out anyway. They bring in albums for me to sign and want to talk rock and roll. Most of 'em are real disappointed when they leave. A lot of 'em can't believe I'm still alive."

Sever smiled. "So you don't talk about the past much?"

"I don't live in the past. Talk to me about bone fishing. Ask me what's hitting out there. Bring me your catch and I'll cook it up for you. It's a simple life, Mick. Like I said, I can't even remember the past. I like this life. It's what I should have been doing a long time ago. I feel good about myself. I don't think that's ever happened to me before."

"You don't have to go that far back for this one. I think somebody in Derrick's band is a killer, and I think it might be Derrick."

A small outboard rounded the bend in the channel and headed toward the landing. Buzz pushed back his chair and stepped off the deck, walking down to the dock. He reached out as one of the fishermen threw him rope. Pulling it tight and tying it off, he helped the two men from their boat onto the rickety wooden landing.

"You guys go on in. Sarah's inside. She'll get you whatever you need."

Buzz came back and sat down, relighting his cigar.

"I booked the band. Most of the guys are still with him. I think the drummer is new. They used to do a lot of cover stuff . . . everything from Harry Belafonte to Marley. Tourist shit for the most part. That pathetic song, "Yellow Bird." God, I got so sick of that. And "Jamaica Farewell." Every fucking band on the island used to have to do that for the old farts. Anyway, they used the club in Negril to work out some of their new stuff, and some of that got a little edgy. You know, you can get away with that shit with the natives, but the heavy money crowd from the resorts didn't understand. Or maybe they did. Derrick started singing songs about hating whitey and stuff, and *whitey* was paying the bills."

Sever tipped his almost empty mug and swallowed the remains of his beer. He pushed the cuffs of his blue denim shirt up to his elbows. "You knew Roland and Randy Jamison?"

"Yeah." Buzz pulled up another chair and propped his sandled feet and bare legs on the vinyl seat. The tan of his skin almost matched the brown of his cutoffs.

"They've got Roland pegged as the guy who's killing all these girls."

"Ginny told me. This guy is like a gentle giant. Not too bright, but just not the type to knife someone to death. I don't see it. Derrick's got a temper, but, to kill someone . . ."

"To kill three someones."

Buzz jumped up and looked down at Sever. "Come on inside, there's somebody I want you to see."

Sever rose slowly, cautiously moving his stiff leg. Buzz opened the squeaky, rusty screen door and ushered him in. The interior was dark and cool. Sever's eyes slowly adjusted to the light. The two fishermen were standing at a pool table in the back, chalking up their cues. Faded neon beer signs hung on the walls along with stuffed and mounted fish. The opposite wall was covered with an assortment of license plates from years past. Sever wondered if they were used to help hold the building together. Fifteen tables were scattered throughout the bar, surrounded by an odd assortment of plastic chairs. An old jukebox stood in the corner, a rack of old 45s stacked under the glass top and ready to play. To the left was the bar, constructed of cheap paneling and Formica. Sever could smell fried fish and hear someone humming in the kitchen behind the bar. He walked to the jukebox and glanced at the selections, mostly country songs, a handful of fifties and sixties classics, a couple of Buffet tunes, and two hits by the Quick.

Buzz called him to the bar. "Mick, let me test your memory. Do you remember this lady?" He shouted back to the kitchen. "Sarah, come out here for a minute."

A short, curvy brunette walked out from the kitchen, tight

shorts and halter top hugging her compact frame. She pushed a strand of graying hair away from her face and walked around the bar.

"Mick Sever. It's been a long time."

Sever stared back, his eyes widening in surprise.

"Sarah D., is that you?"

"It's me."

"Damn, you look good, Sarah, it's been . . ."

"Six years, Mick."

Sever looked at Buzz. "We used to be, well, we were . . ."

Buzz nodded. "I know."

Sever sat on a barstool shaking his head. "So what are you doing here? Working for Buzz?"

"I'm married to Buzz."

Sever froze for a second. "No shit?"

"No shit," she smiled.

"Wow." He looked back and forth at Buzz, then Sarah.

"Funny how things work out, isn't it?" Buzz said.

"Funny," said Sever. Funny.

Just a whisper of an evening breeze ruffled the fronds on the potted palm sitting on the concrete deck. The breeze offered little relief from the humidity of the long afternoon.

Sever and Buzz sat on the deck, both with lit cigars and cold Kalicks in frosted mugs. They set the remains of their grouper dinners on another table and the early evening was quiet except for the water lapping at the dock and the occasional loud voice from the bar.

"James is new. The killings started after they hired him. Could be something to that." Sever puffed on his cigar, watching the pale blue sky as the fingers of sunlight reached for the horizon.

"Can't tell you about him. Rick played the keyboard. A real cock hound. Man, he loved the ladies."

"I watched him in action on Romano's boat. Maybe he's competing with Derrick."

"Sudahd, he and I used to trade licks. I taught him some of the Quick riffs and he'd sneak it into the reggae numbers. I got a kick out of him, but again, I can't see him killing some girl."

"I don't think killers are the ones that you ever suspect. Every news story about a serial killer starts off with a neighbor saying, 'He was such a normal person.' "

"Well, I never said these boys were normal. Flame? Hell, he's Jimmy Washington from Carver, Idaho. I think he was running from something or someone. Acted like he didn't give a shit, but I always thought he was hiding something."

"Flame is from Idaho?"

"Yeah. Where do you learn to play bass guitar like that in Idaho? I never did figure that one out."

"Flame. I thought there was something . . . a little too hip-hop about him. Running from a relationship, or the law?"

"I don't know. He's a bright, friendly guy but I never talked to him about it. I just heard rumors."

"What about Randy?"

Buzz knocked his ash off on the deck floor. "Randy was like the manager. He collected the money, he booked the group, he did the sound checks. . . . I always thought that if he could sing, it would be him up there instead of Derrick."

"But not the type to . . ."

"Nope."

Sarah D. walked out onto the deck, the squeaky screen door

telegraphing her presence. She pulled up a chair and sat down. "This story about the girl and Derrick's bodyguard. It's getting some press down here," she said. She took a sip of Buzz's beer. "News stories say she hung out with a lot of the bands."

Buzz gave her a frown. "There are some other girls I know who used to hang out with a lot of bands."

Sarah smacked his bare leg. "Some things don't change, baby. Like drugs. These guys do ganja all day long. When you're stoned, you do a lot of stupid things." She smiled and nodded at Buzz. "Ask my husband."

Buzz let out a laugh.

"You had some days, didn't you, babe?"

"Hell," the singer smiled, "I had some years." He pushed back his cap.

Sever studied the red tip of his cigar, watching the smoke spiral up and disappear into the early evening light. "What about Marna? She hangs on Derrick but I can't get a real feel for that relationship."

"Don't know Marna. I don't think she was around when I knew the guys. But talk to Randy. He's a bright boy, knows a lot more than he lets on. He might have some ideas, unless Roland did it and Randy wants to cover for him." Buzz glanced at Sarah. "You met Randy the last year I was there."

Sarah reached into Buzz's shirt pocket and pulled out a cigar. Buzz leaned over with his pack of matches and lit it. She took a puff and let the thin trail of smoke escape from the corner of her mouth. "He was the rock. It seemed to me he was the one who held things together for the band."

Sever checked his watch. "There's a rehearsal tonight that I've got to get to. You guys have been great. One more question. Is Derrick as fanatical as he seems? The way he talks, the songs he writes . . . is it an act or is it real?"

There was a flutter as a brown pelican landed on the dock and cocked his head toward the trio. They stared back and he turned and looked up the channel, watching for evening fishermen who might throw him some supper.

"I think he's grown into it. I'm sure he has some strong beliefs, but I'm also sure that he puts on a show. Derrick wants to be a star. It's written all over him. Like I said, some of the songs he sang used to be pretty graphic, but I don't think he really believes the way to Utopia is to kill all the white people, or kill all the girls who are mucking up the system."

"I don't think Roland is the killer. But I'm concerned about Derrick. There's a dark side to him that scares me. The lyrics to some of Derrick's songs are so . . ."

"Mick," Buzz leaned closer to him, "Derrick doesn't write all those songs. They're not his. Randy writes most of them."

"Randy? He writes the songs?"

"He did when I knew him."

"No shit?"

"You know, for a man who makes his living with words, when you're surprised, you seem to have a very limited vocabulary."

Chapter Twenty

The Who mocked him as he crossed Seven Mile Bridge. They sang "Won't Get Fooled Again." He'd been fooled. And maybe Bobby Vane had been fooled too. And maybe it really didn't matter. Maybe it didn't matter any more than it mattered that the killings hadn't started until after James joined the group. But it was a piece of the puzzle.

Sever glanced at the speedometer, easing slightly off the gas. If he wanted to get back for the interview, he didn't need to be slowed down with a speeding ticket. The cops were thick in the Keys and he had four or five pink slips at home to prove it.

He listened to Roger Daltry singing, and remembered the Toronto concert. The Who were wrapping up the outdoor show and even with the heavy rain there were thousands of kids. Townshend beat his guitar against an amplifier until the neck snapped and the head splintered. On cue, the lights went out and the stage was plunged into darkness. Sever had been backstage, watching the spectacle from the wings. Townshend shouted out to him,

"Come on, mate! The birds'll be flockin' up here any bloody second now."

Sever jogged toward the voice, and the lights flashed back on. The girls were everywhere, screaming in shrill voices, clambering up the side steps, lifting each other onto the front of the stage, scrambling to grab, touch, or be in the vicinity of the rock stars. Three stocky men in black T-shirts kept pushing them back but they were overwhelmed. The crowd of young girls shoved them out of the way and ran for the band.

Drummer Keith Moon scrambled out from behind his drums, a bare-chested Daltry tossed his shirt into the throng of young women, and Moon and Sever ran to the edge of the stage. Whatever drugs they had taken that night made them invincible and they both leaped from the stage into the black abyss below.

Sever felt himself floating. It seemed forever, floating through the air, looking up, looking down, it was dark and he was floating. He'd thought maybe this was death . . . just an eerie feeling of suspension. It seemed almost peaceful. There was no sound, no screaming women, no ear-piercing guitars and drums, and then his body crashed into the seats below. His knee twisted beneath him and he could feel warm sticky blood running into his eyes from a gash on his head. It wasn't death, but he passed out from the pain and woke up in a hospital room where they set the leg in three places and Ginny, fresh from a rushed plane trip out of Chicago, intermittently soothed him and screamed at him for all the right reasons.

The accident was probably another chink in the armor of their marriage that helped it come apart. He massaged his knee and tried to stretch it in the confines of the small car.

Sever checked his rearview mirror. Dusk fell over the Keys and headlights illuminated the stretches of highway, few and far between during the evening hours. He listened to the junior jock, talking up the next oldie. Something about the British invasion, and the importance of David Bowie. Hell, this kid's parents weren't even experiencing puberty when David Bowie was in his prime. Historians, all of them. Young punks who never understood the music styles. Kids who tried a 2000 spin on the sixties. They had no understanding of the rebellion of that era. He briefly wondered again why he stayed in the business. It couldn't be for the money. He'd made a fortune, and even though he hadn't been as frugal as he should have been, there was enough stashed away for a lifetime.

Briefing the next generation . . . filling in the gaps for the children of the year 2000-plus, that's what his legacy would be. And with no children of his own, possibly that's why he felt so strongly about telling the story. Or maybe it was habit. He'd known no other life. The life of a scribe was all he knew and if it was habit, then there was no passion, no strong belief. All there was, was a continuation of following the story.

He closed his eyes, clearing his mind of the angry battle between forces. And when he closed his eyes, his mind went into slumber, a quarter-second dream into a battle of the bands. Beatles vs. the Spice Girls. 'NSYNC vs. the Beach Boys. He snapped to attention as the convertible veered right, bumping along the slight ditch that led into the mangroves that laced the side of the roads. Jesus, the two or three beers, the good food, and the warm night were all taking their effect. He breathed deeply, easing back onto the road. A lone pair of headlights hung back, paying strict attention to the speed limit.

The ringing in his ears startled him and he concentrated on it. It stopped and started again. Sever glanced at the passenger seat, noticing the cell phone in the bucket seat where he'd carelessly tossed it before leaving Miami. Only one person would be calling him. He flipped open the black contraption and held it to his ear.

The voice on the other end was decidedly male. "Ginny?"

"No, this is Mick. Who's this?"

"Tony."

"Tony? She's uh, not here. I've got. . . . she gave me her phone for a while and . . ."

"Oh. Mick. You're the ex, right?"

"Yeah. The ex. Who are you?"

"It's not important. Tell her Tony called and we'll get together . . . when she gets her phone back." The line went dead.

Shit. Tony. Fucking Tony. Hey, at least she had a life.

The phone rang again. He considered not answering at all. Three rings and he flipped it open again.

"Mick?"

"No. This is Tony."

She was quiet for a moment. "Having fun, are we?"

"Who's Tony?"

"None of your business. Where are you?"

"About an hour away. Had a nice talk with Buzz and Sarah."

"And apparently with Tony. Any messages?"

"Something about he couldn't wait to see you again. Anyway, I got some information about Randy. Seems he writes a lot of the songs."

Again a long silence.

"So Randy is the one who comes up with the philosophy. And Derrick is his mouthpiece. Is this kind of like Moses and Aaron?"

"Doesn't prove anything, but it does give the story an interesting twist. I don't think Bobby or anyone else outside the group knows. If you're under the impression that Derrick writes and sings the vitriolic lyrics, the whole thing takes on a mystical quality. If you know that he's just voicing someone else's words, it tends to lose some of its punch." He saw the sign up ahead announcing a passing lane in three minutes. There were no cars to pass, just the headlights in his rearview mirror. Another sign announced a small gravel parking lot where tourists could pull over and view the ocean. Not tonight.

"Mick, do you still think Derrick killed the girl?"

"I don't know. He had sex with her. He sings songs about how evil easy women are. . . ."

"And Randy writes lyrics about how evil women are. And Roland is Randy's brother. Kind of like incest in a strange perverted way."

The car behind him had pulled up, now about three lengths back, its bright lights flashing on, glaring in the convertible's side mirror. Sever checked the speedometer. Five miles below the limit so no problem there. He squinted into the mirror, trying to see if the rear car had lights on top. He couldn't make out the car, just the bright, glaring headlights.

"Mick?"

"Yeah, I'm here." He cast a wary glance at the approaching car.

"Do you remember the first time we ever came to Miami? I was a freshman at Loyola. You were doing a story on the Doors, and I was on spring break. You called me, I flew down, and we saw the Doors, March first, 1969. Mick, that was the night . . ."

"I know. The first time you'd ever seen a rock star's genitalia."

"God, I was so spooked. He just opened his pants, right there on stage. I considered what else you might have experienced on the road and wondered if I'd ever be able to accept all of that."

"You weren't that much of a prude. I remember some things you taught me." The car was two lengths back and closing fast. He could see the passing lane a hundred feet ahead.

"In the privacy of my home! There were ten thousand people at the Dinner Key Auditorium. And then, we go backstage and you introduce me to him. And he wanted to shake my hand. I think I remember just walking away."

"He was so fucked up he didn't even remember any of it. I think he and the band took off for the Caribbean that night so they put out a warrant on him. The minute he came into the States they arrested him. Lewd and lascivious behavior in public . . ."

"Indecent exposure, and public profanity and drunkenness. When I got back to school, I told some of the girls in the house I'd seen Jim Morrison's cock. They were so impressed. I think I had a reputation after that. I may have exaggerated the story just a little."

"The story?"

"Well, I may have exaggerated the size of his penis. Anyway, it made a great story."

He moved into the passing area, still only one car in sight. Easing to the far side of the road, he slowed down, waiting for the rear car to pass. He could almost feel the car accelerating behind him, inches from his rear bumper. As he pressed the accelerator to the floor, he felt the bump, jerking him forward. He dropped the phone as his hands gripped the wheel and he fought to steady the lightweight convertible. The car hit him again, this time bouncing him off the road into the narrow ditch. He braked and felt the rough terrain underneath as his car jerked and bounced along. The other car slowed too, now beside him and far to the left. He looked up and saw the red Firebird with the mirrored glass windows. The driver spun the car to the right and came hurtling across the passing lane at Sever's door. Sever jammed the accelerator to the floor and the Firebird missed its mark, glancing off the rear bumper and pushing him further into the ditch.

"Mick? Mick?" He heard the shrill voice coming from the floor. Ginny was still on the phone.

"I'm here!" He was shouting, the adrenaline pumping in his veins. "Someone is trying to kill me, but I'm here."

The convertible whipped through the ditch, the right side of the car scraping scrawny mango trees, ripping off the side-view mirror, and grating at the metal. The Firebird had drifted back now, about three lengths.

"Mick! Are you all right?"

"Stay there. I'm at mile marker . . . shit. There must be one up . . . there it is. One twenty-eight. Stay with me. If this gets any worse, call nine-one-one and tell them to get a cop down here. Never a fucking cop when you need one."

Now the red sports car was closing the gap, racing toward the convertible. At the last second the driver pulled out and went barreling past Sever at breakneck speed. Sever took a long breath and took one hand from the steering wheel, wiping the sweat from his forehead. He eased the car back onto the highway, watching the taillights of the red car in the distance.

"Mick? Jesus! Mick!"

"I'm okay. I think he's gone." He reached down to the floor and picked up the cell phone. "Thanks. I'm glad someone was along for that ride." The taillights spun around and now he could see the headlights coming back. "Oh, shit. This isn't over." Sever dropped the phone in the passenger seat and grabbed the steering wheel. Bright white light glared in his windshield as the driver bore down on him, coming right at him in the right lane.

"He's coming right at me!" One hundred yards, then fifty,

the engine was screaming as the Firebird grew closer. Sever
jammed on the brake, the Chrysler catching, then skidding, the
right rear bumper spinning out. He let off the brake and slammed
his foot on the accelerator, twisting the wheel with all his might.
He did a U-turn in the narrow two-lane road and reversed his
direction as the car leaped ahead. Now the Firebird was chasing
him back down the Keys. He couldn't outrun it. The bend in the
road took him briefly out of sight, and the scenic sign with the
gravel pull-over for ocean viewing was to the left. He braked and
skidded into the lot. Turning the car, he killed the headlights and
aimed it out at the road. He could hear the high-pitched whine
of the red menace as it rounded the curve. Sever waited until he
could see the lights, then flashed on his brights and came roaring
out of the lot. The other driver jerked his wheel, his car skidding
off the road, into the thicket of brush and trees, rolling once,
then twice. Sever spun the wheel to the right, heading toward
Miami, and never looked back.

"Mick?"

"Oh, yeah. You're still there. So, what do you think? Do I
pass the driving test?"

"What the hell happened?"

"I'll tell you when I get back. Right now I've got a rehearsal
to attend, and I can't wait to see who's there and who isn't."

Chapter Twenty-one

Jay Leno had once asked Sever what rock-and-roll music really was. He'd replied, "A powerful outward expression of personal feelings that could change the world." It was a stupid line. Hell, he'd spent most of his life trying to explain rock and roll, and it sure as hell couldn't be summarized in a single quote. He should have stayed with Louis Armstrong's feeling about jazz. When asked what jazz was, the trumpet player had said something like, "If you can't feel it, I can't explain it." But being the scribe, Sever had to define this mystical fire. Most pop songs were loosely defined as rock and roll, and "I love you" always worked better in a pop song. A protest always worked better in a song. Envy, greed, hate, love, distaste, whatever your emotion, it worked better in pop music. Pop psychologists were telling patients to find a pop song that they could identify with, a song that helped validate their existence. A song that could become their mantra. What garbage! College professors were teaching Beatle lyrics. Rock and roll was truly here to stay. Derrick and the Laments were using their brand of rock and roll to teach the masses about Rasta.

Wearing cutoffs and T-shirts, Rick, James, and Sudahd lounged in soft reclining chairs just off the lobby. Derrick and Flame were nowhere to be seen. He was anxious to see if Randy and Roland were helping set up the equipment. The band members nodded to him as he approached.

"Anybody seen Derrick?"

"Derrick?" Rick gave him a grin. "Mon, Derrick don't believe in rehearsals. When you are the star, then you don't need to work with the little people."

"So he won't be here?"

"He will and he won't, he does and he doesn't. Derrick do what Derrick do." The keyboard player closed his eyes and seemed to drift off.

In the large rehearsal hall, two roadies set up the equipment, a small bank of amplifiers, monitors, microphones, and James's drum kit. Vane was pacing in front of the mock stage, yelling into his cell phone. He glanced at Sever and frowned. Folding the slim phone, he pushed it into his bulging pants pocket and said something to the young kids with dreadlocks who were now plugging guitar cords into the amps. He turned and looked again at Sever.

"Shit, two weeks ago the guys did all this themselves. They make a couple bucks, get a recording contract and all of sudden they've got their heads up their asses. Gotta have someone do all the setup for 'em."

"I thought Randy and Roland helped with this," Sever said. "Where is the defendant?"

"He's up in his room. Shit, Mick, he's all right. He was sleeping so I left him up there. Nothin's gonna happen."

"You'd better hope. I want to talk to Randy. Is he around?"

"No. I didn't see any need for him to be here tonight so I told him we didn't need him. I thought he and Roland might get together, a little brother-bonding and consoling kind of thing, but it didn't happen."

"Any idea where he might be?"

"No. Probably went out to eat . . . maybe to see a movie or somethin'."

"What about the red Firebird? Any word on that?"

"I checked. Nobody here claims they know anything about a red Firebird."

"Derrick? And Flame?"

"The fuck. You doin' a roll call here? You've already talked to Derrick. And before you ask, Marna isn't gonna be here either. She isn't involved in the new songs so we don't need her."

Sever took a deep breath. He was tempted to tell Vane about the attempt on his life, if that was what it was. Don't get too close. "Thanks, Bobby. I really want to talk to Roland. If he comes down, ask him to see me, okay?"

"Uh, that's not gonna happen, Mick. Lawyer stuff, you understand. This high-priced mouthpiece I pay, I may as well use some of his expensive advice."

"He doesn't want me to talk to Roland?"

"He doesn't want you to talk to anyone."

"Off the record?"

"The only record we're talking about is the one we're making."

Sever ran a hand over his chin, feeling the rough eleven o'clock shadow. "Then there's no point in doing any more on this story."

"I've begged you, Mick. Write about the music. Write about the show. Write about the social implications of . . ."

"What the hell do you know or care about the social implications?" Sever pushed his finger in Vane's face. "You've made a living putting together teen bands and extorting money from pubescent adolescents. You could give a damn about social implications. What you care about is making a buck, so don't give me shit about looking for the true meaning. The true meaning is, somebody associated with this Jamaican jambalaya is killing young girls. That should scare the hell out of you."

Vane stepped back, eyes wide, surprised, maybe even fearful. "Then leave. There's nobody making you stay. This was your idea, Sever. I was you, I'd be on to the next story, go sell my book somewhere. The lawyer said no contact, so there's no contact. That's the way it is, friend." He brushed by Sever, reached in his pocket for the cell phone, and was connected with someone in seconds. He muttered, swore, and stammered into the mouthpiece as he walked out of the hall into the lobby.

Taking a deep breath, Sever closed his eyes and tried to calm down. It had been one hell of an evening. Vane was right. There was absolutely nothing keeping him here. The book sales were waiting, time for a vacation. Maybe Ginny would agree to get away for a week to Aruba. Or, on the other hand, maybe *Tony* had dibs on that part of her life.

He walked into the lobby, nodded at the band members who were sitting in the same relaxed, rather stoned, state that he'd seen several minutes before.

Flame walked down the hall, bouncing to an unheard rhythm. He glanced at Sever and smiled. "Whassup, man? You don't look so good."

Sever hadn't realized the strain showed. "Hey, Flame. Been back to Idaho recently?"

Silence. Now the affable bass player seemed to be the one who was tense. "That's in the past, man. Way in the past." He focused on the rehearsal hall, then put his head down and walked past Sever without another word.

Before Sever entered the elevator, he checked the desk for any messages. A one-line note on a sheet of hotel stationery.

"Mr. Sever. I need to talk to you about what happened on that boat. Marna."

Sever tucked the paper into the pocket of his jeans and walked into the bar. He purchased an overpriced bottle of cabernet, called Ginny's room, then took an elevator to the fourth floor. Something or someone was tugging at him to stay. He'd have to apologize to Vane and find a way to piece this story together, with or without the help of anybody in the band.

Chapter Twenty-two

Releasing the chain guard on the door, Ginny let him in. He set the bottle of cabernet on the desk and poured two drinking glasses full of the translucent ruby liquid. Handing her a tumbler, he raised it in a toast. "Here's to good times."

"Here's to you coming back alive. For God's sake, Mick, and I do mean for God's sake . . . you're alive. I don't think I would have been more scared if I'd been with you." She sipped the tart wine as she shut down her laptop computer.

"And I still don't know who it was."

"Probably a good thing you didn't stick around to find out. I called the State Patrol and they have no record of anyone having an accident tonight. Actually, they seemed surprised that it was so calm."

"Trust me, it wasn't calm." He took a drink, finished the glass, and poured himself another. "I don't think the car could have gone in the water. The trees are too thick out there."

She walked to the minibar and took out a can of cashews. "Twelve-dollar dinner here. Want some?" Scooping a handful, she handed the tin to Sever. He sat on the edge of the king-sized bed, the wine slowly making its way through his bloodstream and ending up somewhere inside his head. For the first time that evening, he felt some peace and calm. It wasn't the first time he'd relied on chemicals to give him his sense of well-being.

"So, if the cops didn't find the car, it would appear that whoever tried to kill you drove it away."

"Or had it towed away. Can't be that many towing companies around that area."

"Mick, it could have been any towing company in Miami. It's been over two hours since you were out there."

"What were you working on? On the computer?"

"Oh, a piece for a new writer. What else?"

"You're a hell of an editor, did I ever tell you that?"

"Oh, you usually give me some credit. In the new book I think you spelled my name right."

"Who's Tony?" He set the can of nuts on the desk.

"Sever, you are unbelievable." She shook her head in disbelief, her loose blond hair softly moving. "You just went through a near-death crisis, and you're more worried about my social life than anything else."

"Yeah. I know."

"You haven't changed in the least. You want your cake, you want to eat it, and you want more, but let someone else have any piece of it and you go ballistic."

"Hey, I want you to have everything, whatever you want." Sever took another sip of wine and looked away from her, staring at the sailboat painting above the bed. Its sail was full of wind and it appeared to be heading out to open water. "It's just that I always thought we'd have it together."

"Bullshit. Bullshit! You treated our marriage strictly as a convenience." She grabbed a handful of the cashews and glared at him.

"Yeah, I know, but I always thought I'd grow out of that and that we'd grow old together."

"Now I know you're full of it. You never planned on growing old. Remember?" Ginny tossed the nuts into her mouth and chewed furiously.

"Hope I die before I get old?" Sever stepped over to the minibar, rooted through the mini bottles, and pulled out a caramel bottle of Dewar's Scotch. He twisted the top open and poured the liquid into the remaining glass on the desk. Before he drank, he held it to the light as if it were a crystal ball. He gazed at the drink, looking for a fortune and a future. "Don't you believe that people can change?"

"No. I don't. I think the same genetic qualities that shape you at eighteen years shape you at forty, or fifty. It's still there, Sever. You'll *always* be someone who believes that rules were only made for other people. You can do whatever you want, and as long as you keep doing what you're doing . . . immersing yourself in this youth culture that passed you by about twenty years ago, you'll never understand what the real world is like. You will never change. And I'm a fool if I get sucked up into your life again."

"So, I guess we're not spending the night together?"

"Oh, that would be perfect. I actually thought about it. Worrying about you during that chase. I thought, 'If he gets back I'm gonna' . . . but I forget. I forget what an asshole you can be."

Sever sat on the end of the bed, swirling the rest of the Scotch in his tumbler. No future here. Just a cloudless butterscotch-colored fluid and a woman who knew him better than he knew himself.

"I'm sorry." She stood, walked to him, and put her hand on

his shoulder. "We're not a couple anymore. You don't deserve that. I think it's old hostilities coming out. Too much history, Mick." She leaned down and kissed his cheek. "You tell me what I can do, aside from sleeping with you."

He was silent. Too much truth, and the hibiscus scent of her cologne was bringing back memories that he shouldn't touch. "I don't know. I'm at a total impasse. Vane won't let me talk to the band, someone is trying to kill me, and I'm starting to think I should be back on the book tour."

"So go sell the books. Make some money for both of us. I still get a percentage, right?"

"Ginny, if you really want to help, help me straighten it out. I want to do the story. I may be a fossil, and I may be fooling myself, but this is the only thing that gives me a jolt. It's like," he paused, searching for the thought, "it's like, if I don't have a puzzle in front of me, something for me to solve, then what's the point? I'm usually very good at this. And, I'm even better when you're there with me."

"I'm not sleeping with you, Sever!"

"I didn't ask!"

"Okay! Then let's get this figured out."

"So what would you do first?"

"Call Harry Kohls. Tell him about the car."

"Ginny, you know that he . . ."

"I know that he'll have a much better idea of where to start than we do."

"But I . . ."

"Call him, or I will."

Chapter Twenty-three

So maybe you just pissed somebody off. You cut them off, you passed when you shouldn't have, you ran a light . . ." Disdain dripped from Harry Kohls's voice.

"Harry, I know you don't like me, and I know you don't want me getting involved in your case, but . . ."

"Oh no, hotshot. I hope you write another book about how we bungled another case. I'm just a public servant, Sever. Hell, if I can make you look good, that's what I'm here for."

"When we get past the sarcasm, maybe you can take this threat a little more seriously. The Firebird has shown up twice in two days. Both times he tried to ram me, and this last time I seriously think he was trying to kill me." Sever drew a circle on the hotel scratch pad. He added two sad eyes, a nose, and a down-turned mouth. The doodle was constantly changing. Sometimes the eyebrows were arched with surprise, and other times the eyes were slits and the expression was filled with anger. Once in a great while the face had a smile, but never a big one. Ginny called it the Charlie Chaplin smile, always a hint of sadness in the cartoon face.

"All right, so someone's trying to make a point. I suppose that it might be related to this Derrick thing. Give me the mile marker again." The tone of voice had changed to mild disgust.

"One twenty-eight."

"You know, Sever, the judge let our suspect out on bail. I couldn't believe that one. This guy is caught red-handed, knife in hand, and your boys Bobby Vane and Frank Romano get together and post bond. You let a murder suspect like that out and anything is liable to happen."

"Romano was involved too?"

"Oh yeah. And he's sure to be a witness for the prosecution. You're both going to be on that stand, Sever."

"Harry, the first time I got buzzed by this car, Roland was in jail. It couldn't be him."

"How about the other bald brother? Randy? Do you know about him? Seems he was a bouncer in Negril. Beat up a guy one night and almost killed him. He's got a violent temper. You found his brother with the knife in his hand, so maybe he figures if you're out of the way, you can't testify and things might go easier for Roland."

"I hadn't thought about that. But he'd have to bump off Romano, too."

"And the girl, Marna. Three more deaths might not look so good. But I wouldn't rule it out. Criminals are not bright people, Sever. If they were, we'd never catch 'em."

"*Somebody* tried to kill me."

"Why don't you call Romano. See if anyone is trying to run him off the road, put a bomb under his hood, shoot him with a high-powered rifle."

Sever sipped the last of the Scotch, feeling light-headed and relaxed. "I'll do it. In the meantime, is there any way to run a check on the car?"

"There are thousands of red Firebirds down here. If it's somebody from the band, it's probably a rental. The only way we'd know about it is if they don't return it to the agency. Hell, even then these car companies wait forty-eight hours before they report it stolen. I'll have somebody run down the highway and see if there's any sign of the car at one twenty-eight. Could be it's buried in the trees. We might get lucky, but I doubt it."

"Harry, thanks for at least listening."

"You're right about me not liking you, Sever. But I also want to stop these murders. We're taking a lot of heat over that girl on the boat, and if you're involved somehow, then I guess I'll follow up the lead."

"You're a sweetheart, Kohls."

"If I hear anything, I'll call you. Until then, stay off the roads." The line went dead.

Sever turned to Ginny, drinking her second or third glass of wine. Her white blouse was open at the neck, the hint of cleavage showing.

"Uh uh, Mick. Not tonight. Not for all the wine in the Napa Valley."

"You flatter yourself."

"I know that look. I was once your wife, remember?"

Sever stood and pushed the sleeves back on his blue oxford shirt. He straightened the leg. A couple of drinks took some of the pain away. "Marna left me a note. Said she had something to discuss with me. I'll head up to her room, then hit the sack."

"I thought you weren't allowed to talk to anyone in the band."

"I think the point is, they're not supposed to talk to me. So it's up to them."

"Call me," she said. "Let me know what she says."

He turned the handle of the door, then turned to Ginny. "You know, I keep promising that I'm not going to beat myself up over what happened between us, but I do. Every day. And given the chance, I'd screw it up again. I know I would. But, when I look for the one thing in my life that I really believe in . . . when I'm honest with myself about my one great passion, it's you. It's you, Ginny." He opened the door and walked out, just like he had so many times before.

Chapter Twenty-four

Marna didn't answer the knock. He peered through the inverted peephole and saw the room was dark. Sever took the elevator to the lobby and walked into the bar. Bobby Vane held court with two men and three very attractive, diverse ladies. A blonde, a black, and an Asian. A silver bucket sat in a stand next to their booth, the necks of two champagne bottles sticking out of the top.

"Hey, Mick. Over here." Vane waved at him. The smile on his pudgy face seemed evidence that either the argument had been forgotten, or the champagne was flowing through his veins. Probably a little of both.

"Bobby, the rehearsal over so soon?"

"No, no . . . they're working on it right now. Wantcha to meet some people here. Jay Weinstein and Ron Gillian with Mega Records . . . oh, hell, you've met Gillian, haven't you?" He laughed. "Sit down young man, sip some champagne."

Sever sat next to the young Asian lady in the overstuffed booth. Her skirt rode high on her thigh and the look in her eyes was mischievous.

"We're in Lauderdale tomorrow night," Vane spread his arms wide, including the two men in the *we*. "The National Car Rental Center. Do you believe that? Everything has a sponsor's name on it anymore. Anyway, it's big, Mick. Backstreet Boys played there right after that whirlwind continent tour they did. Ticket Master says the Brandy show is sold out. So, the boys here figured it was a good idea to announce the release of the CD at the show tomorrow night. You wanna do a piece on it?"

"A piece?"

"Yeah. You could do a piece about what's gonna be on it, how it sounds, maybe interview the boys here about the sales projections . . .'cause we think this will go half a million on its first go-around. That's not bad for a group nobody here ever heard of 'til last week."

"Bobby, I think you're better off with a press release from Mega. You guys agree?" The two men nodded their heads.

"Well, we're gonna set things on fire tomorrow night and get this show back on track. Got a whole Jamaican contingency comin' down from Miami. Mega records will have, what Ron? About a hundred guests? Gonna have a hospitality tent for Mega, and Red Stripe wants to contribute a little for some advertising. I think they might just spring for their own tour down the road. Gonna have a big-ass sign at the show, Red Stripe Beer. Things are movin' fast, like a locomotive."

"For you they always do."

"A little bit of luck seems to go a long way, Mick." He poured a water glass full of the bubbly champagne and handed it to Sever.

"You've got an eye for talent, Bobby." He took the glass and set it down. "Look, I hate to bring this up, but the police said that Frank Romano posted bail for Roland. Is that true?"

Vane blinked, smiled at the two men and the ladies, hauled his hefty frame out of the booth, and motioned for Sever to follow him. He took about fifteen steps, stopped, and turned as Sever approached him. Vane's heavy hands were clenched into big thick fists and Sever thought he was going to hit him. He approached cautiously, watching Vane's eyes. His father had taught him it was sometimes necessary to fight. When he was fourteen, his dad had come home drunk, screaming at his wife about a multitude of things. When Mick complained about the way his father was yelling at his mother, the old man backhanded him across the face, knocking him to the cheap linoleum floor and cutting his lip. When he struggled to get up, the bastard had kicked him in the ribs. He vowed the son of a bitch would never beat him up again.

Sever started hanging out after school in a neighborhood gym owned by his history teacher. He boxed with kids his own age, then kids in their twenties, and although his punches lacked tremendous power, he learned placement, and how to move. He had a natural ability, and he was light on his feet. When Sever was sixteen, the old man took another swing at him, and spent three days in a hospital with a broken jaw and cracked ribs for his effort. From that point on there was an uneasy truce between the two males of the house.

"Mick, I'm all talked out on this." There was fire in Vane's eyes. "Leave it alone. I'm not gonna tell you again. Don't bring it up again. Not in private, and not in front of my friends and business associates."

"What are you afraid of? You told me yourself that the publicity will do nothing but help sell records. You've got nothing to lose, unless . . . unless you think Derrick is the killer. Is that what's got you scared?"

"Mick, for all the time you've been in the business, you still don't understand." Vane's eyes closed, and when he opened them, they were tired and sad. "I'm the star maker, Mick. I'm the fucking star maker, the Svengali. I'm in charge here. You think these acts are so talented that it's their destiny to be stars? No fucking way! It's the star makers who make it happen, and when I get a group this far, in this position . . . I'm gonna protect the hell out of them. I might get three or four, maybe five shots in my life to really make something happen . . . and this is one of 'em. I'm not gonna let you or anyone else fuck that up." The fat man relaxed his hands. The fire left his eyes. He glanced back at the table, gave Sever a sad smile, and nodded his head. "I think the little Asian honey is perfect for you. She kind of comes with the package if you know what I mean. If you're not busy, come on back and join us. She looks like she's about ready to make a move."

"It's been a rough night, Bobby. I don't know if I'm up for it. Give her my regards."

"Mick . . ." There appeared to be nothing left to say.

Sever took the elevator to his room and stared out at the moonlit parking lot for twenty minutes. He picked up the phone and called Ginny's room. She answered with a distracted tone in her voice.

He hesitated. "Hey, did I wake you?"

"I'm working on this piece. I was going to take the week off, going to put everything aside, but I really need to finish this. I'm sorry, Mick. What do you need?"

"Let's take a break. Both of us. Take a walk, do something. I'm going crazy."

"Okay. We'll take a walk. I'll meet you at the pool. Is there anywhere to walk around here?"

"If there is, we'll find it."

"Give me ten minutes. I'll be there."

Sever fell back on the bed and closed his eyes. He tried to picture the red Firebird, working on the license plate. The car pulling around him and away. He focused on the plate, closer and closer. A Florida plate, with an R and a T . . . RT and three numbers. He looked harder.

Chapter Twenty-five

The phone was ringing, over and over again. He reached out and grabbed the receiver, shaking his head to clear the sleep from his brain. "Yeah?"

"Where the hell are you? I've been down here for half an hour. I said ten minutes, Mick."

"Oh, jeeze, I'm sorry, Ginny. Damn! Fell asleep. Hang tight, I'll be down. Where are you?"

"In the lobby. I'll wait here."

Splashing some water on his face, running his hands through his hair, Sever bolted out the door and took the elevator to the lobby. She was sitting in a leather chair, legs crossed and her foot tapping in midair . . . not a good sign.

"You called me, buddy boy. I've got things to do. If I'm going to put my work on hold for you, you'd better show up."

"Yeah. I'm sorry. I got part of the plate, the license plate. I was working on it and I dozed off."

She stood, and they headed for the lobby door.

"The pool is this way. There's a nice garden that surrounds it. We can walk there."

A thick heavy layer of humidity sucked at the air, as if the overhead clouds could break at any moment, releasing the stored moisture and drenching the parched ground. The heavy air took his breath away. They strolled along a palm-lined walkway, spotlights shining through the ground-ferns, casting mysterious shadows in the trees. A slight breeze rustled the large palm fronds, and Ginny's hair blew softly as she brushed it from her face.

"So you've got a plate number?"

"Partial. That does me no good. I think it'll come to me, but I've got to work on it a little bit more."

"And what about the girl?"

"She wasn't in her room, but I made amends with Vane."

"That's good."

"Then I had another fight with him."

"What the hell is wrong with you?" She stopped and stared at him, looking him right in the eyes and boring through to his brain.

"I don't know. I can't quit asking the questions. I know it sounds crazy, but in a situation like this everything should be on the table. I think Bobby Vane believes that Derrick has been killing the girls. He doesn't want to lose the leader of the band, so I think he wants Roland to take the fall."

Ginny sat on a wrought-iron bench, leaning back as the breeze once again took her long blond hair. She seemed to stare vacantly into the clouded, moonless sky. "Then why did he put up his bail?"

"I haven't figured that out yet. Maybe he wants to keep an eye on him, convince him that he shouldn't protest too much. We already know that Kohls wants to wrap this thing fast. He thinks he's got enough to convict Roland, so now all Vane has to do is keep him under wraps for a few weeks . . . and convince him that with all the evidence, it's best if he just pleads no contest and takes whatever punishment they dole out."

"Which could be death!"

"No, not in Florida. At least I don't think so. And with the right judge, he might get fifteen or twenty years."

"You've studied all this?"

"I have no clue. I'm making it up. It just seems that when I talk to Vane, he's always covering for Derrick."

She stood and they resumed their walk. Hibiscus blooms adorned the walkway, swaying in the moist air. The first drops surprised him, hitting hard, bouncing off the stone walkway and splashing into the foliage on either side. The sky opened and what had seconds ago been heavy, humid air was now a torrential shower. They broke into a run, heading toward the far side of the garden, where they could see the doorway to the rear of the hotel lobby.

As they raced toward the lights of the hotel, they passed the pool, raindrops beating a rapid-fire pattern on the surface of the blue lit water.

"Someone's swimming!" Sever shouted above the relentless pounding of the rain. He slowed, watching the body in the water. Soaked to the skin, water streaming from his forehead into his eyes, Sever wiped at his face and moved closer to the pool. The body was motionless, floating facedown with arms spread wide, little explosions of water bombs beating around the still form.

"Jesus. He's dead."

Ginny stopped, whipping her wet blond mane back over her shoulder and leaning down by the side of the pool. The smell of chlorine gas rose from the blue water, released by the fierce downpour, the surface now looking like it was riled from a shark attack. The body moved gently through the rough water, being pushed by the strong breeze. Sever kneeled and leaned out over the edge, trying to reach the sleeve of the floating man. Ginny grabbed Sever's other hand and held on. The attempt was futile. He rose and spotted a long aluminum pole mounted on a board along with two orange life rings. Yanking the pole from its mounting, he swung it out to the pool, poking at the body and pulling at the same time, bringing the man closer to the edge.

"Get someone," he shouted. She hesitated, then broke into a run toward the hotel lobby doors as the intensity of the rain increased. Sever concentrated on moving the corpse. Slowly the massive body floated within arm's reach. He grabbed the hand, cold and clammy, and tried to pull the man out. The term *deadweight* went through his head. This must be what it meant.

"Mick!" She was running down the stone walk, her feet slipping on the slick flagstone. Behind her was a red-jacketed bellman with an umbrella that was all but useless in the pounding storm. The young man dropped the umbrella and knelt by Sever's side, grabbing at the arm and working with him to pull the body up. Together they dragged him onto the cement.

"You called the cops?" Sever's voice was strained as he fought against the sound of heavy wind and rain.

"They're on their way!" Ginny shouted back. She stood to the side, watching wide-eyed, wiping the streaming water from her eyes as they rolled the man onto his back.

"Shit!" Sever's mouth fell open. He looked into the dead man's face, rain drumming against the open eyes that didn't blink. "Shit!" The accused security guard stared up at him, the look of surprise and terror still on his face, just like the last time Sever had seen him—on a luxury yacht with a knife in his hand and a dead body in front of him. The difference was, this time Roland Jamison was the dead body.

Chapter Twenty-six

Do you have an affinity for dead bodies?" Harry Kohls shook the water from his umbrella as he sat down on the lobby sofa. "It occurs to me that all I've got to do is follow you around and just pick up the bodies. It would save me a lot of work."

Sever sat back in the overstuffed chair, listening to the rain tattoo the ground outside. "So what's your expert opinion, Harry?"

"I never have one. Leave that to the medical guys." He slipped out of his raincoat and threw it over the end of the couch. "Now my *guess* is another story. I think this guy decides he's gonna go down on murder one, and decides to end his life. Jumps in the deep end knowing he can't swim. That's my guess."

"Makes it nice and tidy. We got the killer, he kills himself, and there's no reason to go any further." Sever smiled. "So what do you do when the next girl is killed? Roland comes back from the dead?"

"It's just my guess, Sever."

Out of the corner of his eye, Sever watched Vane and Randy

come striding in. Vane immediately saw Sever, shot a severe look
at Randy, and strode over to the chair.

"You found him? Damn! Where's the . . ."

"They took him away. Medical examiner is doing the autopsy
right now," said Kohls.

"Damn! I just don't understand." Vane appeared to be genuinely shaken, wiping his hands on his shirt with trembling hands.

Randy touched Vane's shoulder. "Easy, Mr. Vane. We all
should have paid more attention to him."

The bald black man walked to Sever and offered his hand.
Sever stood up to take it, noticing the fresh cut on the dark flesh
of his lower arm. The wound ran from his wrist to his elbow, not
deep, but still a nasty-looking cut. He shook the offered hand.

"I thank you for finding him, and trying to save his life."

"I was too late for that. I just got him out of the pool."

"I don't believe my brother is a killer, Mr. Sever."

"For what it's worth, I don't either, but the police," he nodded at Kohls, "they've got a different view of things." He
searched Randy's face, noticing a deep bruise on his right cheek-
bone. "Looks like you've been in a fight."

"I was. Someone tried to mug me earlier, a man with a knife.
I held my own."

Sever reached up and lightly touched the bruise. Randy
winced. "This wasn't down in the Keys, was it?"

"I have never been to the Keys, Mr. Sever."

"I'm sorry for your loss."

"Thank you, mon." He turned and walked away, out of the
lobby, into the hallway, and toward the elevator.

Kohls stood up as two patrolmen walked in, rain dripping off
the slickers and clear vinyl-covered hats.

"We've talked to most of the guests. The ones who aren't
here have messages at the desk to call us." The tall one brushed

at his slicker, sending a shower down on the thick green-and-white-patterned carpet. "No one saw or heard anything."

Kohls nodded, looking past the two policemen, out the glass doors to the pool area. Half an hour ago there had been a bright portable searchlight highlighting the area, and ten patrolmen and detectives looking for whatever police look for after a murder. "Whatever clues might be out there, they're going to be washed away. You guys may as well head back. We'll wrap it up for the night and see what happens tomorrow."

Sever watched him, cool, calm, handling the situation like the pro that he was. "So is it officially a suicide or a murder?"

"I told you, Sever, no official comment. We'll have an answer for you sometime this morning. Until then, you've got nothing."

The doors swung open as a young lady in a vinyl raincoat strode through the door, followed by a skinny kid with bad acne wearing a Motley Crüe T-shirt and carrying a video camera on his shoulder.

"Hi, Harry."

"Hey, Liz, you're number one. I compliment the timeliness of Channel Four, but I just finished telling Mr. Sever over there that we have no official word. As of now, we've got a body in a swimming pool. That's it."

The twenty-something female took off her coat, draping it over the edge of a vinyl chair. Sever admired her legs protruding from the short red dress. "You're the same Sever that writes for *Spin*? The MTV Mr. Sever?"

He smiled. "Yeah."

"So, I'm number two. Mr. Sever has already got a story." She gave him a coy look, squinting her eyes.

"Mr. Sever found the body . . . but, I'm giving you fair warning. He is prone to exaggeration and out-and-out lies, so if you decide to interview him, don't take a thing he says as gospel."

"When will you have a cause of death?" She shot the comment to Kohls, never letting her eyes leave Sever.

"Sometime in the morning. That's the best I can do."

"Mr. Sever, can we go one-on-one?"

Sever thought he caught a hidden message but ignored it. "I don't think so. I don't have any more information than you do, so I'm afraid you'd be wasting your time."

"I think you know a whole lot more than I do. I would really appreciate it if you'd talk to me. We can get you some great exposure on the early morning news and tomorrow night if the story has legs."

He let his eyes glide over *her* legs. "No. But thanks."

Ginny strolled into the lobby, hair blown dry and a pair of skintight jeans hugging her curvy frame. Surveying the scene, she gave Sever a wry smile. "Well, Mick, it doesn't take you long."

"This is . . . Liz, from . . ."

"Channel Four," she muttered. "Harry, where's the pool? Tim, get some footage of the pool and let's get some b-roll of the hotel." Strictly business. No more coy looks, or flirting.

"Talk to whoever you want, Sever," Kohls stood up and picked up the umbrella, "but remember, you don't have a clue as to what happened. As of now, our official position is that we think this guy was the killer. When I know anything else, I'll be happy to share it with you. Now, considering that we've pretty much wrapped everything up here that can be wrapped, I'm going home. Night, everyone!" He walked to the door and out into the downpour.

The female reporter disappeared with her cameraman.

"Dead bodies and pretty girls," Ginny said. "Maybe that should be the title of your next book."

"Not to change the subject, but do you think this is a suicide?"

"Just wait it out, Mick. We'll get an answer by morning."

"Who would have killed him? Randy? Derrick? Flame? How about Vane? Maybe somebody who wanted to avenge the girl's death. I think somebody is protecting himself."

"Where was Derrick?"

"Meditating? I don't know. The guy seems to disappear every time someone gets killed."

"You know, Mick, right now might be a good time to talk to him, and maybe to Randy. Now that Roland is dead, you should be able to interview anyone you want to."

Sever walked to the window, watching the sheets of rain pouring from the black sky. "Did you see the way Randy looked? Got banged up pretty good. Claims he got mugged. Now who the hell would be stupid enough to try and mug a guy who looks like he does?"

Ginny walked up behind him, putting her hands on his shoulders and gently squeezing. "Randy must be mixed up in this somehow. He's relegated to the grunt work while Derrick gets all the glory. . . ."

"And all the girls."

"That too, but, Mick, he didn't kill his brother. I just can't believe that. . . ."

"Somebody did. That wasn't suicide and you know it." He spun around and headed for the elevator.

"Where are you going?"

"Marna. She wanted to talk. I've got to find her."

"Be careful. There's a killer loose out there." She followed him down the hall.

Chapter Twenty-seven

He knocked on her door, gently. Two A.M. was not a good time to go pounding on doors. He waited patiently, then knocked again a little louder. He had decided to go down to his room and call her just when the door opened. She smiled at him over the chain guard.

"Mr. Sever. You came."

"Marna . . . it's Mick."

She shut the door, then opened it, the chain removed. She motioned for him to come in. Music played softly on the radio, a Latin music station. Only one light was on, above the bed. A paperback book was lying on the bedspread, Jack Kerouac's *On the Road.*

"Studying your American history, I see."

"We're on the road, Mr. Sever. At least we will be tomorrow. We're obviously having a different adventure than Mr. Kerouac did."

She sat on the end of the bed, a white terry-cloth robe wrapped around her, a glimpse of her caramel thigh showing as if she was waiting for him to notice, watching him with what seemed to be amusement. She seemed to be watching to see where he would sit. Beside her? On the other bed? On the desk chair? Possibly his final destination would give her some insight into his character. He studied his options, then sat next to her, apparently surprising the dark-haired beauty. She shifted and scooted farther away.

"You said you had something you wanted to talk about."

"Things have changed."

"So you don't want to talk?"

"It's just that things are different. Mr. Sever, it is rumored that you believe either Derrick or Randy killed the young girls. With all of the stress that everyone is under, it is not good for the morale of the band to have someone of your stature accusing members of our group as murderers."

"Who is the murderer? Why don't you just tell me, and we can put the whole thing to rest."

"Now you make fun of me. I believe Roland was the killer. I believe he either took his own life, or someone may have pushed him into the water. Someone who felt it would be better if he died and paid for his sins, rather than making the whole band pay for them. We must get on with our work. Derrick and Randy both believe it is time to move on."

"For God's sake, Randy is his brother. You can't tell me that he wanted him dead."

"Randy wants what is right. Derrick wants what is right."

"The songs. Randy writes them and Derrick . . ."

"Randy writes what?" She stood up and glared down at him.

"The lyrics, the music."

"Derrick writes the music." Her brown eyes were wide, and her brow creased, genuinely puzzled.

"I was told that Randy writes the music. Whoever writes it,

much of it is extremely violent. Very antiwomen. There are direct references to killing young girls. So why wouldn't someone suspect the writer and maybe the singer of acting on these lyrics? Roland had nothing to do with the songs or the violent lyrics."

She pulled the robe tighter around her slim body, hugging herself. Turning away from him, she walked to the door and opened it. "It's time for you to go."

Sever slowly stood, feeling the deep throb in his tender knee. He winced, glancing at her for a sign of sympathy. Her stare was cold and hard.

"I can assure you that Derrick writes and sings the songs. If you study the publishing contracts, you'll see that. I can also assure you that neither he nor Randy are the killers. There may be passion in his lyrics, in his voice, and in his actions, but Derrick is a man of peace. Roland was the killer, and now it is over. Please, Mr. Sever, stop your divisiveness. There is more here than just a group of musicians. There is a chance for something truly great to happen. It happened with Bob Marley, and it can happen for Derrick."

The jangling phone broke the tension. Holding the robe tightly around her, Marna answered it. She turned around and offered it to Sever.

"Mick?"

"Ginny?"

"It didn't take them long. Kohls called from his car. It appears that Roland was hit with a heavy object before he went into the pool. The blow would have knocked him unconscious, and death was due to drowning. He was murdered, Mick. You were right."

He handed the phone back to Marna.

"Mr. Sever, I asked you before if you had a passion. Derrick doesn't believe a man is full until he is passionate about something or someone. Do you feel that way?"

He studied her for a moment, the fine lines of her jaw and cheekbones, the way her nostrils slightly flared when she was angry, the bare legs showing from the short robe. He didn't want to confuse passion for lust.

"I'm not sure I understand your definition of passion."

"To have passion for something means you would die for it. Is that simple enough to understand? What would you die for? Do you believe in anything that strongly?"

A chill went down his spine and his stomach felt weak, not like a sickness, but like standing on a balcony of a forty-story apartment building and forcing yourself to lean over the railing. There was a moment of panic, then it was gone.

"I'd have to think about . . ."

She interrupted as if she had already anticipated his hesitation. "No! There is no thinking. You know instinctively if you have that kind of passion. You don't. You are not yet a full man. You may never become one. I think you are probably a self-consumed man, and since you would not voluntarily die for yourself, then you have no passion for your life." She walked to the dresser, now more subdued. Picking up a turquoise-handled hairbrush, she started running it through her coal black hair.

"And you? You are passionate about something?"

"Oh, yes. I can truly tell you that I have passion."

The man of words had nothing left to say. No parting shot, no sharp retort, no sarcastic farewell. He turned to the door, speechless. There was an emptiness in him that he couldn't shake. He put it off to the lateness of the hour and the fact that he'd skipped dinner. About now, he could get almost passionate for a really good steak dinner.

Chapter Twenty-eight

Look at it, Mick. Twenty thousand seats, give or take a few. Gonna pack 'em in tonight." Vane's eyes were darting around the arena as they walked toward the stage. Men in orange uniforms set up wooden folding chairs on the temporary floor, a cold sheet of hockey ice directly underneath. With the trained observance of a seasoned promoter he watched the afternoon activities. He pointed up, motioning to Sever as the techs adjusted large can lights, pin spots, and an assortment of other stage lights from a narrow catwalk. Below, Derrick stood stage center, waiting patiently for a cue to move. "They did Brandy earlier," Vane said. "Once they set Derrick, they'll just leave 'em 'til the show." He spread his arms wide. "Gonna be packed," he repeated. "Our boy is gonna set 'em on fire, Mick. Got a call from Bono. He's gonna be here. And Barry Gibb. I think he lives somewhere down in Miami. Gonna be a night for stars."

The lighting crew passed commands down to the stage with small wireless microphones and headsets as the band dutifully moved to different positions.

"Press is gonna be at the hotel at five. I'd like to think we're gonna talk about the tour and the new CD, but we'll probably end up talkin' about Roland."

"Who's doing the conference?"

"Derrick wants to handle it. He says he needs to recapture the tone of his message. He figures it got off track these last few days. . . ."

"Before it ever got on track."

Suddenly Derrick's voice boomed from the stage, "We testing." A huge stack of speakers amplified his voice and shook the wooden chairs on the floor like a clap of summer thunder.

"Now they'll do the mike checks." Vane seemed to be talking to himself as if checking off the list of duties before the show could go on. "Oh, I've been meaning to ask you," his eyes roamed the hall, avoiding a direct look at Sever. "Marna said you've been writing a piece about the murders, and, uh, she seems to be under the impression you're gonna try and implicate Randy or Derrick." He seemed to be exhausted, as if the accusation had drained him of all his energy.

"Come on, Bobby, we've been through this way too many times."

"Yeah," he paused and scratched his stomach, "I thought so, too. Any plans on running with it?"

Sever started to speak as the musicians broke into a new number. He stifled his comment as the band music rattled through the nearly empty hall. A ragged, up-tempo beat, with bass and drums punching the indoor arena atmosphere. Derrick, loose and limber, prowled along the lip of the stage. Flame, a.k.a. Jerry Washington from Idaho, riffed on the bass and Sever swore he caught Sudahd playing a lick from one of the Quick's songs. Buzz's influence, no doubt. Then the keyboards and finally Derrick.

"Don't think that anyone will take your blame, no no. . . . If you blow out the candle and you blow out the flame, no no . . . I got to tell you that, no one here gonna take the fall, no no . . . they just go bout their business and they build up a wall . . . no, no. . . ."

A tech walked onstage and stopped the song, resetting a mike stand and two stage monitors.

"Bobby, I'm just following the story. You probably know more than I do."

"I'll tell you what. It's just damned stressful, that's all. This band is edgy as it is. They're workin' with some sort of voodoo message, then you factor in that they're over here from a foreign country, and the murder thing. . . ."

The keyboard kicked in with a mournful organ sound, cutting off Vane's final words. Marna walked onstage in tight black slacks and a sheer white top. A small black bra was prominently displayed beneath the garment. Derrick glanced at her, mouthed something off-mike, then picked up a guitar and struck a chord.

"Whatcha gonna do when dey come for you?" Derrick stopped and laughed out loud, the sound rolling through the arena. Mick recognized the line from the popular television show *Cops*. The band settled in again, chunk-a-chunk rhythm.

"Take de blame for what you do, yeah . . . take de blame it's up to you, yeah yeah . . . Stand up, stand tall, take de blame and take it all, yeah yeah . . ."

"Your room okay?" Vane shouted to be heard. Sever nodded. Again a tech motioned to the band to give it a rest.

"Sure, it's fine."

"And the ex, she's happy? Got her own room, right?"

"Yes, Bobby . . . she's got her own room."

Randy approached from the rear of the stage, briskly walking toward them. He ignored Sever, putting a hand on Vane's shoulder and steering him away. They conversed for a minute, then broke.

"Randy," Sever called after him. The large bald man turned. "I'm confused. I talked to a friend of yours a couple days ago who told me that you write most of the songs for Derrick and the Laments, but Marna says it's all Derrick. She seems to have seen the publishing contracts with his name only."

"Who is your friend?" He seemed surly, a frown causing a crease in his forehead as deep as a canyon.

"Buzz."

"Ah, the Buzz man. And he has firsthand knowledge of my many talents?"

"Seems to."

Randy paused, briefly looking at the stage, Derrick and Marna close together, talking . . . she, touching his arm and looking into his eyes with an intimate gaze.

"Don't believe everything you hear, Mr. Sever. Don't believe everything that you see. It seems to me you've been makin' up far too many stories as it is!" He glowered at him.

Sever noticed that the bruise on his face seemed darker, more sinister. The friendly man who had thanked him for trying to save his brother's life was gone. In his place was a large bar bouncer who had almost killed a man, and had possibly killed three women. Sever didn't want to be next on his list.

Randy spun on one heel, an agile step for such a big man, then trudged off to the stage.

"He's got a lot of pressure, Mick. You're not makin' things easier for him. Police are holdin' his brother's body 'til they do some more tests, and then we got to arrange for him and Roland to go home for the funeral, and in the meantime he's workin' here, and . . ." His voice trailed off. "Say, it's three o'clock. Why don't you and me and Ginny grab a bite to eat and then we can go back to the hotel for the press conference. I'll get Mega Records to pick up the tab . . . whaddaya say?"

"Nah, I'm not really hungry right now. I'll see you at the conference."

"Mick, we're gonna get this straightened out, and then we're gonna rock the world. Rock it! Life is good, buddy boy, life is good."

Sever headed toward the exit.

"Mick . . . come on." He shouted after him. "Let me buy dinner. Tell ya what. Frank Romano is stayin' at the hotel. Hell, he's probably checked in by now . . . gonna see the show tonight. So I'll call him on the cell, and the three of us can grab a bite to eat. How 'bout it?" There was urgency in his voice, a plea asking for more than a bite to eat, but Sever couldn't figure out what it was.

"Not interested, Bobby. We'll get together later." He left the arena, drove the beat-up rental to the new hotel, and handed the keys to the doorman. Strolling into the lobby, he could feel his muscles relax. An energy drain, Ginny had called it. An energy drain. All the stored-up, pent-up energy from the day's activities seemed to evaporate as he walked into the strange hotel. This was home.

Chapter Twenty-nine

*H*otel and motel rooms were an homogenized blur. The ones Sever stayed in were usually a step up from average. The carpets were a little thicker, the generic prints on the walls were touched up with two or three original brush strokes, the armoire with the thirty-two-inch television and drawers and the standard minibar with extravagantly overpriced drinks and snacks were standard fare. A king-sized bed, uncomfortable sofa, tables, stiff chair, and a writing desk rounded out the living area. In the bathroom was the cheap basket of fruity-smelling soaps and lotions, and washcloths folded into fancy triangles or seashell shapes. Finally there was always the room service and a *USA Today* outside your door. Sever figured that he could live forever in an upscale motel room. The thought frightened him.

Some days he woke up not knowing where he was, and some nights he would walk into his strange room and experience déjà vu. He likened it to a cruise ship, where you could be in a different country every day, and in the same room every night. It was a very weird feeling.

Slipping his card into the door, he felt his energy evaporate, as if all his ambition had taken wing and simply flown away. The green light flickered, and he turned the handle and opened the door. The room was black, looking like evening had come early. The maids had apparently closed the heavy curtains, and the only light in the room was the soft glow from his laptop, sitting on the desk.

He hadn't left the laptop on the desk. It had been stowed away safely in his leather travel bag. Yet there it was, the soft white light emanating from the small screen. He paused and looked back at the door. Maybe this was another mind deception. Maybe he had left the computer on. Maybe he'd been writing in this room and he'd forgotten to turn off the computer. No. As much as the days, the rooms, the assignments blurred together, he remembered this one. He'd put the laptop to bed, in his travel case, and here it was, as if by magic, glowing in the dark room, probably spilling its secrets to the blackness. Sever rubbed his temples, tired and slightly confused. He stepped backward, one, two, three steps. Staring straight ahead at the softly lit screen, he brushed his hand over the wall, searching for the light switch. From the right, near the bathroom, he sensed the presence of someone else. The sour, stale breath of garlic and tomato and a rustle as the person moved quickly. A split second later a whisper of air caressed him and he felt a fist slam into his solar plexus, driving up into the sternum. He gasped and doubled over, the pain and an overwhelming urge to throw up everything in his stomach coming at once. A fist passed centimeters above his head, where it had been a half second before.

Sever took one more deep breath, grimaced from the excruciating pain in his midsection, and rocketed up from his crouched position, driving his head and fists forward. Without a clear view of the shadowy figure he felt like he'd caught the intruder high

on the chest and maybe on the chin. He heard the grunt as the
stranger banged against the wall. Sever's second nature took over
as he crouched, guarded his face with a fist, and lashed out, now
hitting the trespasser on the cheek. A right caught him again on
the face. He bobbed and weaved, pretending the man was Billy
Dukes at the Bayfront Gym in Chicago, and they were sparring
in the dark. The punches found their mark but stopped the
stranger for only a moment. The larger man struck again, a powerful roundhouse to the head, and Sever felt himself fading to
black. He closed his eyes and rocked back on his heels. He
breathed deeply, seeing the stars in his eyes disappear. The sound
of the two men, breathing hard, grunting, and cautiously moving
in a tight semicircle, was broken by the jangling of the telephone.
Seeing better in the dark, Sever watched the figure turn his head
toward the phone, then snap back. Sever cocked his arm and let
go with a powerhouse left hook. He caught the man as he was
turning back, hard on the chin. The intruder held his position
for three to four seconds, then crumpled to the floor, sighing as
he collapsed.

There was no movement. Sever froze, waiting to see if the
man got up. Nothing. Once again, he felt the wall, finding the
switch and flipping it on. Nothing. Either the overhead bulb had
burned out or someone had removed it. If the man got up again,
Sever wasn't sure he could take him a second time. He backed
up to the door and opened it, easing himself out. He shot one
more look at the body, now bathed in the light from the hall.
The dark man with the bald head lay almost in a fetal position
and Sever hoped he was still alive. He'd had enough of this family's death. Ever so slightly he could see Randy's chest expand as
he drew in shallow breaths. Sever winced as he walked down the
hall and around the corner to Ginny's room. Battered and
bruised, hunched over in pain, he looked like he'd been on an

all-night binge, and it wasn't even early evening yet.

She opened the door, the chain in place. When she gazed at the bruised face, the discolored skin around the left eye, and the bent-over body, she released the chain and cautiously hugged him, helping him into the room, and laying him out on the bed.

"Randy?"

"Yeah. Randy. In my room. Looking for God knows what."

"Looking for whatever it is you're writing. Either trying to protect himself, Derrick, or the reputation of his brother."

For every breath he took, there was a reaction of sharp pain in the ribs. He groaned and tried to sit up.

"Just lie there." She reached for the phone.

"He's unconscious in my room. Call Kohls."

She called the hotel operator and asked for the Miami Police. Thirty seconds later she was connected. Kohls was in the field, but she was assured that they would be in touch with hotel security and they would contact the Broward County sheriff's office. If Randy was still in the room, immediate action would be taken.

"Vane tried to take me to dinner." Sever spoke with short breaths and a rasp. Not exactly in fighting form tonight. "I think Randy wanted him to keep me occupied."

"So, did he find anything?"

Sever breathed more deeply. "He'd never find it, but it's there. Thoughts, observations, our conversations." He gazed up at her. "Even the bit about Tony and the cell phone. Who the hell is Tony?"

"Sever, you are truly one fucked-up man. Shouldn't we be worried about what the hell just happened?" Her eyes blazed.

He struggled into a sitting position, holding himself upright on the bed with his arms. His entire body ached, except for his knee. Strange.

"Do me a favor," he said. "Call Vane. Let's get him to your room and see what he says."

"I can't call Bobby out of the blue. If he knows that Randy was in your room, he sure as hell isn't going to come up here."

The sharp knock at the door caught them both by surprise.

"Easy," Sever said. He could hear Ginny attach the chain again and slowly open the heavy hotel room door. The voice was gruff, angry.

"Open the Goddamned door!"

It was Bobby Vane, sounding somewhat profane.

"Well," Sever muttered, "ask and it shall be granted."

Vane's gut preceded him into the room. The heavyset man entered with his head hanging low. He glanced at Sever and frowned. "And how's the other guy?" he asked.

"Believe it or not, Bobby, I got the better end of the deal. Sit down and tell us exactly what the hell is going on."

Vane pulled up the desk chair and sat down as if the weight of the world were in his large stomach. He ran a pudgy hand over his forehead, wiping away the perspiration that beaded up on portions of his face.

"I knew he wanted to see what you'd written. That was all. You haven't called the cops, have you? Come on, Mick, you haven't called the fuckin' cops? This thing isn't gonna die down 'til you leave it alone!"

The rapping at the door interrupted him. This time Ginny called out. "Who's there?"

"Hotel security, ma'am. Did you call about a fight?"

"Shit!" Vane gave Sever a disgusted look. "Had to go and do it. Damn! Sever, you're more trouble than you're worth."

"Look, Bobby," he took short breaths, his rib cage still hurting, "what the hell I write is not subject to your scrutiny."

Ginny stroked his shoulder, as if her touch would heal the

pain in his body. He had to admit it helped. "Did we call anyone about a fight?" She looked into Sever's eyes.

"The guy tried to kill me, Bobby."

"If the guy wanted to kill you, you wouldn't be here right now." Vane looked at him with those pleading eyes.

"Tell him there's been a mistake." Ginny stood and opened the door.

"I'm sorry. There was a misunderstanding, but I think it's been cleared up. Can we call you if there are any other problems?" She glanced back at Vane with a stern look.

"Yes, ma'am. If you have any problems, please call the front desk immediately."

"Randy is goin' through a rough time." Vane's eyes were riveted to the carpet, unable to make eye contact with anyone. "Hell, his brother gets accused of murder, then his brother gets murdered. That's not easy to take, Mick. Jesus, I don't know what family you have, but can you picture this? Now, you're tryin' to prove that Derrick or Randy is really the murderer. Well, hell, he's gonna' defend himself, and if you're goin' after Derrick, that's his good friend."

"And his meal ticket."

"Now what's that supposed to mean? Because he works for Derrick? Well, then, maybe that's what it is. But this is how it's playing downtown. Roland killed the girls. There's not much question about that. The cops have pretty much told me that case is closed." He wiped perspiration from his forehead with his meaty hand, wiping the hand on his black polo shirt. "As far as who killed Roland, they've got some ideas, but he had no identification on him when you pulled him from the water. No watch, no jewelry, no money. There wasn't anything in my room either, so the guess is he was mugged and someone took everything that was on him."

"Mugged? Like his brother? Do you think that runs in the family?"

"Yeah. Like his brother. Somebody hit him, took his wallet, his watch, his rings, and split. Miami is dangerous, Mick. Lots of people die here. Lots of crime, muggings, carjackings. And lots of unsolved murders. Ask your friend Detective Kohls."

"That's too easy, Bobby." He struggled to stand up, grabbing the back of the desk chair for support. Vane reached out and helped him up.

"You and me, we go back, Mick. Before either of us was anything. Back when Frankie Romano was the only success story we knew. Friendship has privileges. You can use a friend to your advantage . . . once in a while. You can count on a friend when there's trouble. And you can tell a friend off for his own good. But you can't—you don't ever dis a friend in public."

"And that's what you think I'm doing to you?"

"It's what you're doin', not what I think you're doin'."

"You've got a job to do and so do I. There's nothing in this friendship code that says either one of us should stop doing our job."

"There are a million things you could be doin' right now, Mick. You could be doin' personal appearances on that million-dollar book. You could be travelin' with any damned band you want to . . . the best parties, gettin' laid every . . ." He paused and looked at Ginny, sitting on the bed. "God, I'm sorry. That just slipped."

She was quiet. She glanced at Sever as he looked into her eyes. Sever took some hesitant steps to the window, hurting, but feeling restless, caged. He almost smelled desperation in the room. Helplessness from a strong man. It was not pleasant.

Vane reached out to take Ginny's hand, but she shook him off. "Again, I'm sorry, Ginny." He turned to Sever. "Randy wanted to see what you wrote. He thought he could get into your laptop and get a heads-up where you were goin' with your story. You weren't supposed to walk in when you did."

"I was supposed to be eating dinner with you. So now you're an accomplice?"

"Shit! I'm gonna tell you this, Sever, and if you ever, fucking . . . excuse me, Ginny . . . if you ever fucking repeat this, so help me I'll do whatever I can to bring your shining career to a screeching halt. . . ."

"You're threatening me?" Sever was surprised at how loud his voice was. He felt the blood pounding through his veins, beating inside his bruised body, and he was acutely aware of every ache and pain.

"I'm gonna' tell you something. I think somebody in the band killed those girls. I think Roland was too," he hesitated, searching for the right word, "simple, nice, or not aggressive. I don't think the boy did it. I don't know who did it. Might have been James, Rick, or maybe Flame. I've got some suspicions, but as long as it doesn't happen again, the cops are happy with the outcome. Their suspect is dead, and the case can just go away. That's off-the-record. I'm happy with the outcome if we can just move on. Okay?"

Sever watched the parking lot as the Channel Four news van from Miami pulled in. The same team got out of the car. The punk camera kid and the leggy brunette reporter. Two more television vans pulled in behind them.

"I can't believe you're comfortable with a killer in the band! But I'm going to tell *you* something." He turned from the picture window and looked daggers at Vane. "I think Randy tried to kill me down in the Keys. And I damned well know he tried to take my head off about thirty minutes ago. I can't prove a thing, but tell him to keep away. I'm staying with the tour, and I'm not going to press charges, but you let Randy know that everything is out in the open. All the cards are on the table, and tell him to keep his distance."

Vane stood up, easing his bulk out of the wooden chair. "There's somethin' else you probably should know. See, Roland had a reason to keep clean . . . not get his hands dirty. He needed this job. Roland is married and he's got a one-year-old daughter back in Jamaica. It destroyed him when that resort fired him. There's no way he would have screwed this job up. He loved his little girl."

"And now?"

"I don't know. I honestly don't know. As of now, that little girl's daddy is a killer. And I think they got it wrong!"

Sever rubbed his aching knee. "It gets stranger by the hour." He gazed at the floor for a moment, not seeing anything. Finally he looked up at the big man. "Keep Randy away from me.

"Thanks, Mick. I'll tell him. I promise you, I'll keep a tight rein on him. I don't want anything happening to you."

Sever shook his head. "You've got it wrong, Bobby. *I* was the one who walked out of that room. You need to worry about what I'm going to do to *him*."

Chapter Thirty

The coffee shop was shiny vinyl and china. The clink of saucers and cups bounced around the room, interrupted occasionally by the ting of forks or spoons hitting plates. Kohls sniffed the aroma from his strong black Cuban coffee, letting it cool before he took a sip. "So you're not pressing charges? Since when did you become a nice guy?"

"Hell, Harry, you know it wouldn't go anywhere. The maid let him in, so it's not exactly like breaking and entering."

"Well, they could have found some charges. I'm sure I'll get all the details from one of their fine detectives at this press conference."

Sever smiled. "And why did you decide to come to this press conference?"

"Because as a Miami detective, I'm also involved in public relations, and I want to see how we come off. The last time I trusted the press to be kind, you tore us a new asshole. We want to be ready this time." He gave Sever a sarcastic smile. "Are you sure you want this guy running around loose?"

"If I'm right about him, I'll get more information while he's running around loose than if he was in jail, and let's face it, now he owes me one."

"I'm not sure he'll see it that way." Kohls stirred the dark liquid, steam still rising. "What Vane told you is pretty much the way we're dealing with it. Our suspect is dead, so the case is closed. Roland Jamison's murder is still under investigation, but I've got to be honest with you, there isn't a lot of interest in it. I don't sense a lot of public outrage. I think that the people feel it was an eye for an eye, and they're happy he's gone."

"You know, I've got enough for a book right now. This is great stuff. Derrick and the Rasta thing, three young girls murdered, then the suspected killer is killed and thrown into a swimming pool, and the band played on."

"But you're not gonna stop. And you're probably gonna drag the Miami P.D. into your sordid little story."

"Yeah, I probably am."

"Well, this isn't our jurisdiction so don't blame me for whatever happens here."

"Since this isn't your jurisdiction, and since you aren't working the case anymore, let me ask you a couple of questions."

"Off the record!"

"Off the record." Sever wanted to take notes, badly, but resisted the temptation. He would have to relive the conversation back in his room. "This won't take long. That press conference is coming up in about fifteen minutes, and I want to see what Derrick says. You've heard me say that I don't believe Roland did it. My money's on Derrick or Randy. I may not have solid reasons, and God knows I don't have proof, but the way Derrick attacks women in his songs . . ."

"Now wait a minute." Kohls sampled the coffee, then took a deep swallow. "If we were to suspect every singer, songwriter, movie director who took on violence as a theme, we'd have more suspects than victims. Francis Ford Coppola directed three *Godfathers*. Does that make him a suspect in every gangland-style murder?"

Sever spread his hands. "Harry, the songs almost telegraph the murders. That's a little different than the *Godfather* movies."

"And you were one of those kids who grew up believing the grassy knoll theory. Lee Harvey Oswald had help, right? Conspiracies everywhere. I'd tell you to give it a rest, Sever, but you've got to sell another book, so I suppose you'll keep digging until you run out of dirt." He took another gulp of coffee and set the mug down. "If we want to get a good seat, we probably ought to get going."

"Harry, you're going to have to open the case again. Trust me. I've got a very strong feeling."

Chapter Thirty-one

Derrick looked almost regal, like a tribal chief, his dark skin shining in the TV lights, a royal blue shirt open halfway down his chest. He wore dark jeans and sandals, and what appeared to be a permanent frown. Sever noticed the dreads seemed to change color when he moved his head. From light brown to dark brown, then coal black. There was no mistaking the electricity that seemed to flow from the man. His eyes were penetrating and he seemed to look *at* everyone and *through* everyone at once. He stood up from a table and the twenty-some reporters and camera people quieted down. Bobby Vane walked to a small podium and cleared his throat.

"We're really pleased to announce that Derrick and the Laments have signed with Mega Records, and they're rushing the release of the first CD to coincide with the middle of our summer tour. Derrick has agreed to answer questions, so I'll turn it over to the Jamaican Music Mon. Derrick . . ."

There was a smattering of applause. The lanky black man moved behind the podium as a reporter asked him, "Do you believe that Roland Jamison killed those three girls?"

Derrick kept his frown in place. "Let me tell you one time. We are here to make music and to spread the word of Jah. Roland was a friend. Once a man is dead, I pass no judgment on his life and what he's done. But I tell you this. The killings must stop. The violence must come to a halt."

The reporter continued. "Violence is a strong part of your message. We've heard the lyrics to some of your songs, and you seem to promote violence."

"When there is purpose, then violence may be useful. Many great causes used force to win. Jah in his infinite wisdom used force throughout the Bible. We are here to concentrate on the music and the message. The people will hear the message in the music. That is all I have to say on this matter."

The Channel Four news reporter spoke up. "You've been compared to Bob Marley. Do you see similarities?"

Derrick broke the frown, letting the corners of his mouth relax. "Yes, many times I've taken offense at that comparison. However, he believed in the Rastafarian faith as I do. We have the same cause . . . to bring the black man back to his roots."

She pressed her advantage. "Marley had a rather traumatic experience in Miami."

"Yah," Derrick reverted to his frown. "He died in Miami. Cedars Lebanon Hospital. Of cancer."

"Wasn't there an assassination attempt?"

"Yah."

"Do you fear an assassination attempt? Based on the violence your music seems to have caused?"

Vane moved to the podium, leaning into the mike. "I've been in this business for a while now," he said, grabbing the neck of the microphone with a death grip. "I don't think I've ever seen a press conference get off on such a negative note. We've got some exciting news here. The boys are starting their first tour, they're about to release their first album, and all you can do is talk about killings and assassinations. Jesus, people, let's get back to what we're all about. Entertainment!" He backed off, but by then Derrick had returned to his seat.

Another reporter shouted out, "You've played one show in the States. How did you find the crowd?" Derrick sat still, making no effort at all to answer the question. An uneasiness filtered through the room as he looked beyond the assembled members of the press. Finally the young singer stood and walked out the door.

Sever watched Randy ease himself out of a chair in the front row and follow him, Marna close behind. The big bald man turned his head for a moment and looked directly at him, his eyes piercing into Sever's. Sever made a mental note not to ever be alone in a room with the big guy again.

Chapter Thirty-two

The speakers onstage pumped out an old Jackson Browne tune, "Running on Empty." Swarms of people crowded the aisles, searching for their seats. Ginny squeezed into the chair next to him, looking a little flushed but radiant, her golden hair flowing around her shoulders. "I've got some news that should interest you," she said. "I ran into James and Sudahd in the hall outside their room and I wished them good luck. They must have been smoking a ton of junk in there because the halls reeked. Anyway, they're both really stoned and James says, 'Wish Mr. Derrick all the luck, missus. He'll need it.' So I asked him why that was. Sudahd tells me they just found out that the official name on the new CD will be *Derrick*."

"*Derrick?* That's it? The name of the CD?"

"*Derrick.* The name of the CD and the name of the artist. No mention of the Laments. I assume they'll get individual credits for their performances but they were not happy, Mick. James seems to be the leader of the opposition. He says the group just about walked out on tonight's show. He told Derrick that if there was no group, just Derrick, then Derrick could just perform by himself."

Sever jotted down the information on his steno pad, Jackson Browne still singing about wearing out. The last he'd heard from Jackson was that he didn't even have a record label. As far as the record companies were concerned, Jackson Browne was washed up. Here was a guy who'd sold millions of records. "Doctor, My Eyes," "Got To Be Somebody's Baby," "Stay," and "Runnin' on Empty," and now he couldn't even get a record deal. Derrick and the Laments, or just plain Derrick, were on the verge of their first record deal and major stardom and they were ready to throw it all away. There was no justice in the world.

"Who made the decision on the CD?"

"They assume it was the label. James was really messed up and really pissed. He said that they're all tired of Derrick's preaching and his holier-than-thou attitude. It sounds like they could all walk away from this at any second."

He'd seen it before. Dozens of times. Artists who'd worked long and hard to get their first big break and busted their ass to perfect the act and make the connections, suddenly afraid that they wouldn't measure up. Or, afraid that they would. They'd freeze, and rather than take the break they'd been praying for, would walk away from it all. Sever had often wondered how they felt the next day, or week, or ten years down the road, when they realized that the break would never come again. Groups quarreled, girlfriends and boyfriends got involved, families interfered, or just the fear of the unknown played on their minds and they would break up and just walk away from it all. The next time he was looking for a story, this was one he'd consider.

"Are they okay for tonight?"

"Sudahd said that Bobby was giving them all a little pep talk before the show."

Sever felt a hand grip his shoulder and he turned to see Jimmy Buffet smiling down on him.

"Hey, amigo. How's it hangin'?" Buffet's warm voice cheered him.

"Jimmy!" he exclaimed.

"Gonna see what this Music Mon is all about tonight, Mick. I heard you're pretty jazzed about him."

"Hell, don't rely on my taste. I'm pretty jazzed about you."

Buffet laughed and moved down the row. The reserved seats for celebrities seemed to be filling up fast. Gloria Estefan and her husband were sitting just four seats down and three members of some current boy band, he couldn't remember which one, were sitting one row up. Two of the Gibb brothers had arrived during Sever's brief conversation with Buffet, and he stood up to let the BeeGees into the row. They exchanged pleasantries, and Sever remained standing, stretching his knee. He closed his eyes for a brief moment, listening to the din of the crowd and the incessant pulse of the music pounding into the large arena. "Who let the dogs out? Who let the dogs out? Who let the dogs out?" Catchy lyrics. He opened his eyes and Frankie Romano was standing beside him.

"Hey, Mick. How's the boy?"

"Frankie."

"I think I'm sitting . . ." he glanced at his ticket, "right next to the lovely Virginia here," he beamed a bright smile to Ginny. She looked up and gave him a cool nod. She was no Frank Romano fan. Hadn't been since the boat incident with the two blondes. Sever had tried to reason with her, that it was the situation, not Romano, but she was always a little standoffish to the short stocky man.

"Ginny," Sever put his hand on her wrist, "let me talk to Frank for a minute."

Frowning, she stood up and moved to the next seat. Romano squeezed in and sat down.

"What's up, Mick?"

Sever turned his head, watching the steady stream of concertgoers pour into the building. He looked back at the stage, where the roadies were fine-tuning the guitars onstage. Randy walked out, supervising the final check. Apparently the band was going to perform. Turning to Romano, Sever looked him straight in the eyes.

"Why did you help bail out Roland?"

Romano was quiet for a moment. Finally he spoke. "Why is that a concern of yours?"

"Because I'm writing a story. It's what I do. I ask questions, questions that might be relevant to the story."

Romano looked at the stage, clasping his hands over his rotund belly. His earring caught the light and sparkled. "I helped out as a friend. For Bobby. He wanted the kid out of jail, and I wanted to help."

"Frankie," he raised his voice over the growing clamor of voices. They'd jacked up the volume of the speakers, and the decibels this close to the stage were giving him a headache. The song was by a Jamaican singer named Shaggy. Something about "Cheating with the girl next door, bangin' on the bathroom floor." "Frankie, you and I walked into that room together. Do you think that Roland killed that girl?"

"Yes!" There was no hesitation.

"So you believe that it's all over and almost all the loose ends have been tied up except . . ."

"Except who killed Roland. Yeah, and being the bulldog that you are, you won't rest until that one is solved." Romano ran his hand over his bald head, lingering for a moment, stalling. Finally he spoke. "He killed three girls, Mick. There's no question about that. This guy was on the scene right before each girl died, and right after each girl died. That wasn't just a coincidence. And somebody decided to put an end to it."

"Wouldn't it have been better to leave him in jail? With your theory, Frank, it sounds like you and Bobby got him out to make sure somebody finished the job."

Romano's eyes shut, then snapped open. "Listen, you little shit bird, even in jest you'd better not accuse me of anything like murder, or complicity of murder. You want to know the truth? I'll tell you the truth. Bobby and I are partners in Derrick. I'm working the promotion end and when we looked at the big picture, it didn't seem like a good PR move to have one of our guys locked up in jail." Sever swore steam was coming out of Romano's ears. "Anything else, Clarence Darrow?"

"Yeah, who decided to change the name from Derrick and the Laments to Derrick?"

"I did." Romano stood up and motioned to Ginny. She moved back to her seat and leaned into Sever.

"What was that all about?"

"I'll tell you later. Did the guys in the hall say anything else?"

"Yeah. They said that Randy was as overbearing as Derrick. They liked Roland. Apparently he was down-to-earth, easy to get along with. They're a little concerned about someone trying to kill other members of the band."

"These guys must have talked for hours. You got all of this in a brief conversation in the hall?"

"I told you. They were stoned, Mick. And then they took off on Marna."

"It doesn't sound as if they like anybody."

"James said that Marna contributes almost nothing, gets a full cut and Randy watches out for her more than anybody else." A tapping over the speakers caught their attention and they turned to the stage. Randy was bouncing his fingers off each microphone then giving a thumbs-up to a sound technician working with an eight-foot mixing board halfway down the center aisle. "Everything they said sounds to me like a case of presuccess jitters. How many times have you seen that before?" she asked.

"There are just some little things I've noticed, but I think Randy's got the hots for the girl."

"Just some glances and a couple of things you've said, but I think you do, too."

A voice blared over the speaker system. "Whassup?" Again, the voice shouted, "Whassup?" The crowd roared back. "Whassup?"

"Hey, this is Rick Riot from WZZP, and along with Coke and Red Stripe Beer, we're glad to be a part of this show. In just a little while we're gonna bring out little Moesha," he referred to the television character played by Brandy, "but right now we're about ready to introduce you to Jamaica's Music Mon! Whassup?"

· The crowd came back one more time. "Whassup?"

"Ladies and gentlemen, let's give a rousing WZZP welcome to Mega recording artist Derrick!"

The enthusiastic revelers screamed and applauded, waves of sound washing up to the stage like high tide. Sever was amused. Only a handful of the thousands of people had ever heard the first note from Derrick, but this crowd was plugged in. The publicity machine was alive and kicking and with just one stateside concert and an unreleased CD, Derrick Lyman was already living the dream. And with just one stateside concert and one unreleased CD, the Jamaican Rastafarian had accomplished what it took Frank Sinatra, Elvis Presley, Cher Bono, and others dozens of years to accomplish. Everybody now knew him by his first name only. Derrick. Derrick had arrived. Now the question was, could he survive?

Chapter Thirty-three

The band sauntered out, slowly and deliberately, as the crowd applauded. Mick recognized the opening as they settled into the rhythm. Derrick was starting with "You." As the lanky singer sauntered onto the stage, a large Ethiopian flag unfolded behind him. Two large video screens, one on either side of the stage, flashed on and a portrait of Emperor Selassie filled them. Derrick swayed with the beat, pacing back and forth, waiting for his moment.

"You, you got de power. Jah, he give it to you. You, no one can take it. You, I tell you true." He shouted, "You," then held the microphone out toward the crowd. They caught on quickly and shouted back, "You." He pointed to them and again they responded, "You."

Moving like a prizefighter, he worked the stage. "You, de second coming, You as Jah has said, You, the chosen people, You the white man dread." He pointed to the crowd, made up of mostly middle-income Caucasians, and they shouted, "You." They had no clue.

The second number was "Moonlight Lady" and Marna joined him onstage, dressed in a colorful flowing skirt, her hair done up high on her head. It was a different look, very native, and Sever thought she'd never looked more beautiful. Ginny nudged him. "She's got class, Mick. I've got to give her that."

The next song was a new ballad from the latest recording session. A haunting, free-flowing story, with no percussion. Derrick moved fluidly across the stage, the tall angular singer appearing to be performing a tribal dance.

Ginny leaned over. "It's got to be the Binghi."

He looked at her, puzzled.

"It's an African dance . . . look, it's so deliberate."

"For what? Crops? Fertility? Rain?"

"Death to black and white oppressors."

Sever studied her face to see if she was kidding. She wasn't.

Rick was playing a free-form jazz-back as Derrick repeated his lyric. "Look to Africa, The crowning of a king. Know that your redemption is near."

Sever looked at Ginny. "Marcus Garvey . . . black freedom fighter from the twenties."

"I'm impressed, Mick. You've been doing your homework."

"No. I saw the notes at the recording studio when they were laying down the tracks."

Derrick continued to weave his message with lyrics from Garvey's writings. The same message he'd used in almost all his songs. Unite, throw off the white man's tyranny, and head back to Ethiopia, heaven on earth.

The set lasted about forty minutes, and even though they'd never heard him before, Derrick controlled the audience from the moment he walked onstage until the end. As he strutted and prowled the parameters of the platform, the crowd screamed its approval, standing up numerous times, many of them raising their fists in a power salute. Sever was impressed. It was one thing for a band to have sway over a crowd on their own turf, but to control this crowd was a major accomplishment.

Several times during the show he glanced at Frankie Romano, watching for his reaction. The little man just smiled. It took a lot to excite him. Something like accusing him of being involved in a murder. That seemed to shake him up a little.

When the set was finished, the group simply walked offstage. There was no farewell, no encore, as the crowd roared its approval. There seemed to be a sense that they were all in on the ground floor of something big, and they shouted and applauded for another four minutes, not wanting to let go. Finally Rick Riot came onstage to a loud chorus of boos.

"Hey, whassup?" They booed louder than before. There was no response except the catcalls and shouting. "Hey, guys, we'll be back in about half an hour with the main show. Brandy will be out shortly!" He jogged off the stage, obviously not looking forward to his next appearance in front of this group.

Sever stood up and moved out to the aisle, Ginny by his side. They walked to the side door and exited into the sticky Florida night. Brandy's tour bus was parked by the building, ready for a fast getaway. Three police cars sat side by side, blue and red lights flashing, throwing strange purple shadows on the side of the large building.

Sever stepped closer to the cars. The door to the first vehicle was open, and he glanced in. Someone seemed to be cuffed in the backseat, arms pulled back and head down. There were always problems at the concerts. Kids high on all kinds of drugs, alcohol, and the phenomenon called concert rage. A person would feel he'd been slighted by someone standing up in front of him, or spilling beer on him, or any number of other perceived injuries and he'd go crazy, beating someone up, throwing chairs, trying to set someone on fire.

Two burly cops stood outside the car, one talking on a hand-held radio. Sever pulled a press pass from his wallet and flashed it to the second policeman. "Any chance you can tell me what happened?" The cop glanced at the pass for the *Florida Sun Coast*. Even though he hadn't written for Romano's paper for probably seven years, Sever kept the pass as a calling card for cases just like this.

Glancing at his partner, then at the prisoner in the rear of the car, he nodded. "Yeah. We've got a suspect on a murder charge. Miami police want to question this guy about a guy who drowned in a pool in some hotel down in Dade."

Sever ducked down and once again observed the large man in the rear. He'd raised his head, and from the backseat, Randy glared at Sever, the fire in his eyes hot and intense.

Chapter Thirty-four

The concept of killing a relative wasn't all that foreign to Sever. He'd dreamed about it, actually considered it, and finally wished he'd done it. The time he'd beaten his father, he thought he could do it. As the man lay on the ground, Sever thought about kicking him in the head until blood poured from his ears. Not just to kill him, but to make him suffer. Suffer at least as much as he and his mother had suffered over the years. But it wasn't in him. He'd accepted the fact that in humiliation, his father was probably suffering enough already. So, he'd walked away. But he understood that someone could be motivated to kill kin.

"You tell me, hotshot." Kohls propped his feet on the gunmetal gray desk and blew imaginary smoke rings toward the fluorescent lights. "What do you think made us dig a little deeper? Should be good for your ego."

Sever watched the man tap an unlit cigarette on the desk. The squad room was strangely quiet at this hour of the night.

"Harry, I don't know why you had him arrested but it means you've still got the case open."

"Well, Sever, I'm going to share some information with you. First of all, the *case* isn't open. We're not looking for the guy who killed the girl. At this time we still feel we know who killed *her*, but," Kohls took a deep drag on the unfiltered cigarette and blew out an imaginary steady stream of smoke, "we picked this guy up because of you."

Sever's eyes widened. He brushed the hair back from his forehead thinking he should probably get a haircut in the next couple of days. "You picked him up because of me?"

"You've been pitchin' a bitch ever since your boat party. You thought we had the wrong guy. You thought that this Derrick or Randy had more reasons than the drowning victim to kill that girl. Then you thought this guy Randy tried to kill you down in the Keys."

"You didn't want to hear it. You kept blowing me off."

"Sever, if we ran down every cockamamie accusation that people gave us, we'd do nothing except . . ." he paused.

"Chase down cockamamie accusations." Sever stood up from his folding chair and walked to the coffee dispenser. He poured himself a Styrofoam cup of the stale black liquid and walked back to the desk. "Let me guess. When I reported the break-in at my hotel room and the fight, you figured I might be on to something."

"Yeah. And don't flatter yourself. This thing has a long way to go before we can prove anything."

"So, can you tell me what actually triggered the arrest?"

"I'm going to tell you. You're not a day-to-day reporter so I assume you'll keep this quiet until you do your weekly or whatever article you're working on. It doesn't really matter because eventually we'll let it out. We found the weapon." He swung his legs down from the desk and eased out of the padded chair. He traced the path to the coffee machine and poured himself a cup. Pouring in a huge spoonful of powdered cream, he stirred it thoughtfully. "We still think that Bald Brother One killed the girl. All the evidence points in that direction. We think Bald Brother Two killed Bald Brother One. Got that?"

"What's the motive?"

"In this case, we don't have one. We may get it, we may not. Doesn't matter, if the evidence holds up."

"And the evidence is?"

"Today we called Broward County and had them get a search warrant for Randy's room."

"On what grounds?"

"We found the Firebird. Your buddy rented it, and if your story holds, it explains the way that car looks. He put it through the ringer!" Kohls walked back to the desk and resumed his position, the worn soles of his shoes on the desk facing Sever.

"Harry, what did you find?"

"Just settle down. We took into account the break-in to your room, and," he gave the sentence a dramatic pause, "we got an eyewitness at the hotel in Miami."

"An eyewitness?"

"Derrick Lyman."

"What? Derrick saw the murder?"

"No. That would be too easy. Doesn't seem to happen like that very often. Derrick saw the perp and the victim at approximately the time of death. He said they were walking together in that courtyard. Took him a while to make the statement, but we decided to take it at face value."

"So you searched the room?"

"We had Broward search the room."

"I can't believe you weren't there."

"Oh, hell, Sever. I was there. You can believe I was there."

"You've stretched it far enough, Harry. What did you find?"

"What did *they* find. Remember, hotshot, I have no jurisdiction up there."

"All right, Harry. What did they find?"

Kohls smiled at him, seeming to enjoy the anticipation.

"We didn't have to look too far. It was in his closet."

"Are we going to play twenty questions all night here? What the hell was in his closet?"

"You know, Sever, you get to write these books and build up the suspense. Then, when someone else does it, you get pissed off. Let me tell the damned story in my own time, okay?"

Sever smiled. The cop was once again going to play a major role in Sever's next book.

"All right. You tell it your way."

"We opened the closet and it was right there, in the corner."

"What was in the corner, the reporter asked?"

"The baseball bat."

"*The* baseball bat?"

"We think it's probably the same one he used to beat that guy with in Jamaica. Seems it's kind of his signature. When he was a club bouncer, he had it with him all the time. It's this wooden bat, with the name of some local team stenciled on the side. It's sitting upright in the corner of his closet."

"And you assumed that this was the murder weapon?"

"Oh, we're more sophisticated than the last time you took us to task, Mr. Sever. We actually use scientific methods and everything." His voice dripped with sarcasm.

"So what did you find?"

"*We* didn't find anything."

"Oh, yeah, this was Broward's find."

"They did an analysis, and even though this bat had been

wiped down, they found traces of blood. Took a while, but we found it."

"So you've got the blood that matches Roland's?"

"Have you ever thought about writing a book? You've got a very good grasp of the obvious. We feel pretty certain that the lab results will show a match."

"But you haven't got enough to hold him for long?"

"Oh, hell, Roland got out on bail after two of you caught him with the knife in his hand. A little thing like forensic evidence probably won't hold him forever. Didn't get O.J. convicted, did it? But if we get the scientific stuff verified, we think we've got a case."

"So what happens now?"

Kohls snapped his unlit cigarette in two, the tobacco spilling onto his desk. He brushed the halves into his hand and tossed them into the wastebasket next to his desk. "Damned smoke-free laws!" He rubbed his hands together and continued. "Broward shipped the evidence to us, and we're going to extradite Bald Brother One to Dade. We'll try to hold him. . . . Vane will try to get him out, Vane will probably prevail, and God only knows what will happen when Derrick and Randy get together again."

Sever stretched his leg slowly. "What's the reason, Harry?"

"I don't have a clue."

"Oh? I remember your scenario several days ago. Randy and Roland scout the girls and hook them up with Derrick. Derrick has a thirty-minute fling with the girl on the boat. They get tired of playing the pimp so one of them goes down and tries to get some of the action. She refuses and he kills her. Maybe it was Randy who killed her, not his brother."

Kohls looked at him through slit eyes. "Great imagination, Sever."

"He asks Roland to clean up his mess, then leaves . . . or, Roland walks in right afterward. He sees the girl, picks up the knife in disbelief and Marna walks in. She screams and he freezes. Romano and I stumble in and, well, that's as far as it goes."

"Could have happened. But nobody saw it that way."

"Harry, I think you've got the killer, and if you don't, you've got the killer's protector."

"For now, Sherlock, we've got Bald Brother Two's killer. That's all. We're on record that Roland Jamison killed the girl. We think Randy Jamison killed Roland. That's all you get." He swung his feet off the desk and stood up. The interview was over.

Chapter Thirty-five

Red symbolized the blood of the martyrs. Yellow was the wealth of the homeland. Green was the beauty of Ethiopia, and black was the color of the Rastafarian's skin. Derrick sat in a wooden deck chair, resplendent in his multicolored shirt, watching a distant light offshore and carefully preserving the smoke from his cigarette. Taking a deep lungful of the Jamaican weed, he held it for a long time, then slowly let the precious herb escape through his lips. " 'He cause grass for the cattle and herb for the service of man.' Psalm One-oh-four, Mr. Sever. Herb is a good thing. I believe that herb be truly Jah's way to make you whole."

Sever sat facing him, watching the serene face of the normally emotional man. It was as if he'd shut down, like a powerful generator that always pumped energy into everything around it and suddenly someone had thrown the switch to off. Tranquil, peaceful, Derrick seemed to be floating. "When do they release the CD?" He wanted to ease into this gradually. He was surprised that the singer had asked to talk with him. He'd assumed he was persona non grata around Derrick ever since the first interview, but Vane had called him. Just an hour ago. He'd been getting ready to go to bed, exhausted after the day's, and night's, activities. He'd left Kohls in Miami and headed back to his motel in Lauderdale. Vane called the second he'd walked into his room. Romano had moved the boat, the yacht, up to Lauderdale and it was in the harbor at the Bajia Mar Hotel. Derrick wanted to talk.

Now the distant lights glittered on the water like pinpoints of stars, and the early morning calls of birds, creaking boats, and the gentle water lapping at the docks echoed across the marina.

"I did not contact you to talk about de CD. I want you to help save a friend."

"Randy?"

"Randy. We are brothers . . . more than his own. We feel the same, have the same mission. When one is hurt, the other is hurt as well. Randy and I would die for each other."

Sever paused. There it was again, the passion for something or someone that was so strong a person would die for it. Derrick would die for Randy.

Romano stepped onto the deck from below, balancing two cups of coffee. He handed one to Sever, then walked to the forward cabin, never saying a word.

"My friend has been arrested for the killing of Roland. Cain and Abel these two. I need him by my side. The journey we embark on will be pointless without him."

Tempted to stay silent and let him talk, Sever couldn't resist the opening. "Other than friendship, what does he offer? You can always get security. What else does he bring to the table?"

Lazy puffs of ganja smoke drifted out over the edge of the deck and Sever could hear the song "Smoke on the Water" in his head. The sweet smell of the cigarette brought back memories. He hadn't had a joint in years.

"It is only important that he brings stability and meaning to the music. You have asked if he writes the songs. Isn't it so?" He was quiet for a minute. "It seems that everyone is concerned about how Mr. Sever sees things. What Mr. Sever say, what Mr. Sever believe, what Mr. Sever write about, the questions Mr. Sever ask."

"I'm a reporter. A journalist. I ask questions, I have thoughts." He felt stiff, unsure of himself. This twenty-something kid had him off-balance. There was an aura, a mystic feel, about the way Derrick talked and held himself. Even in the state of drugged euphoria he seemed to have a blessed presence.

"If you have the power to make people worry about what you say, what you think, what you ask, then I think you have the power to help Randy."

"How do you think I can help? It sounds to me like there's strong evidence that Randy killed his brother. You're the one who reported that they were together right before he died. As you said, Cain and Abel."

"The influence of the pen, the power of the press. You have influence beyond most writers. When we first met, I did not understand your touch. Now I may know more about it than you do."

"So you want me to try to prove his innocence?"

"If you raise the questions, if you show the doubt, it could go away."

Sever looked at him, uncertain. "I can't change the evidence."

"Evidence did not convict O.J. Simpson. It does not have to convict Randy."

"Do you think Randy killed Roland?"

Derrick was silent.

"Do you think Randy killed the girls?"

"What I think is for no one but myself."

"Did you kill the girl on the boat?" He expected a reaction.

He watched for a fit of rage or a total shutdown. There was no reaction. The Jamaican weed must have medicated the man.

"Mr. Sever, I may have called the wrong mon." He kept his eyes on the water and points along the distant shore.

"I think you did. If I believe that Randy didn't kill his brother, then that's what I'll write about. I can't tell stories that I don't believe. If I feel that he was the killer, then I'll probably go with that."

"We are about to embark on an exciting journey. We have only to ask and it shall be given. Whatever we want will be ours. No one can stand in our way. To defy us, to deny us, would destroy the mission. You are with us, Mr. Sever, or against us. There be no middle ground."

Sever stood, looking into the dark sky, the horizon just starting to turn a tinge of orange from the still unseen sun. A hint of blue sky touched the horizon. Not a Jamaican blue, but a southern Florida blue. The humidity and heat were already stifling. It was going to be a scorcher.

Chapter Thirty-six

He *tried to capture the* fraction of a second between consciousness and sleep, an almost magical moment when he could glimpse other worlds. There were images that reminded him of his drug hallucinations, simply wildly colorful patterns with geometric shapes in oranges and purples and always gold . . . lots of gold. And there were times when he saw his mother. She was at the kitchen sink, cutting something, vegetables perhaps, and she would look over her shoulder at him. There was a bruise on her cheek, not a deep purple bruise but a fiery red mark that started just below the eye and covered half her cheek. He knew the bruise, knew its origin, and felt remorse at being powerless to stop it. But he'd lost all respect for his mother . . . a woman who'd been so dependent on her spouse that she let him not only control her in a strong abusive fashion, but had let her husband demoralize and intimidate an impressionable young boy. He'd stood up to the old man and from that point on he'd never needed either of them.

He'd made a better living as a teenager than his father did

as an adult, and at the first opportunity, he left home and never looked back. He needed no one. He trusted no one. Not even Ginny. He wasn't sure he was incapable of trust, but he wasn't sure how to achieve it. Even his ex-wife had suggested professional help, but the perception of weakness was something he refused to show in public. In private, he sought it out. There was probably a wonderful professional explanation why the human mind often seeks out memories that torture the soul, but he couldn't explain it. And maybe, just maybe he was alone in this quest. Maybe he was the only freak of nature who reveled in his own anxiety. He doubted it.

Sometimes that split second before sleep brought wonderful revelations. The moment before sleep, the minute fraction of time between conscious awareness and unconscious awareness, was a magical mystery tour, and he never knew quite what to expect.

This morning, this late or very early hour, 4:00 A.M., he captured the moment. It was Frankie Romano's boat, and he knew immediately the reason for the image. He'd left the yacht and the reggae singer just a short time ago. But the image focused on the night of the murder. He saw Derrick Lyman, on deck, yelling back at the beautiful Marna. Derrick, dressed in loose-fitting slacks with a rope tie in the front and a T-shirt with marijuana leaves on the front, seemed angry. Marna, in a long, flowing white dress and sandals, was pointing a finger in his face. Derrick turned on his heel and walked away as she shouted after him. That was the moment he saw. It was the moment she had explained to him. Derrick did not seek out the public and had to be prodded into mingling with the people. The scene bothered him. He felt uneasy as the Jamaican singer disappeared in a dreamless sleep.

Four hours later he woke with only a vague recollection of

the mystical moment. He splashed water on his face and felt the skin slowly tighten. Turning on the shower, he stripped off his underwear and stood under the pounding hot water, breathing deeply the steam that billowed off the tiled walls. When he was done and towel-dried, he pulled on a pair of faded jeans and a soft, cotton, open-collared shirt. Barefoot, he opened the closet and pulled out his precious bag. He removed the laptop and opened it, turning it on. He pulled up the chair to the desk and for the next hour took notes. He wrote dozens of pages of notes before writing even the smallest of articles. Sever liked to review the facts, the thoughts, the impressions, the feelings, before he ever wrote the first word for publication. This morning he had a lot to remember.

Chapter Thirty-seven

I'm going to Jamaica. Want to come along?"

Ginny looked up from her magazine, pulling down the sunglasses that sat perched on top of her blond hair, the sun reflecting off of the almost perfect golden strands. She absent-mindedly touched the strap of her orange bikini bra to make sure it was secure. Sever caught a whiff of toasted coconut, the oil she used when she was getting sun. He remembered the first time they'd gone to the beach, she was what? Twenty-three? South Beach, Miami. She spread out the blanket, sat down, and took off her top. Those perky little breasts with the dusty rose-colored nipples were out there for all the world to see. She'd looked up at him, standing there with his mouth open, and she'd laughed. "What's wrong, baby? Afraid I'll get noticed?"

"Why?" She brought him back to the present.

He squinted and found himself looking at his miniature picture in the dark lenses of her glasses. "Because this thing just gets weirder and weirder. Because I think there's an answer over there." Two young boys about twelve years old raced by and dove into the shallow end of the large pool, splashing Ginny and Sever.

She lay the magazine down on the plastic table and tugged at the bottom of her two-piece. "Mick, what can you possibly find over there?"

"I don't know. I called the police in Negril and they're willing to talk to me. They'd like to solve the case, too. They don't like murders at tourist establishments."

"So talk to them on the phone."

"Not the same. If I'm going to do the book, I need to see where they died. I need to talk to the staff at the resort, maybe the owner of the bar where Randy and the band worked. You know better than anyone. It's the only way I'm going to get a feel for this."

"I can't go. I've got to work with . . ." she paused, "an author I'm working with." She seemed to fumble for the right words. "I have a job, Mick. *You* create your work. I have to go where they send me."

"Will you be here when I get back? Two, three days tops."

"I don't know. I should have been back already."

"Look, I'd like you to go."

"You want a gopher."

He looked out over the large pool to the tall palms that surrounded the area. "Is that all you think I want from you?"

"Mick, you used me from the moment we met. You mistook that for affection and romance and maybe even love, but it was convenience. That's what mattered most. 'Ginny will be there when I need her.' " She pushed the sunglasses back on her head and settled back into the lounge chair. Picking up the magazine, she continued to read an article, acting as if the conversation had never taken place.

"Okay. Maybe I deserved that, but you hit me with these

zingers every once in a while without any warning. I'd like some time to prepare my defense."

She was silent. Sever ran his hand through her thick blond hair, admiring the golden tan on her long legs and upper torso.

She kept her eyes on the magazine. "Derrick wants to talk to me."

"What the hell does he want with you?"

"I'm guessing he's no different than you. He wants me to be his gopher."

"I'm not following this."

"He didn't feel he got his message through to you, so he wants to get through to me. Then I can convince you to do . . . whatever. I'm tired of it, Mick. I need to get back to sanity. I need to get back to Chicago."

"I have no idea what his message was. He turned Randy in, then wants me to use some influence to get him off. It makes no sense."

"I'm going to talk to him this evening. I'm going to be your gopher again and hopefully bring back a piece of the puzzle, okay?"

"Only if you're comfortable with the situation. And if you're going to meet him, do it in a public place."

"For my reputation, or for my life?"

He said nothing.

"You're not worried about my virtue, are you? As long as I come back with a story."

"Ginny, what would you die for?"

"Come again?"

"What are you passionate enough about that you would die for it?"

"A family . . . if I had one."

"But you don't. What about religion?"

"I'd like to think that, but I'm not that religious."

"Is there anything you would die for?"

The sounds of the children's laughter hung in the air. A reverberating echo of a diving board springing a young girl into the water, and the splashes of bodies breaking the smooth surface of the placid, chlorinated water, were crystal clear. Amid the noise and activity he heard her voice, soft but sincere.

"You. I'd probably give up my life for you."

Chapter Thirty-eight

The flight was commercial, not the private entrance to the island that he and Vane had experienced, with the close-up view of towering palms and lush green hillsides. The plane stayed far above the hills and valleys and picturesque palms that he'd seen only weeks before. Romantic views aside, the ride was comfortable and one of the young female attendants caught his eye several times during the brief flight. When they landed, she asked if he knew the island well. He felt certain she would offer him a guided tour if he desired. He didn't.

A three-seater flew him to a deserted airstrip just outside Negril. A small cement block building and a fuel pump were its only fixtures. He called a taxi from there. An hour later, he and Det. Sgt. Dennis Alison were walking barefoot on warm Jamaican sand, just out of reach of the gentle blue water that lapped the edges of the beach.

"We have our share of problems, but I'm not sure they are worse than yours." The tall detective bent down to pick up an empty beer can that lay in his path. "I know that we are accused of corruption, and that is never good, but in the United States you have the Los Angeles Police, the New York Police, the Key West Police, Miami Police ... there is always corruption. Can you name a police force that doesn't have corruption?"

Sever smiled. "Power corrupts."

"And can you name a police force that isn't understaffed? Mr. Sever, Jamaica has an abundance of pickpockets, purse snatchers, shoplifters, common thieves, and high-scale robbers. We do not have an abundance of police. The tourism business is a double-edged sword for our island. It is our livelihood, but it brings out the worst in us. We are not equipped to handle the problems. It's like someone from the States once told me, 'trying to stuff ten pounds of shit into a five-pound bag.' "

"And what about murder?" Sever dug his toes into the sand, feeling the warmth through his entire body.

"Your specific murder?"

"Murder in general."

"Jamaica has the third-highest murder rate in the world. The third. Are you impressed?"

"I'm not sure impressed is the right word. I'm surprised."

"We have three detectives here in Negril, Mr. Sever. We are stretched very very thin, like a fine wire that could snap at any time. Often we rely on outside help. You have heard of the travel writer from the States? She disappeared from a resort near here?"

Sever nodded. The story had major press back home. A young attractive travel writer had come to Jamaica to write a piece about the resorts in Jamaica and Cuba. She had vanished. Her passport, her clothes, her personal items were all left behind in her room but she was nowhere to be found.

"Your FBI, our government, and other outside sources have all gotten involved. We can't even say it's murder yet, but obviously the indications are that she was abducted and probably killed. And the native girls who you inquire about. We have two victims, but not a perpetrator."

"And no motive?"

The black detective tossed the empty can into a plastic trash container. He stopped and surveyed the beach, white tourists littering the sand with blankets, towels, umbrellas, and all the trappings of a sun-filled vacation.

"None we can prove. Who knows? We have turf wars by rival drug gangs, we have domestic disputes, we have jealousy, and we have these rich tourists who are a very tempting target for people who have nothing. All these things can be reasons for murder."

Sever squinted as the sun climbed higher in the sky, reflecting its blinding rays off the white sand. "You spent a lot of time looking at the security guard, Roland Jamison. Now the Miami Police believe he killed a girl there. Did you miss something?"

Dennis Alison stopped and pointed toward a row of whitewashed buildings. "Up there." He motioned with a sweep of his arm toward a pool. "That's where the one girl was killed."

Dozens of naked and semi-clothed bodies lay thirty feet from the two men. As they approached the pool, a uniformed security guard dressed in a white short-sleeved shirt and shorts walked down to meet them. The gold badge pinned on his breast pocket shone brightly in the sun. Somewhere in the twenty-some steps he took he recognized Alison. "Ah, one of Negril's finest. How are you, Detective?"

"It's Robert, right?" Alison smiled and offered his hand.

"Robert it is. I hope this is a social call. Our manager can only handle so much stress."

Alison laughed, a deep, rolling, down-in-your-chest laugh. Sever felt a genuine affection for the man, a man who took his job very seriously but realized his limitations of effectiveness.

"Robert, I want you to meet Mick Sever. Mr. Sever is a journalist from the United States. I'm tryin' to bring him up to speed
on the young lady who was killed here several months ago."

Robert nodded. "I wasn't workin' the shift. One of my men,
Roland Jamison, was here. He found the body. I'm certain that
the fine detective has told you they took Mr. Jamison into custody. They found no proof that he had committed the crime. I
personally know the man and feel certain that he had nothin' to
do with the murder. However, I will not condone what he did."

While Sever waited for the explanation, a totally nude
woman, about twenty-five years old, walked by him, and continued down to the water's edge. Her figure was perfect. Her nipples
were hard, her tan was even, and her pubic area was shaved clean.
Sever felt his heart rate increase. It took all of his strength, every
fiber in his being, to avoid following her with his gaze. Instead,
he bit the inside of his lip and stared at the young security guard.

"Roland smoked a joint."

Sever closed his eyes, clearing the vision of the gorgeous
blonde with the shaved body. "He smoked a joint? And what does
that have to do with the murder?"

"Mr. . . ." he paused, forgetting the name.

"Sever. Just call me Mick."

"Mr. Sever, I am very sorry. I am the head of security here.
Drugs are available everywhere in Jamaica. Tourists come here
expectin' a drug culture. We don't disappoint them." He glanced
at Alison. "Detective, I am sorry. Bein' a journalist, I'm sure he
wants the truth."

Alison kept his mouth shut, his thick lips sealed tight.

"Roland was not unlike other employees we have. He used
drugs recreationally. However, there is a strict rule that you cannot . . . cannot use drugs while you are on duty. Roland smoked
a joint."

"What about breaks?"

"We would prefer that they don't use them the entire time they are on duty. Once in a while an employee will smoke while he's on break. In this case, a security guard took an unauthorized break and smoked. Mr. Sever, every one of my security guards has done the same thin'. Every one of them! However, only one of them had a murder occur while they were supposed to be on duty. Roland Jamison."

"So he was supposed to be watching the area?"

"He left this area for about five minutes. When he returned, the damage had been done."

"The person who committed the murder . . . how would they know that he would slip away for several minutes?"

Detective Alison watched with cool detachment the nude bodies lying by the pool, as if his eyes saw, but remained unfocused, as he concentrated on the questions at hand. "We thought of that, of course. There seemed to be no distraction. The killer simply was at the right place at the most opportune time."

"Where did Roland get the joint?" Sever noticed the shaved blonde returning from the ocean. She glanced at him and smiled, a sleepy smile with her bedroom eyes lazily looking him over. He shivered.

"He told us he had it with him when he came to work."

"If someone had offered it to him, they might have guessed he'd be distracted."

"He told us he brought it with him."

"It just seems strange. . . ."

The detective chuckled. "Mr. Sever, as small as our staff is and as backward as you may think we are, all these things were considered. However, we have no witnesses, we have no murder weapon, and we have no perp. The case is still open but it's hard to be aggressive in the light of no new evidence."

"Do you know the band?" Sever decided to move on. He didn't want to offend the man. There was a fine line between digging and pushing. A reporter could dig, could ask probing questions, but when he started to push, often the interview was over. And once a source decided to shut down, there was no turning him back on.

"I've seen them perform. I've interviewed them."

"Any thoughts about them?"

"I'm not sure what your question is."

"Did you suspect any one of them? Derrick? Randy? James?"

Alison nodded to Robert. "Robert had some thoughts about that."

Robert looked confused, his brow creased. He looked to Alison for clarification.

"You knew of some relationships the band had with the girl?"

"Ah," he smiled. "Yes. She was a regular here. A fixture, so to speak. You see, Mr. Sever, drugs are prevalent here in Jamaica, but some American tourists also expect some sexual freedom. The women come here with a dream of rolling in the sand with a Jamaican man. The men come here to meet exotic women. It's a fact. The lady in question provided male tourists with an exotic pleasure. In return, she received not only money, but a certain freedom at many of the resorts. Her presence, and the presence of others like her, are important to the atmosphere here."

"She was a prostitute."

"I'm sure the young ladies try not to think of themselves as prostitutes. I'm sure we would rather think of them as social entertainment. But the fact is, they are a necessary part of doing business. She had spent some time with a wealthy American, a day or two perhaps. But he was asleep in his bungalow when the murder occurred."

"What about relationships with the band?"

"Derrick Lyman spent time with her. He was aware of her adventures, but he would often meet her here or at other properties. It's only my observation, but she seemed very attracted to him."

"But there was no reason to suspect that he was involved in her murder?"

Alison dug the toe of his shoe in the sand. "We suspected everyone, but he had an alibi that evening."

"What about Randy Jamison? Roland's brother?"

"That was Derrick's alibi. They were together writing music. Other members of the band said they saw them."

"So Randy Jamison does write some of the music for the band?"

"It was the alibi," Alison said. "I don't know who writes what."

"The lyrics," Sever said, "the hatred toward women. It seems to me that someone who writes down those thoughts may very well be a suspect. I keep coming back to that."

"To be perfectly frank, I'm inclined to agree with you. I don't care much care for what they do."

"So you accepted the alibi and that was the end of it?"

"She was a native of Jamaica. We spent time on the case; however, we had to move on. There are wealthy American tourists who make great demands on our limited resources." He smiled condescendingly at Sever.

Robert looked back at the pool. "Mr. Sever, I'd be happy to give you a tour of our property. I think you would find it very interestin' and I did notice some serious eye contact with one of our guests. Would you be interested?"

Wondering if Robert's job was pimping, matchmaking, or security, Sever declined. He and Detective Alison walked back along the beach until they came to a small dirt path that led to the road. Alison's car was parked where they left it.

"We'll drive from here," Alison said as he started the patrol car. "The other girl was found in the parkin' lot of a club. The Palm Breeze. They make a rum drink called the Palm Breeze that is delicious and powerful. It was our findin' that she had left the club after closin', then was dropped off to pick up her car. Sometime later she was killed."

"And the band that played here was . . ."

"Derrick and the Laments. They have a very big followin' here."

Sever sat back as the car bumped along the pockmarked winding road. Small wooden shacks dotted the landscape, some with open fronts and some type of merchandise displayed on tables. To Sever it looked like cans and assorted junk. In green fields, slope-backed cows tiredly munched grass while white egrets flew onto their backs looking for bugs. Occasionally they would pass a young woman or several children walking along the side of the road. The women were dressed in brightly colored skirts or wraps of purples, reds, oranges, and yellows, the children in loose cotton shirts and shorts. Everyone seemed happy, waving as the squad car went by in a cloud of dust.

"Did Derrick have an affair with this young lady too?"

Alison kept his eyes on the narrow street, sliding around a curve and hugging the inside of the road as a rusted rattle-trap pickup belching gray smoke came sputtering around the corner. The old man driving waved as he went by with inches to spare. "We were never able to prove that. She spent time with the band, and was here almost every night they played. There were rumors that she and Derrick spent the night together once or twice, but no one will witness that."

"Who started the rumors?"

"Again, I don't know. When it comes to friends and relatives, these people keep a very tight lip on their secrets. They will back each other up, lie for each other, and keep secrets for each other. When the police are involved, there is much distrust."

"You know it's not any different in our country. People would rather do anything than talk to the police."

"Sometimes I think we have given them a reason for their fears."

Sever massaged his leg. "Power corrupts."

Small stucco shops appeared more frequently now, and the road narrowed. Signs for soft drinks and Red Stripe Beer were plastered on·the side of one- and two-story buildings.

They rounded another curve, and the detective turned a hard right, pulling into a gravel parking lot. There were no palm trees in sight and as Sever exited the car, he felt the hot, still stickiness of the Jamaican climate. The Palm Breeze had no palms and no breeze.

"Wait until you get inside," said Alison. "It's not much to look at, but mon, you've got to try a Palm Breeze."

Inside, a noisy room–air conditioner rattled and wheezed and the air was slightly more tolerable. Alison ordered two Palm Breezes and the old bartender refused to take any payment. "On de house, mon. Fo you, on de house." He smiled a toothless grin, figuring he'd just purchased some favors down the road.

The drink was smooth and sweet. Rum, coconut, and a fruit juice that was hard to define. He took a long swallow and sat back in a worn wooden booth. "Tell me, Detective, who do you think killed the girls? Do you have any suspicions at all?"

"Certainly. I have drawn my own conclusion, but it would be speculation and if I tell you anythin', it must be strictly off-the-record. It would not be wise for me to be quoted about my personal feelin's." ·

"Off-the-record then. Who did it?"

"Randy Jamison. And it appears he will finally pay for the crime of murder."

"Randy? Why?"

The lanky detective took a drink of his rum, wiped his mouth with the back of his large black hand, and watched the door. Sever had noticed he took the seat facing the entrance. It was the Wild Bill Hickok syndrome. The Old West lawman always sat in a bar facing the door so he could see his enemies when they walked in. One time, and one time only, he'd made the mistake of sitting with his back to the door and had not seen the gunman who entered the bar and shot him. Or so the legend was told. There was also something about the poker cards he had in his hand at the time, aces and eights, the dead man's hand.

"It is only speculation, Mr. Sever. There are several reasons I think he is responsible for the deaths. First of all, I believe he is a man of faith. I believe that he is a true Rastafarian. I also believe he writes much of the music and his strong ideals come through the mouth of Derrick Lyman. That man is a mouthpiece only. So, I believe that Randy Jamison does not approve of the young ladies and their conduct with Derrick."

"So he kills them to protect Derrick's reputation?"

"Possibly. In his own mind, he may think this is justifiable. Possibly he kills them to protect his religion. There are some Rastafarians who believe a woman should have no social contact at all and should show complete deference to males. The women that have died are very social, and very demanding of males."

"But if your theory holds, Derrick is responsible too."

"Ah, but males are dominant. They are allowed transgressions. Women are punished for their transgressions. And don't forget, Mr. Sever, if I'm right, Derrick is the prophet. Much like John the Baptist cried God's message to the wilderness, Randy looks at Derrick as the prophet. Randy Jamison is God. Derrick Lyman is John."

Sever was silent for a moment, somewhat satisfied that some of his ideas were shared by the detective. He sipped the rum drink, working the puzzle in his head. "You said there were several reasons you thought Randy was the killer."

"The primary reason I believe he killed the girls was to protect the message. Assuming he writes the songs . . . you have heard the lyrics. You've felt the power and emotion and the strong feeling about women. These women stand in the way of the message."

"So was he going to go around killing every woman that Derrick slept with? Rock stars sleep with hundreds . . . thousands of women. We could have had a real bloodbath on our hands once this group got famous."

"You ask for my own opinion. It's all I have. If I was sure of the answer, this case would be solved. Finish your drink, it's time I return to work." The interview was over. There was no opening up the door. Dennis Alison remained silent as he drove Sever back to the Barn Bon Hotel. Sever shook his hand, thanked him for his time, and headed up to his room. He wanted to get the notes down on the computer before they left his head. He had a strange feeling that the detective had left out a very important part of the puzzle, almost as if he'd wanted Sever to find it for himself. Protecting the message was only part of it. There also had to be a reason he'd killed his brother. Every time he thought he had an answer, things got more confusing. Alison had more information, but Sever had pushed too hard and the source had shut down. Oh, well, you win some, you lose some.

Chapter Thirty-nine

You're still there." He **cradled** the phone between his shoulder and his ear and flipped on the computer.

"I'm still here, Mick. I'm going back tomorrow."

"Tony?"

"He's a new writer, Mick. It's my job, okay?"

Sever pecked at his keyboard. He'd turned the lights off and the glow from the screen comforted him, like a candle in the dark night.

"I talked to Derrick. Actually, we had dinner."

"Whoa. This is the same guy who hates women and journalists, in that order?"

"He . . . I don't know how to describe him. He is a very engaging young man. I think he's deeper than almost anyone I've ever met in the industry. I was very impressed."

"And everything I'm finding out about him is that he's a phony."

"He's very convincing."

"What did he convince you of?"

"His sincerity. He has strong moral convictions," she paused.

"Oh? He has sexual affairs with these ladies, he spouts messages of death and destruction of women and every Caucasian in the world, and he believes that drugs are a birthright for his religion. And you think he has moral convictions?"

"In his own mind, Mick, and he believes that he and Randy are soul brothers. He says that he was forced to tell the police that Randy and his brother were together that night."

"Forced?"

"He says he saw the two of them talking outside. It was all very simple. When the police interviewed him, for the third or fourth time, he happened to mention it. They got him to talk about some of the sibling rivalries that took place between the Jamison brothers. He says it was all harmless. They decided it was murder."

"And what do you say?" A good journalist learned never to trust a first interview. The interviewee would, without question, say what he or she thought the interviewer wanted. Even Derrick, in his initial interview with Sever, told him what he wanted to hear. That he was a rebel, untamed, defiant. A good journalist learned never to trust the subject. You could go with the story, or you could question it, but in your heart, you knew that the initial interview was only what they thought you wanted to hear. He assumed the police felt the same way, never trust the first interview. Maybe that was why it took three or four interviews to find out that the Jamison brothers were together the night of Roland's murder.

"I don't know what to believe. He wants *you* to believe that Randy is innocent, but he hasn't got another suspect in mind. He doesn't have an alibi for Randy, he just doesn't believe that man would kill his brother."

"But they fought a lot?" He stared at the computer screen, wishing the story would write itself.

"Typical sibling rivalries."

"You didn't have a sibling and neither did I. How would we know typical?"

"Yeah, you're right. Derrick Lyman casts a spell, Mick."

"Anything else?"

"While we were having dinner, Randy's little friend walked into the restaurant."

"Marna?"

"Marna. She pulled Derrick away, seemed very agitated, and had about a five-minute conversation with him. I had the impression she was very upset. Derrick seems to have a remarkable effect on women. I can't exactly put my finger on it, but he seemed to push her buttons."

"If Randy is her boyfriend, it makes sense. The love of your life is up for murder one, you're not going to be jumping for joy."

"I was thinking about what the guys told me before the concert. They think she's dead weight. Now that Randy is in jail, I wonder if she has a future with the band. Seeing the show, I agree. Unless she sews, cooks, and blows the boys in the band, I don't think she contributes a hell of a lot."

Sever rubbed the back of his neck. He was tired, frustrated, and getting nowhere. "I visited the resort and the bar where the two girls were killed. It turns out that Roland Jamison was taking an unauthorized break when the second girl was killed. Smoking a joint behind a building. There are all kinds of pieces to this puzzle, but I'll be damned if I can put any of them together."

"Mick, you know it's possible that Roland killed the girls and Randy killed Roland. As you said before, it still makes a hell of a story, and it appears that the cops are going with that scenario. Why keep fighting this?"

"Because I don't believe it. I think Derrick or Randy killed the girls. Roland was a stooge. And I'm not sure that Vane and Romano aren't involved somewhere."

"Vane and Romano?"

"Why not? They may have more to lose than anyone. Someone is trying to protect the group . . . maybe from itself."

"For God's sake, you *are* a conspiracy freak. You've got absolutely nothing to base that on. Why are you trying so hard to prove something that seems to have no proof?"

"Ginny, what was your biggest criticism of me? When we were dating, when we were married. What did you always say was my biggest fault?"

"Other than your vanity?"

"Hey!"

"You got too involved in your stories."

"*You* said that. And what did you always tell me was my biggest strength?"

"That you got too involved in your stories."

They were both quiet. The air conditioner hummed in the wall and a couple next door raised their voices, laughing or yelling at each other, he couldn't tell which. Maybe it didn't make any difference. Laughing, or yelling. Both showed passion. And what good was a relationship, or a profession, if you didn't show passion?

"I'll be home tomorrow."

"Home?"

"Home is wherever I'm living at the moment. I'd like you to be there when I get back."

"I need to go home, Mick. My real home, but I'll see what I can do."

"Ginny, I'll get to the end of this story. Maybe we could go away, no story, no Tony."

"Yeah. Maybe. 'Night, Mick." He heard the click in his ear. He'd pushed too hard and the source had shut down.

Standing, he walked to the window, the same clear pane that looked out on the same still night that seemed to haunt his every night. There was no home, there was no passion, there was no Ginny. Fuck 'em. He was Mick Sever and he'd really been alone most of his life. The story was the thing. He wanted to tell a good story, and he wasn't moving on until he told it.

Chapter Forty

*P*ower was a strong aphrodisiac. Rock stars had power, and they had women. Sever'd dreamed of it as a young man. He'd written about it, seen it firsthand, and experienced it. Women threw themselves at rock stars. Sometimes they would throw themselves at the roadies, the equipment managers, the managers themselves, just to get to the lead guitarist or the singer. Whatever it took. They wanted a piece of that power. They would do things that they would never do with their boyfriends, lovers, or husbands. In later years they would go into heavy self-denial. They had never done those perverted, disgusting, humiliating acts. But Sever knew that in a corner of their mind they remembered. They remembered, just like the lady who looked up Buzz in the Keys. She'd told Buzz that a night with a rock-and-roll man in Cincinnati, Ohio, had been the highlight of her life.

He figured that the ones who had experienced the aphrodisiac of power could go on with their normal lives. They'd experienced an ultimate thrill, like one time on the biggest roller coaster in the world. Like an astronaut's one shot at a moon landing, or a football player's kickoff return touchdown. They had experienced the ultimate thrill, fifteen minutes of a brush with fame, and they could now go back to normal, mundane lives. But then there were those ladies who kept coming back for more. They couldn't get enough, and the thrill and danger were like a drug. You needed more and more to get high.

He'd been there, seen it, and experienced it. And maybe that was what he was like. A groupie who could never get enough. The stories had to get more detailed, more graphic, more involved and darker, because God knows there was a dark side to the fascinating world of pop celebrity. Writing was like a drug. The more he wrote, the more he needed to write. The smart thing would be to stop right now. The smart thing would be to write the story and take six months off. Maybe have a disgusting affair with a young lady and go someplace he'd never been before. Maybe hook up with Ginny and see if they could rekindle anything at all. Maybe. But the lure of the next story kept calling.

He watched the television, realizing that CNN must be everywhere, even in Jamaica. A news anchor announced that rap star and producer Puffy Combs had just been found innocent on a gun and shooting charge in southern California. Maybe Puffy was innocent, but maybe the money, the power, the glamour, and glory of rock and roll made the rules different for the players. The world of rock and roll was a different world.

Sever lay back on the hotel bed with the stiff foam-rubber pillow, hands clasped behind his head. He started to drift, realizing he was between consciousness and sleep. Ginny floated into view along with Romano and Vane. There was no clear message, just faces and feelings about the relationships he had with them. Everyone was on edge. Maybe Derrick had been right. People worried too much about what Mr. Sever thought, what Mr. Sever wrote, what Mr. Sever did. But if people didn't worry about Mr.

Sever, then possibly Mr. Sever wouldn't be selling millions of books and be in such demand. He had power, and power was a strong aphrodisiac. So why was he sleeping alone?

The magical moment, the mystical second, he tried to capture was before him. Marna, dressed in her brightly flowered dress, was screaming, asking for help. He stood in the doorway not knowing what to do. He saw nothing except the lovely Jamaican girl, in the loose flowing gown, covered with brightly colored red, orange, and yellow tropical flowers. She looked at him, pleadingly, asking him to make this all go away. Could there be a possible relationship there? After what they had shared, possibly there was a chance to work through it and come out as more than friends. He felt something for her, but couldn't quite put his finger on it. The look and the plea disturbed him. She was trying to tell him something. She knew a secret, but couldn't share it. He sat up and took a deep breath, trying to capture sleep before it escaped. It was gone.

He lay still for another three minutes, random thoughts running through his head, then got up, massaged his stiff knee, and flipped on the desk light. He turned on the computer and opened his minibar. Choosing a small airline-sized bottle of Dewar's Scotch, he poured it into a drinking glass and added half a tumbler of water. He slugged it back and poured another. The alcohol worked its way through his body, relaxing him as he studied the screen, anxious to get some of his scrambled thoughts down before they drifted away.

"Entertainers, rock-and-roll musicians, even writers may be true to a standard, true to an art form, but they are compromised at every turn by a public that treats them with," he struggled for the word, then settled for two. *Undeserved adulation.* When you can't find one word, use two.

He'd made the case before, lately in his book about the murder of Job Jobiah. There was far too much importance given to the lifestyles of rock-and-roll musicians. That fact would never change, just as the lifestyles of these musicians, bloated with underachievements and overindulgence, would never change. They would be prisoners to their own success and excess as long as an over-adoring public continued to heap praises upon them. Not a bad life if you've got to be in prison. Joe Walsh, who'd been the leader of the James Gang in the seventies and played guitar with the Eagles in the nineties, had written a song titled "Life's Been Good to Me So Far," mocking the rock-star persona. The story was probably his own, about a rock star who had too much of everything. Sever had to agree. As a journalist, he had to be critical of the phenomenon. As someone who fed off of it, and fed very well, he had to respect it. Maybe writing about it and exposing the underbelly of the glamorized monster was his rationalization. Just like Joe Walsh. Life had been good to him . . . so far.

On the other hand, he envied Buzz. A bar down in the Keys, where the biggest event of the day was cooking up a fisherman's fresh catch. He pictured Buzz and Sarah on the deck, sipping beers and smoking cigars. Deep inside he knew he'd never be happy with that scenario, and that hurt worse than anything. Deep inside he craved the power. He was in some ways no better than the personalities that he took to task. He'd taken full advantage of the lifestyle and the retarded maturation process that it fostered. He wasn't ready to grow up anytime soon.

He considered calling Ginny back, even at this late hour. Apologizing for pushing too hard. He wanted to talk to someone and there was always Ginny. And who the hell was this Tony anyway?

Chapter Forty-one

He'd drifted off in the chair, waking slowly to an agonizing pain in his neck. His chin had been pressed tightly into his chest and the neck muscles strained. He carefully raised his head and looked at the screen. The story had not progressed at all. It refused to write itself, and now at three o'clock in the morning it beckoned him to come to closure. He refused. He would work to that end, but until he was convinced of an ending, he couldn't write it.

Scrolling though his notes, he found the time line, an outline of dates, times, and happenings. Hurrying through the details, he found the evening on Romano's yacht. Romano introduces Vane. Vane introduces the band. The boys in the band start hustling the ladies on the boat, or vice versa. He and Romano catch up on old times, and then they hear the screaming. Obviously Derrick had experienced his moment of ecstasy earlier that evening. How much earlier he wasn't sure. Within an hour, Derrick would have had sexual relations with the girl, then possibly killed her. No one had seen him leave the boat. No one had seen what he was wearing, or anything. He'd just disappeared. The time line didn't seem to help. He read the notes carefully, remembering his flashback several hours ago. He and Romano had walked into the room. Roland Jamison stood over Sabrena, the young mulatto girl, knife in hand. The security guard had looked helplessly lost. He was wearing a white T-shirt and jeans. The T-shirt had a smear of blood across the front. In the corner, huddled and shivering with terror, was Marna. She was genuinely frightened and had to be sedated and taken to the home of one of Romano's friends. If it was all laid out in front of him, why couldn't he put it all together? Randy Jamison was still on the boat, or was he? Sever flipped back through the notes. Vane had introduced only the band members. There was no mention of Randy, Roland, or Marna. They may have been with the crowd, or possibly Randy was down below. He'd have to see if Romano or Vane had seen either of them. He couldn't remember. Closing his eyes, he pictured the introduction. The band members stood directly behind Bobby Vane. No Randy anywhere, and no Roland. He let his memory stroll across the deck, watching Rick and someone's very pretty wife gently stroke each other through their clothes. No Randy, no Roland. And no Derrick. Immediately after the introduction, Derrick had disappeared, too.

He pushed the laptop aside and stretched, yawning and wishing he could go back to sleep. He'd scheduled just one interview today with the owner of the Palm Breeze. He was hoping the man would give him some background. As soon as he got back to the States, he wanted to call Buzz again too. Now that both of the Jamison brothers were accused of murder, Buzz could possibly shed some new light on the situation.

He lay back on the bed and nodded off. He woke up at 6:30, took a hot steamy shower, and went down to the hotel restaurant for an early breakfast. He felt a sense of urgency, as if he needed to resolve his conflicts now. He was alive and focused, with a sense of purpose. A good feeling.

The little bartender with the missing teeth wasn't there. The owner of the club was a young guy, Sever guessed about twenty-eight years old, who looked like he'd once been a bouncer himself. Arms like tree trunks, big chest, big neck and starting to go a little soft in the gut. Probably too many Red Stripes and Palm Breezes. Sever unconsciously sucked in his own stomach as he shook the man's hand. The grip was strong and the greeting warm.

"Just call me Greg, Mr. Sever. I've owned the Palm Breeze for six years. Whatever I can share with you I'll be happy to do so."

"Greg, call me Mick. It seems like everyone here is a little too formal with my name. You know Buzz?"

"Certainly. Buzz worked here for several years. He managed the property." Sever smiled. Calling the place a property seemed a little serious for a run-down bar and restaurant.

"I'm not sure what information I'm looking for," he said. "I want some impressions of some of the players."

"The players?"

"Randy and Roland Jamison, Derrick Lyman, Flame? Did an American kid from Idaho playing in a Rasta group raise any eyebrows?"

"One at a time. Randy was a bouncer here. We do occasionally attract a rough element to the club. There is an even mix of tourists from the surrounding resorts and locals, and we have to be careful that they get along. In many cases, it's the haves and the have-nots."

"It seems like there's a lot of that here."

"Mr., Mick . . . Jamaica is a very poor country. Tourists come here from wealthy homelands and say, 'How bad can this be? You have sun every day, you have fruit that grows on trees, fish that swim in the sea, Red Stripe beer and rum, so how much do you need?' And to some extent they are right. We have a paradise here. However, that same wealthy tourist builds a beautiful home on a cliff, a pristine golf course on farmland, a luxurious resort on one of our fabulous beaches and then is able to reap financial rewards from our country. After a while our people grow weary of having our faces rubbed in the wealth and opulence." Greg stood up from the table where they sat and poured himself a cup of deep brown coffee. "Would you like some? Jamaica's finest."

"Sure," Sever said. "So, you do have fights in here from time to time."

"Tell me a liquor establishment that doesn't. However," he handed a mug of the steaming beverage to Sever and sat down, "it's our own special kind of fights. Sometimes it is a tourist lady who is interested in a Jamaican man and a boyfriend or husband becomes upset. Sometimes it is a tourist who comes across as too pushy, too insistent on being treated properly."

Sever sipped the coffee, wondering if it could just step out of the cup and walk into his mouth. It was that strong. "So it's always the tourist's fault?"

"It's always that perception. And, it is usually the locals who get thrown out because we are told by our city government to treat the tourists with the utmost respect. We want you to come back and take advantage of our hospitality. We want you to come back and bring your friends." Greg peered over the top of his oversized mug, as if measuring Sever's reaction to his baited comment.

"I get the impression you aren't fond of the tourists," Sever said.

"On the contrary, Mick. I depend on them. However, as a Jamaican, it becomes tiresome to see natives in their own land treated like second-class citizens. And that's what we have become."

Sever steered the conversation back to Randy. "So, Randy was a bouncer. Was he here before the band started?"

"It seems to me he was the one who suggested we hire Derrick. He and the Music Mon had been friends from their youth."

"And his brother, Roland?"

"I saw him from time to time. He was working security at a resort on the beach. I understand he was in the club the night the girl was killed in our parking lot, but I wasn't here that evening."

"Is there anything else you can tell me about either of them?"

"Randy Jamison did a good job for us. He was a polite, sincere employee. I don't think he would ever steal from me, or deliberately offend a customer. However, on at least one occasion he almost killed a man with his baseball bat."

"A native?"

"No. Interestingly enough, an American tourist. A young college boy on his spring break. The young man was here with a group of fraternity brothers. They were very drunk. This young boy became increasingly rude to other customers and especially to one young lady."

Sever took another sip of the hot coffee and longed for a cigarette. "Tourist?"

"Native. He forced himself upon her, kept insisting that she go home with him. His friends were belligerent as well. But this boy was all over the girl. She tried to leave and he forced her to stay. Finally Randy tried to escort him out. The six fraternity brothers and the young man turned on Randy and started beating on him. He took the bat and began to swing it, cracking this boy's head open and once the boy was down, he hit him several more times. The college boy was in intensive care for several weeks and left here with some paralysis in his left side. I'm not sure he will ever fully recover full motion of his body."

"And there was never any retaliation?"

"Oh, there were threats from his wealthy family. But we assured them that the boy was in possession of a quantity of drugs and we would not only bring charges of attempted rape and murder, but trafficking as well. I think they decided to take their boy back in his current condition rather than have his reputation ruined even more."

"Wow. Randy got that riled up?"

"It was his job to protect people in the club. In this case, the young lady was in jeopardy."

"Randy has been accused of using the bat in the murder of his brother. They've found blood samples on the bat that they feel will match Roland's."

"He can be provoked. It's strange that he would kill one of his relations, when he almost killed someone to protect his relative."

"The girl?"

"The girl."

"Who was she?"

"His sister. Marna. She was a beautiful young lady."

Chapter Forty-two

"His sister?"

"Their sister!"

"It's an amazing story and turn of events, but does it change the facts?"

"The facts? Or the suppositions?" Sever doodled on a pad of paper, a face with a sad smile, as he sat back in the easy chair, a rum and cola on the table by his side. "Ginny, I really need you there. I'll pay you whatever it takes. Tell them you're picking up a freelance job for a couple more days. I'm coming back but I've changed the itinerary. I'm flying into Key West and meeting Buzz. He's meeting some fishing guide down there to talk business and he's got a couple of hours this afternoon. I'll rent a car and drive up from there. Can you stay? One more day?"

"I'll try, Mick. Let me make a couple of calls." She sounded distracted.

"It's no wonder Randy was so protective of her, and my guess is that she got the gig with the band solely because of her big brother," he said, watching the television with the sound turned off. John Phillips, leader of the Mamas and the Papas, had just died of heart failure. CNN ran a caption under the picture. Phillips, his wife Michelle, and Mama Cass had partied on several occasions with Sever and Ginny. He remembered John Phillips living large. Drugs, alcohol, a perfect example of excesses far beyond most mortals' dreams. "John Phillips died."

"Yeah, I heard about it an hour ago. Should we send flowers?"

"There will be thousands of them. No one would ever know."

"We were on that road. Could have been you."

"It still could be. I think there's a residual effect with all that shit. Anyway, let's talk about Marna."

"I don't see what changes."

Sever took a drink of the syrupy liquid and studied his scratch pad. "I wrote down a couple of ideas. If we're to believe the police, she walked in on her own brother right after he stabbed the girl on the boat. If Randy was the killer, then Roland was taking the rap for him and he and Marna both knew it."

"And if it was somebody else? Remember, you even said it could have been anyone on that yacht."

"But it wasn't *anyone* and you know it. We've got it narrowed down. If Derrick killed the girl, then Roland, Randy, and Marna all were protecting him. This guy would have to have something really big to hold over their heads."

"You're assuming Marna knew that Derrick was the killer. She may not know who the killer is."

"She knows that Randy can be provoked. She watched it happen at the Palm Breeze. The owner of this place says that the kid should have been dead. And this is with six college guys beating on him, he swings the bat and takes the kid down. It didn't sound pretty."

"But you're forgetting something. The beating of the frat kid and the clubbing of Roland were both done with a bat. Stabbing someone with a knife would seem to me to be an entirely different type of attack. It doesn't sound like him. He's more physical. You can attest to that. I mean, he tried to beat the crap out of you."

"I don't know. This information seems like it should have made a difference, and now I'm not sure it did. I'm hoping Buzz will think of something that we're overlooking."

"You and Buzz getting to be good friends, are you?" He heard a smirk in her voice.

"We both have exquisite taste in women."

"Yes, you do. I'll try to be here, Mick. And I'll ask some questions if it's appropriate. And remember what you said about paying me. I was never cheap. Remember? High maintenance and total control? That's the line you always used."

A smile played at the corners of his mouth. He'd accused her of that, and a friend of his had even written a song about her. "'Tall and good lookin' with long hair, legs that don't know where to stop, silky fine skin, she's sure to win, the heart of every guy on the block. Dressed up lookin' so sexy, *high maintenance and total control*, give her a country tune and old barroom and she takes on a different roll. . . . She is just one of the boys, cuttin' up, makin' some noise, and all of the guys who try to give her the eye, she can put 'em down and give 'em all a reason to cry, well she laughs at all the barroom humor, she's got a treasure chest of stories of her own, she is just one of the boys, 'til some boy is takin' her home." It fit Ginny perfectly.

"How much?"

"I'll get back to you, but it won't be cheap. And, Mick, I'm serious."

"I know you are. And so am I."

"I hate to say this," she said, "but I'd probably do it for free if you'd asked. It's just that I know you can afford it. And, I want some credit when the new book is released. Got it?"

"I've got it. See what you can find out and I'll call you when I get to Key West."

"The drive back to Miami should be a little smoother. The last guy who gave you a rough time down there is in jail."

"Ginny, be careful. I have no idea what's triggering these murders but I sure as hell don't want you to be number five."

He heard the click on the other end of the line. The finality of the conversation bothered him. As worldly as she was on the outside, there was still a trusting, innocent girl trying to get out.

Chapter Forty-three

The airport at Key West consists of just a few runways and a low one-story building. Sever stepped off the plane into the heat and humidity and walked over the tarmac to the gate. A sign welcomed him to the Conch Republic. Buzz was waiting, two Coronas in hand.

"Hey, Mick. Have a cold one."

Sever sipped the beer and followed him to the rental car waiting outside. The Chevy convertible had the top down and the breeze in his face cooled him down as they drove across the island. Past the deteriorating houseboats that sat offshore, emptying sewage into the blue bay, past the Holiday Inn and the entrance to A1A that ran up the Keys to Miami, and past Mount Trashmore, in the distance, the huge pile of trash that the navy had dumped up on Stock Island. Buzz headed up to the Bight, where the shrimp boats used to dock until the rent got too stiff. Now, expensive yachts and charter boats shimmered in the southern sun, rolling gently on the oily water. He drove past PT's Late Night Bar and Diner and Pepe's Cuban Restaurant, the oldest restaurant on the island, where Sever and Ginny had spent some quality time. They pulled into a new restaurant called the Conch Republic Seafood Company and Buzz got out and led him up to the sprawling waterside restaurant. Sever remembered the building as an old sail factory. Buffet's studio, a nondescript cement block building, was just ahead on the other side of the restaurant. The last time he'd been there, Jimmy had a bestselling book, *A Pirate Looks at Fifty*, and they'd talked about the publishing business. He remembered the area well.

"I don't mind rehashing the old days, but I've told you just about everything I can remember," Buzz said. "I never met the sister. Didn't even know they had one. I watched Randy beat another guy up, a native, but the thing with his sister I don't remember."

Sever took a swallow of his second Corona and gazed past Buzz at the aquarium that ran across the restaurant. Blue and red fish swam lazily back and forth. He and Buzz had settled into a booth and he felt strangely relaxed and comfortable. Key West always did that to him. "Did Roland come into the bar very often?"

"Nah. I don't think so. You know, I wasn't paying attention. I was into the band, the music, and the girls. Derrick got his share of pussy. I mean they all attracted the white girls. I swear, Mick, we had hit records and I never got that much action. I told you that Sudahd . . . the guy had two, three girls a night. Rumor was he was hung like a horse. And Derrick, he'd get high and drunk every night and never went home alone."

"He got drunk? I thought our choirboy wasn't into alcohol."

"All I can tell you is that he'd drink rum straight from the bottle the whole time he was onstage, then go outside and smoke a ton of shit." Buzz pulled a small Cohiba from his shirt pocket, glanced around the room at the handful of afternoon people, and lit up. "Nobody here to offend." He sounded disappointed.

"What about Randy?"

"Did his job. I don't remember him being a real party animal. Always stayed pretty straight and kept to himself. I could see him being protective of somebody. Guy was very protective of the band."

An airplane came in low over the building, heading into the airport, and the roar of the engines sounded like a hive of angry bees. They were silent for a moment.

Sever drained his beer. "I've got this theory. Randy writes the songs, and they pretty much reflect his beliefs. Then he goes out, picks up this bar band, and turns the lead singer into a spokesperson for his religion."

"Go on," Buzz said.

"Well, Derrick decides it's better than doing makeovers of old sixties tunes, so he buys into it. Gets a little rap going about Rasta and ganja and starts spouting the line. Starts eating Ital food, lays off the booze, and in the meantime . . ."

Buzz jumped in. "In the meantime, Randy is still not exactly happy with his prophet. He finds that the womanizing and whatnot are not exactly the way he wants his spokesperson to act."

Waving at the waitress, Sever held up two fingers and she nodded, heading for the bar to get two more Mexican beers. "So they're getting bigger and bigger and the message is spreading and Randy doesn't want Derrick screwing things up."

"But he can't shoot the piano player."

Sever blinked. "Huh?"

"The old Elton John album. *Don't Shoot Me, I'm Only the Piano Player*. Derrick is just the messenger. Randy's the message. But he's behind the scenes and can't tell anyone. So he has to go out and take care of Derrick's screwups."

"So I'm not crazy? It makes sense?"

"Well," Buzz sucked in a mouthful of smoke and let it slowly escape. He waited until it was drifting in the still air above them. "I don't know if it makes sense, but I suppose it's possible. So Randy kills the girls. But he also pimps for Derrick. Didn't you tell me that he and his brother were out scouting talent in the audience?"

"Yeah, I haven't figured that out yet. Let's say Randy knows Derrick is going to score anyway, so he has a better shot at controlling it afterward if he knows who the girls are."

"It's so—perverted. I know this guy. He's not the kind who goes out and kills girls because they sleep with his friend."

Sever stood up, stretching his stiff leg. He headed to the can, and when he returned, Buzz was standing. "Let's take a walk down by the water." They strolled along the water's edge, watching the pelicans on the edge of the docks waiting for someone to throw them a fish. "You know, I don't think Randy could kill anyone."

"Apparently he's tried."

"Defending someone."

"In this case, maybe defending something. Who else? James? Flame? You said you thought Flame was on the run from something. What? He seems to be keeping his roots a secret. Or maybe it all stems from the band's jealousy. Maybe they're so tired of the Derrick domination that they are trying to set him up."

"Makes no sense. The band without Derrick wouldn't work. They know that."

"I'm not sure they do. Possibly going back to being a bar band with a new lead singer would be preferable to putting up with a prima donna like Derrick."

Sever watched a seagull swoop down between two moored fishing charter boats, and come up with a small fish in his bill. The silver fish wriggled, flipping back and forth, but the bird took a steady course and never seemed to be distracted. "Buzz, do you believe in something so passionately that you would die for it?"

"What the hell does that have to do with anything?"

"I don't know. Marna said that Derrick believes a man is not a man unless he has something so important in his life that he would die for it."

"That's some pretty heavy shit. You think that comes from Randy?"

"If Randy's putting words in Derrick's mouth, it could be."

"I like it. It's macho but sensitive at the same time. Girls would love it."

"Yeah, but *do* you?"

"Believe in something so strongly that I'd die for it? Probably. But I don't know what."

"That's not very definite. She says you have to know it up front. You've already made the decision that you'll die for this."

Buzz thought for a moment. "You know, if somebody attacked Sarah, maybe. Hell, I don't believe in too much, Mick. I don't own anything that's really important to me. Two Stratocasters and a Paul Reed Smith with a sunburst on the front. That's a sweet guitar, man. Dicky Betts gave that to me. Other than that, I guess I'm not a real man."

"I thought about this a lot," Sever said. "Bob Marley, regardless if Randy and Derrick like the comparison, almost died for his faith. There was that assassination attempt, and the guy always knew people were out to get him. But he kept preaching."

Buzz nodded. "But you forget one thing. Marley gave up sacraments to save his life. He believed that you had to wear your dreadlocks, and he believed you had to smoke your ganja. When he got the big C, he cut off the locks and quit toking. Anathema to a man of the Rastafarian faith. Scared to death for his life."

"I didn't know that. You're right, it's a macho thing. You can say you'd die for something but when it comes down to it . . ."

"Man, go back to the Bible. Peter tells Jesus he'll stand up for him, and within eight hours he denies him three times. The man wants to save his life."

They walked along in silence, past a rowdy crowd sitting in an open-air bar. Raucous laughter punctuated the late afternoon. Drunken revelers staggered from the exit, one of them stumbling and landing facedown in the gravel.

"There's a guy who would die for no purpose at all," Mick said.

"Could have been us, man. Should have been. Somethin' kept us alive all those years. Maybe wanting to stay alive, having a strong passion to live, is more important than having something to die for."

"It gets too deep."

"Or wait a minute. How about this. You have to believe in something so strongly, so passionately, that you would *kill* for it. How about that?"

Sever stopped. He glanced back at the fallen drunk, watching the man's friends pick him up and support him between two of them, dragging him into the parking lot. "Say it again."

"What?"

"What you just said. Say it again."

"What if you have to believe in something so passionately that you would *kill* for it?"

"Is that harder? To kill for your belief."

"Seems to me it's more productive. More effective. You can be a martyr but if you stay alive you can still influence whatever it is you believe in. And you can kill people who get in your way. Hey, don't look at me like that. It's not like I've ever killed anyone. I'm just playing your little game."

Sever stared at him. Through him. "Hell, that's what's happening. Whoever it is believes in something so strongly that they would kill for it. Maybe they believe in the band, a relationship . . . so strongly that they would kill to keep it. The question is, would they die for it?"

"If they get caught, you're gonna find out."

Chapter Forty-four

The book had slipped. Number five on the *New York Times* bestseller list this week. Hell, there were only so many people who were going to read about the death of an over-the-hill rock-and-roll singer. He read the list from the paper with little interest, sipping a Dewar's and soda on the deck of the Pier House. The late sun was dangerously close to touching the water and the crowds of tourists were out in force to watch the phenomenon.

He'd visited his good friend Clay at the Last Flight Out store across from Sloppy Joe's bar with its airplane memorabilia and collection of T-shirts. Clay carried the book and told him sales were still strong. He called his accountant's office from a pay phone by the pool. The checks were coming in on a regular basis and his bank balance had never been healthier. He checked his service and found eighty-four messages from just about everyone, including his mother. She lived in a nursing care facility in Elgin, Illinois, and although he hadn't seen her in two years, he sent the check every quarter. Once in a while she'd call to complain that the service wasn't exactly to her liking. Sever figured that at least no one was smacking her around every night. He assumed that she was safe from physical abuse.

His agent wanted to know when he could resume his book tour. The publisher wanted to milk it for everything he could. And he had about twenty offers to write anything he wanted if he would just publish it with this company and that company, and there were another twenty requests for one-on-one interviews, people who wanted to peel away the layers and expose the real Mick Sever. He was afraid they might find nothing.

He hadn't listened to his messages for several weeks and found that most of the concerns that had piled up were taken care of.

Message 5: "Hey, Mick. *Spin* needs you to do a thousand-word piece on the demise of the Seattle rock craze. The pay looks really good. Need an answer by next Monday."

Message 18: "Hey, Mick, *Spin* got a writer from Seattle to do that piece. Never mind."

Message 36: "Mr. Sever, we haven't received payment on your American Express bill for over thirty days. We will be requiring payment immediately. Please call us today."

Message 47: "Mr. Sever, this is Stephanie. I'm Mr. Blair's new secretary. I'm afraid I have to apologize. I'm in charge of taking care of your bills, and being new and all I overlooked two of them. We've made payment on your American Express card and your MasterCard bill. We also called these companies and apologized for any inconvenience. I'm very sorry, Mr. Sever. Thank you."

Sever had read that Napoleon, the little general from France, had a habit of waiting six weeks before he would check his growing pile of mail. He found that 90 percent of all the problems that people had contacted him about had been taken care of by the time he opened the mail. Sever thought the world would be a better place if everyone had a little Napoleon in him.

Message 84: "Mick, I'm staying. For a while anyway. I don't know if it's safe to say anything about Marna being a Jamison, but Derrick asked if he could see me again, so I agreed to meet him for coffee tonight. I thought about mentioning her just to get a reaction. Anyway, they play Orlando tomorrow night and tonight he's free. I'll see what I can learn. Be careful on the drive into Lauderdale, baby. No car chases, okay?"

Twenty minutes of messages and this was the last one. Not a good way to end. He hung up the receiver and immediately picked it up and redialed. The phone in her room rang twelve times before the operator came back, informing him that no one appeared to be in the room. He closed his eyes and massaged his temples, trying to remember the cell phone number. No luck.

Long blasts from boat horns and sirens split the early-evening air, and revelers' shouts floated over the water as the sun slowly sunk in the horizon, appearing to be swallowed by the sea.

Grabbing the receiver once more, Sever punched in his calling card number and tried Bobby Vane's room. No answer. He wanted to warn her off the meeting. It didn't feel right. But she was a big girl and had been in tough positions before. Hell, he'd put her in some tough positions. The rental car company was picking him up in half an hour and within the hour he'd be headed for Lauderdale, so he should be back by eleven or twelve. Not too late. He hoped.

He made one more call. There was one more flight off the island to Miami, and yes they had several available seats. He booked a reservation on the last flight out and caught a cab outside the hotel desk. The airport was only fifteen minutes if the traffic was light and it was.

Checking in, he handed his leather bag to a flight attendant

Chapter Forty-five

No first-class, just a small coach section, and the cramped space made it difficult to stretch his knee. He closed his eyes, but the pain kept him from dozing off. Somewhere in the rear of the aircraft a baby whimpered and the captain wanted to talk forever. Sever didn't care how high they were flying, or what the weather was like a couple of hundred miles to the north. He didn't care how the ocean currents in the Keys affected the air currents or anything else. He cared about Ginny and what might happen tonight with Derrick. The forty-five-minute flight seemed like an eternity.

White billowy clouds like thousands of giant cotton balls blanketed the sky beneath the plane. Sever gazed into the white mass, picturing wispy animals, faces, and buildings. Child's play. He watched a floating moon-face turn into a lazy smile and a dragon with a fat tail. Leaning into the window and looking ahead, he saw a long, flowing, virginal, white dress, sleeveless, the type of summer dress that Marna wore on the boat. The gown seemed to float through the rest of the clouds. Sever watched it for several seconds and was vaguely aware that he was slowly drifting into an unconscious state. Exhaustion was taking its toll, his knee was now numb, and he rested his head on the wall of the plane, gradually giving in to the welcome sleep.

He saw her again. Huddled in the corner of the room, softly sobbing, watching her brother hold the knife. She must have thought he'd killed the girl. How hard it must have been, thinking her brother was a murderer. And she looked so helpless in her flowing white summer dress. He dreamed that a cloud was drifting by, and woke with a start, something playing at the back of his mind, just barely out of reach. His breathing was ragged and his heart was racing, as if he'd taken that leap from the stage and come crashing down into the seats below. Holding his breath for a moment, he willed himself into a more relaxed state. Something was terribly wrong. A sudden jerk, then a sensation of the bottom dropping out of the plane, and he caught his stomach up where his heart should have been. Around him passengers were trying to appear cool and composed while their white knuckles gripped the arms of the seats, leaving lasting impressions in the vinyl. The lone flight attendant picked herself up from the aisle floor just three rows up and staggered to the front of the plane holding onto the backs of seats as she moved.

"Ladies and gentlemen," the captain again, "we're experiencing some slight turbulence at the moment," *No shit*, thought Sever, "and we would appreciate it if you would return to your seats and . . ." the plane took another dip, seemed to level out, then shook like a rattle. An overhead bin popped open and several bags came tumbling out, bouncing off a seat in front of him and rolling down the aisle. Sever wished the captain would quit the damned talking and try to get the plane under control. The baby in the rear was now in full scream mode and the flight attendant was strapped into her private seat at the front of the aircraft, head down and hands clasped between her legs.

"Please fasten your seat belts." There were no more words from the cockpit. The violent jolts seemed to subside and the plane settled into an uneasy trajectory, occasionally buffeted by a strong current.

It was still there, in a corner of his mind. He'd thought it was the jolt of the plane that woke him but now he knew it was something else. Something equally disturbing. He looked out the window again, trying to recapture the thought. Now and then the clouds broke, affording him brief glimpses of white-capped foamy water far below. Small boats appeared as dots on the surface, and deep green shadows of bottom formations colored the turquoise blue sea. Not Jamaican blue, but Florida blue.

It would come to him when he least expected it. That was always the way it worked. The thought would work itself through his intricate computerlike brain and print out the answer at any time, day or night. He closed his eyes again but sleep wouldn't come. The plane landed twenty minutes later without further incident and after massaging the stiffness from his knee he walked to the gate and retrieved his bag. A quick call to the hotel confirmed she hadn't returned to the room, so he rented a convertible, popped the top, and headed for Lauderdale. There was probably nothing to worry about, but he sure didn't want to take any chances.

Chapter Forty-six

Walking into the hotel lobby, Sever fought his way through a mob of conventioneers, men and women in Hawaiian-styled shirts, cutoffs, and name tags hanging around their necks. The colorful, unruly mob had tropical drinks in their hands in plastic cups that spelled out BOCCO in bold blue letters. He angrily pushed two of the boisterous party animals aside and headed toward the elevators. On the third floor he knocked loudly on her door. No answer. He spun on his heel and walked down to his room. There were no messages on the hotel answering service. He checked Vane's room and Derrick's room, too, but no one was home. On a hunch he called Marna but there was no answer there, either.

He checked the restaurant at the hotel, but no one had seen them that evening. As he hurried out to his car, he almost ran into James, walking just as quickly around the corner from the bar.

"Hey, mon. How you been?"

"Have you seen Ginny and Derrick?" Sever asked.

"The Music Mon and your pretty wife? Yah, they be sittin' in the bar up two, three blocks from here. Marna be askin' the same question 'bout half an hour ago."

"Marna?"

"Ya, mon. I told her the same. Bar called Flaggler's Folly. You walk up the street and cannot miss it. Flame and I was there, talkin' to some ladies. They was in the corner talkin'. Better go get your lady from Mr. Derrick. Ya never know what the man may be thinkin'."

"Thanks, James. I owe you one."

"Oh, somethin' else you may want to know. Randy is out on bail. He'll be doin' the show in Tampa tomorrow night."

Sever sprinted to the car and drove the three blocks in under a minute, traffic lights be damned. He drove up the fourth block and thought he'd missed it altogether, then saw the sign jutting from a building still one block up. Garish flashing red neon, like a sign out of the fifties on the side of a brick building. Flaggler's Folly. He pulled into a parking spot two doors down, and jumped from the car.

The room was dark and musty with the foul odor of stale cigars hanging in the air. Why they'd picked this place he had no idea. The atmosphere reminded him of a seedy saloon on Chicago's South Side where his dad used to hang out. He'd taken Mick with him when the boy was about twelve. Sat him down at a pinball machine, gave him four quarters, bought him a Coke, and left him alone for an hour. The rough talk and boisterous laughter, the strong smell of alcohol and tobacco, and the accusing eyes of the surly patrons stuck with him to this day.

He scanned the dark areas and couldn't find them. The bartender remembered the gorgeous blonde and the freaky black guy with braids. But then, you see all kinds in this area. They'd left about twenty minutes ago.

He wished for a cell phone but none materialized. He dropped thirty-five cents into the pay phone on the wall and dialed the hotel once again. There was no answer in any of the rooms. Punching in his calling card number, he called the Miami-Dade police. The bored, monotoned lady on the other end told him that Detective Kohls was not on duty this evening. He could try back tomorrow between the hours of eight and five.

Frustrated, he slammed the phone into its cradle. There was nowhere else to go. He drove back to the hotel, where at least he could establish a base of operation. There was a phone, and sooner or later there would be someone who knew something.

He slammed his fist into the room door, the pain shooting up his arm. He checked for messages and the service was empty. The fully stocked minibar beckoned with miniature bottles of Dewar's, and he poured one into a tumbler filled with water. Throwing down a healthy swallow and throwing himself back on the bed, Sever closed his eyes. Marna wore a flowered dress that night when he and Romano burst into the room. She cowered in the corner of the room in a flowered dress. She was sobbing, moaning, afraid and confused in a flowered dress. Marna wore a white summer dress when she stuck her finger in Derrick Lyman's face on the deck not more than forty-five minutes before. A white summer dress. God, she was beautiful. She changed her clothes. Women changed clothes, changed hairstyles, changed makeup and jewelry . . . at the drop of a hat. In fact, in the twenties and thirties, they probably changed hats. At the drop of a . . . whatever. She changed her clothes.

Why? She didn't need a reason. She spilled something on the white dress. Jerk chicken. That red sauce would permanently stain anything. A glass of wine. Red wine was not something to be drinking when you wore white. So she went below and changed. Walked in on Roland, he slammed the door shut, she was afraid . . . why did she bring a change of clothes on board? She didn't live there. She had a room at the hotel. To bring maybe a pair of jeans and a top would be one thing. Maybe she was going to slum it, but to wear a white dress and bring a flowered dress too . . . what was that all about? Two dresses?

He sat up, gulped down the rest of the Scotch and water, and walked into the bathroom, running the water cold and splashing it on his face. You changed your clothes because of your situation. If you were home, you put on sweats, jeans, something casual. But you didn't change jeans to put on other jeans unless there was something wrong with the first pair. If you spilled a drink, if you got blood on a dress, then you changed dresses. There, he'd thought it. So there was blood on the dress. And she had time to change. And yet, there was Roland with the knife in his hand. And again, why did she have a change of clothes? And where was Randy?

Randy was out on bail. Derrick was out with Ginny. Marna was asking questions about Derrick and Ginny, and he couldn't find any of them. He called her room again but there was no answer. He left a message telling her to stay put when she got in, and he went back to the lobby. The party was in full swing and a forty-something peroxide blonde with a size-forty chest grabbed him as he passed through. She hugged him and whispered in his ear some slurred words about joining the party. He shoved her aside and walked out the door.

He drove in the opposite direction, heading toward the Bajia Mar and the *Christy Lee*. Romano's boat was the beginning, where he'd first entered the story. Romano's boat was where another of his stories had ended several years ago. The irony intrigued him. He moved through the late-evening traffic with ease, passing slower-moving vehicles and running yellow lights with regularity. It took him fifteen minutes to get there, and after he'd parked, another five to get to the boat. There were no expectations, just a gut feeling that the *Christy Lee* had a prominent place in the Derrick Lyman story.

Derrick was with Ginny, Marna was looking for them both, and Randy was out on bail. If he was right, the players were all onstage. Flame, or Jimmy Washington from Idaho . . . Romano, the benefactor, and Vane, Sudahd, James, and Rick didn't seem to be true players. He had to go with his gut feeling. Now he had to find their locations. He stepped on deck, the halogen lights on the dock burning through a light mist so he could see everything. The front deck was vacant, with lounge chairs and small drink tables scattered around. He gave the bar a cursory glance and his eye caught the ashtray and cigar, still burning. He walked over and blew gently on the tip, a fine line of smoke drifting up to the sky. A full drink glass sat next to the ashtray and he sniffed the clear liquid. Vodka with a twist. Quietly he stepped into the main cabin. No sign of anyone. He expected Frank Romano to come out at any moment and slap him on the back, offer him a drink, and tell him about some new venture. The last venture if he remembered correctly was a romantic encounter with a young girl. He'd mentioned it on boat at the party, just before they'd been interrupted.

He walked softly, aware of the soft, shuffling sound of his deck shoes stepping on the teakwood and then on the carpeting in the main room. Someone was on board or had just stepped off and the prudent thing to do would be to shout out his arrival. However, he didn't feel like alerting someone at this exact moment. He stepped into the head, and what was this *head* stuff anyway? It was a damned bathroom and that was all. No one was there. The second head was below, along with the two bedrooms. Sever walked into the galley and again there was no sign of anyone. Quietly he opened the door to the stairs and descended. The

sound of waves slapping the bow echoed in the narrow passage-
way and he felt the boat gently rock. He grasped the handrail for
support and stepped onto the tiny landing. There was a chance
he might walk in on someone in an embarrassing situation, but
he turned the handle of the first room anyway. Easing the door
open, he slipped inside. This was the same room, the one where
the bloody corpse had been sprawled on the bed. This was the
room that he and Romano had burst into, where Roland Jamison
had stood with a knife in his hand, and where Marna had collapsed into Romano's arms. This was it.

There was no one there. The room smelled as if someone
had recently sprayed it with disinfectant. The antiseptic odor
burned his nostrils. He stepped out and shut the door. He pushed
the door of the second room and for a moment it seemed to be
jammed. Pushing his shoulder into the wood, he forced it open.
The curtains had been pulled shut and the room was pitch black.
Sever stepped back, remembering the last time he'd walked into
a dark room. He fumbled for a light switch on the wall and
flipped it on, as a warm glow bathed the small room. Frank Romano lay crumpled on the bedspread, blood seeping from the
side of his head where a dark purple bruise had formed. He
looked for all the world like he'd dreamed his last dream.

Chapter Forty-seven

His father had curled up in a ball on the floor, trying to protect his body. One punch to the jaw and he'd gone down, crumpling in front of his son like cheap lawn furniture. Sever wanted more, and as the man lay there, he kicked him in the head, then in the ribs. And then he'd just walked away. There was nothing else to do. The abusive father, the abusing spouse huddled in a fetal position until his stunned wife helped him up, poured him into the family station wagon, and drove him to the hospital. Later, she told Sever that he'd just whimpered the entire trip, never saying a word. Sever had kicked all the bravado out of him, and all he had left was the coward inside.

He shuddered to see Romano lying there, then noticed the ever-so-slight movement of his chest as he took in shallow breaths.

"Frankie. Can you hear me?"

Romano grunted, his eyes fluttering. He tried to take a deeper breath and it caught in the back of his throat. He choked and began coughing, finally bringing it under control. His eyes were open wide now and he looked at Sever as if looking at a stranger. "Mick? What the fuck?"

"Frankie, what happened?"

He grunted and tried to sit up. Sever grabbed his arms and pulled him upright as the older man propped himself up with a pillow. "I'm an old fool, Mick. Shit, I'm too damned old to play this game." He gently touched the bruise on his head and brought his hand away, observing the blood. "Randy's out on bail."

"Randy did this?"

"Yeah. Trying to protect his little sister." He moved his head, turning it slowly and gently touching the bruise again. "Must have banged my head on the deck after he hit me. I should know better, partner! You'd think after all these years I'd know better."

"So, Marna was the *young lady* that . . . Jesus. Marna?" He tried to comprehend it. Romano had had an affair with Marna. He didn't know whether to be proud of the old man or jealous.

"Yeah. Hey, I knew exactly why it happened. She wanted something for the band. I could help. That old trade-off, but hell, I'm gettin' too old for this shit, man. Can you get me something to drink?"

Sever climbed the stairs and brought back the glass of vodka. He handed the drink to Romano, who sipped at it sparingly.

"Seems he has a couple of things to clear up before he gets the hell out of town, and I was one of them."

"You're alive."

"Oh, I don't think he wanted to kill me. Didn't have a bat or anything. Said something about me fucking around with his sister, asked me to tell him where she was, then he popped me a couple of times. Next thing I know you're here and I'm down below."

"And Marna?"

"That's the sad part. Shit, we haven't been together since I invested in the group. That was all she wanted. . . ."

"You got what you wanted too. A roll in the hay with a twenty-year-old. You just had to pay a bigger price than you thought you would." He noticed Romano wince every time he moved his head. "Why don't we get you to a hospital?"

"Nah, I'm tough. I'll be all right."

"So where is Randy now?"

"I don't have a clue. I don't think he's gonna stick around to stand trial for the death of his brother. I got the distinct impression he was moving on."

"So he did it? He killed Roland?"

"I think so. I think he felt he had to."

"I'm lost, Frank. If he's the killer, why did he have to kill his brother?"

"I haven't put it all together yet, but my guess is Roland was going to turn him in. There was no way Roland was going to take the rap for those three girls, and he knew his brother was the killer. Randy had to get rid of him. It's the only thing that makes any sense."

"So Derrick is innocent in all of this? Just a pawn?"

"Oh, I think he knows. He may have been a party to the whole thing. It just seems to me that somebody's going to have to find this boy and get him back behind bars before he kills again."

The creaking of the deck silenced them both. Sever strained to hear more. Soft footsteps directly overhead, then off to the right. Someone was in the main cabin. Everything was still for a moment, then the soft padding sound moved off to the bar area and again all was still.

Romano pointed to a dresser. "There's a gun, top drawer." Sever opened the top drawer and sifted through the man's boxer shorts and socks. The pistol was buried in the back corner, small and black, a Walther PPK. The same gun that James Bond used, and the same manufacturer who made guns for the Nazis in World War Two.

"The clip is in it. Just pull the damned trigger," Romano whispered.

Sever grasped the rough steel handle, getting used to the weight in his hand. He'd never owned a gun, fired only a few, but was surprised at the feel of the weapon. Surprisingly, it felt comfortable, like it was a part of him. There was a certain degree of confidence with this gun. He slipped his finger through the trigger guard and held it in front of him as he eased toward the door. It was then he heard the footsteps on the stairs. He froze and stood to the side. The steps were cautious, someone slowly moving down the stairway. Sever flattened himself against the wall of the room and held his breath. The footsteps found the landing and a shiver went through his spine. He heard the door handle to the room across the way turn. Again, an eerie silence. He had no idea what had happened to the person. Twenty seconds, thirty seconds turned into an eternity.

Sever glanced at Romano. He'd closed his eyes and again looked as if he'd expired where he lay. He heard a shuffling sound as if the intruder were rummaging through clothes. Finally the footsteps came closer and he knew the next step was through the door. He held the gun at eye level, grasped it with both hands, and as the body moved through the doorway, he screamed, "Freeze!" It just seemed like the right thing to say.

The tall, rail-thin body froze. Derrick Lyman's profile filled the frame and he didn't move a muscle.

Chapter Forty-eight

Sever *wasn't sure how anyone* kept his cool under these circumstances, and he wasn't sure how James Bond could confidently say, "Bond, James Bond." The fear of who it could be, what he would do, and what he himself might do with the gun in his hand was frightening. He was trembling as he stepped in front of the singer and pointed the pistol at a spot between his eyes.

"Where the hell is Ginny? And what are you doing here?" He had a litany of questions, but those two seemed pertinent.

"Mon, put down the weapon. I mean no harm. Please, mon, put down the gun. I don't wish to die this way." He folded. The bravado and the macho attitude faded away and the skeleton remained.

Sever lowered the gun, slowly bringing it down, finally letting it hang by his side. Derrick stayed glued to the spot, obviously not trusting Sever. "Where's Gin?"

"I dropped her off in the lobby of the hotel. I don't know where she goes after that."

Sever considered the possibility. "What did you talk about?"

"The same thing I tell you. Randy is not a murderer. I beg her to communicate with you. Let him be." For the first time he noticed Romano, now sitting up on the bed. Derrick's eyes narrowed into slits. "Ah, Mr. Romano, the kindly patron saint of all musicians. It appears that the two of you have been in battle." His grim expression surprised Sever.

"Randy beat him up. Frankie and I both think you're wrong about him. He's certifiable. The best scenario seems to be that Roland was going to tell the authorities about Randy. Randy had to kill his brother to protect himself."

"I'm tellin' you, he's not the murderer. Randy is many things. He be a writer, a mon of infinite wisdom, someone who has a vision, someone who knows the true meaning of life. But he is not a killer." He finally seemed to relax, and as he stepped into the room, Sever once again raised the pistol.

"Just sit down." He motioned to the wicker chair by the dresser.

"Go easy, mon. I don't think you understand the entire story."

Sever watched him warily. "Okay. You tell me the entire story because I'm certainly not figuring it out for myself."

"You might ask Mr. Romano about part of the story. He's not tellin' you everything he knows."

Sever looked over at Romano. Frank glowered at the Music Mon. "I don't think you want everyone to know the whole story. What I will say is this. I think that Roland was protecting Randy, and when he finally decided to watch out for his own ass, Randy had to kill him."

"Mr. Romano, you know the truth when it comes to my music. Randy Jamison put words in my mouth. Strong words. Words with passion. I became a new mon, someone who believed in the words I spoke. Now they are my words. I speak for Randy Jamison now, not him for me. The mon is innocent. He beat Mr. Romano for very personal reasons. They should be quite evident."

Sever shook his head. "I found out that Marna is Randy's sister. Blood is thicker than water and all that horseshit. He was looking out for her, and her little dalliance with Frank Romano pissed him off."

"Yah. It pissed off other people as well. So Mr. Romano took a couple of blows. It could have been much worse." He turned on his heel and headed back up the stairs. Sever walked into the landing and shouted up after him. "Do you have any idea where Marna is right now?"

"I believe she is with your wife, Mr. Sever. She was lookin' for her the last time we talked."

"Marna and Ginny?"

"Yah!"

"Hey, I've got a couple more questions for you." Without thinking he raised the gun. Derrick turned and glared back at him. His attitude was back.

"I came to look for Marna. She is not here, and I am leaving. If you want to shoot me for that, do it now."

Sever sheepishly lowered the pistol and watched the man leave. It was impossible to tell who to believe.

He turned to Romano. "What the hell is going on?"

"This gets pretty deep, Mick."

"Frankie, you and I have always been straight with each other or at least I think we have. If anyone understands a reporter's perspective, you do. Derrick says you're holding back information. Why not tell me? What the hell do you know that I don't?"

"Several things." Romano again touched the side of his head. The purple bruise was swelling and his head had a cartoonish appearance, one side larger than the other. "You heard Derrick. Randy writes the songs. He's known Derrick for years—hell, they grew up together, and when Derrick started the band, Randy started writing songs. The guy can't sing, can't play an instrument . . . can't dance . . ."

"I know the feeling." Sever dropped into the chair in front of the bed and set the gun on the dresser. "That's why I write."

"Anyway, so does Randy."

"So I'm right. Randy is the writer, Derrick is the spokesperson."

"Randy is the Rastafarian. Without the dreads. He has a scalp disease and can't even grow hair. Can you imagine? A Rastafarian without dreads? Anyway, he's had an amazing influence on Derrick. I think that Derrick idolizes him. But the charisma that Derrick Lyman shows, the persona he projects onstage, are overwhelming. That's what makes them a fabulous team. If this could ever work, it would be a phenomenon even by all the show-business standards."

"Frankie, I don't think it's going to work. We've got a killer as part of the team, remember? Sooner or later that's going to come out." He gave Romano an exasperated look. "Let's start addressing the real world here. What happens when Randy ends up on death row?"

"I haven't gotten that far, Mick. However, I would imagine that Jamison can write from jail. It doesn't change things."

"Jesus, you're totally self-involved. All you care about is whether the band plays on."

"Is that any different than the way you are? All you care about is if the story comes out the way you want it to. You're not happy if there's a *happy* ending, so you're going to promote the most negative ending possible."

"What else do you know that I don't?"

Romano pushed down on the bed with his arms and forced himself into an upright position. He swung his legs out and lifted himself from the bed, delicately trying to balance himself. He fell back once, and Sever moved forward to give him a hand.

"I can take care of myself." He stood up, wobbled slightly, and headed for the head. About two minutes later he returned. "You know that Marna is the sister." He fell back on the bed, exhausted.

"I found out today. That never entered the equation."

"But now it does. Her relationships with the band were kept a secret. I didn't know it, Vane didn't know it, and the only member of the band that knew it was Derrick. He'd grown up with Randy and Roland, and he knew Marna better than anyone."

Sever nodded. "All right, so Marna is the sister and she has a fling with you to get your support for the band. Is that all there is to this?"

"No."

"Then what else is there?"

"You find Marna. Tonight. Let her tell you."

Sever frowned, watching Romano's head sink back into the pillows. "You need to see somebody, Frankie. Could be a concussion."

"Leave me alone, Mick. I've gotten along fine without you as my nursemaid for all these years, and I'll get along fine now." He closed his eyes and seemed to drift into sleep.

Sever placed the gun back in the drawer and climbed the steps to the deck. Derrick was nowhere to be seen.

Chapter Forty-nine

Sever walked slowly to his car. His second car. He'd never had two rental cars at the same time. One at the hotel and one he'd rented at the Miami airport. Better sell a story to pay for all these expenses.

Marna was screwing Romano the night of the murder. Chances are she had a change of clothes on board because she was staying overnight, so it all made sense. Randy was finishing unfinished business, and Sever was afraid *he* might be part of that business. He wished he'd kept the gun. Something about it just felt right. Glancing over his shoulder, he picked up the pace. Marna and Ginny were somewhere together in this dark night and a murderer was on the loose. Scared the hell out of him.

He drove back to the hotel and called a local twenty-four-hour emergency medical group from the hotel lobby. He had them dispatch a team to Romano's boat, charging it to his American Express card. He cared a lot for the little guy.

The red light was blinking on his phone when he entered the room. He wanted a drink, but the incessant flashing got the better of him and he picked up the phone. Punching in the required code, he waited for the sequence to kick in.

"Thank you for calling *room message*. You have . . . four unplayed messages. To hear these messages . . . press two."

He pushed two.

"Playing message . . . one."

"Hey, Mick, you there? It's Bobby. We got Randy out on bail. They haven't been able to make that DNA thing stick yet, so they had to let him out. Been a nightmare, Mick, a real fuckin' bad dream, but we got him out and it's on with the show. Give me a call when you get in, man."

"End of message. Press two to play your next message."

He pushed two.

"Playing message . . . two."

"Sever, you and I need to talk. We've had our little moments. Now it's time to sit down one-on-one. I'll call back later tonight."

"End of message. Press two to play your next message."

He pushed two.

"Playing message . . . three."

"Hi, Mick. Long time no see. Had an enlightning conversation with Derrick. I got your message about staying here, but Marna wants to talk to me now. Says it's very important, so I'm meeting her in the lobby. I should be back in a while. Hey, buddy boy, I'm on your payroll now, so if the players want to talk to me, I'd better be available. This is gonna' cost you."

"End of message. Press two to play your next message."

He pressed two.

"Playing message . . . four."

"Mick Sever. Dennis Alison here. I have some information for you that you may find interestin'. Call me. You have my cell phone number so any time is fine."

Sever looked at the phone, debating whether to call Vane's

room or the detective first. He pulled out his calling card and punched in the numbers. Three rings later Dennis Alison answered the phone, sounding somewhat drowsy. Sever apologized for the late-night call.

"Ah, I told you to call. Some new things have come to light since last we spoke. I thought you may be able to use this information. Do you know that Marna is Randy and Roland Jamison's sister?"

"I'm ahead of you on that one. I've been trying to run a number of scenarios with that information, and I'm not sure it really matters. It's probably the reason she's with the band."

"Maybe. But there could be another reason."

"It's not the talent. She doesn't do more than play tambourine. And, the other band members don't seem to be too happy that she shares in the money."

"Mick, we've done a little more background checkin' on the band members. And, on Marna. Two years ago Marna was married."

Sever was silent.

"We missed it before. And even if we'd caught it, it wouldn't have made much difference. Now, it still may not make a difference, but we're lookin' at it much more seriously. I called the Miami police with this information and I will share it with you. Marna is married to Robert D. Lyman. Want to guess what the D stands for?"

"Jesus!"

"No. That starts with a J. D stands for Derrick. They are Mr. and Mrs. When they come back home, we have some more questions for the happily married couple."

Chapter Fifty

Bobby, you've been holding out on me. And, I would guess you've been holding out on the police as well."

"Mick, what the hell are you talkin' about?" The paunchy man rubbed the sleep from his eyes and tugged his pajama bottoms up, trying to cover the expanse of his broad gut. He pulled the white hotel robe around his sizable middle and sat down on the bed.

"First of all, you didn't tell me about Marna being Randy and Roland's sister, and second of . . ."

"Now wait a minute. It's not my job to fill you in on all the relationships that happen in this little band of troubadours."

"What about the relationship our little Marna has with Robert Lyman?"

His eyes widened, obviously surprised that Sever had uncovered the secret. "Robert? Well, that gets a little messy. It's kind of an on-again, off-again thing, but we decided to keep it a secret. Derrick has an effect on women, almost like he's able to hypnotize them into doing just about anything, and we don't want to mess that up right now. Maybe after the band has had a year or two of exposure, then we announce that he's married, but right now . . ."

"Right now Derrick is screwing someone in every city he visits. Right now, Frank Romano is nursing a bruised face and bruised ego because he slept with Marna and her brother beat the shit out of him. Do you think it's possible that relationships might have been a factor in all of this?"

"What the hell happened to Frank?"

"I think you should have kept Randy in jail. He visited Romano tonight and smacked him around a little. I sent some paramedics out to check up on him."

"And this is because . . ."

"Because Randy found out that Romano was having an affair with Marna."

"And why should that bother Randy?"

Sever pushed back the sleeves of his shirt and straddled the desk chair. "You tell me."

"Honest to God, Mick, I don't have a clue. Hell, Romano is money in the bank for these guys. Why would Randy beat up Frankie?"

"For one, the guy was messing around with his sister. Do you have a sister?"

"No."

"Neither do I, but I'm guessing that if you're a protective brother, you'd be a little pissed off. Number two, the guy was messing around with the wife of his business partner and best friend, and . . ."

"Romano didn't know she was married. He really didn't know."

"Doesn't really matter. If the brother is upset, then he's upset. Number three, it goes against everything he believes in. I'm not going to pretend to understand the Rastafarian faith because, like every other religion, it seems to suit whatever purpose you want it to, but in Randy Jamison's mind, women are to be pretty much servants to men, especially their spouses. Women are to be chaste, pure, and not out tempting the men."

"Which is why you think Randy is behind all the murders? Because all these women are out tempting Derrick and the rest of the band?" A challenge surfaced in the tone of his voice.

"That's obviously been one of my scenarios."

"Then why is Randy out picking up the girls for Derrick? There's the question! He picks 'em up so he can kill 'em later? Come on, Mick. Makes no sense at all."

Sever stood up. "Are you familiar with the murder of the girl at the resort?"

"Sure. They pulled Roland in for questioning on that one. Guy was pretty shook up. He took an unauthorized break and somebody stabbed the girl while he was gone."

"The cops think that Roland was behind the murders because he was physically present at every murder scene. There was someone else who was present at every murder scene, too."

"And who the hell was that?"

"Whoever offered Roland the joint on the beach that afternoon."

"He claimed he took it with him."

"Somebody knew he'd take that break. Somebody set him up. Could have been the guy selling drugs. That makes sense. But I don't think it was. I don't think Roland Jamison could buy a joint from the drug salesman in front of all those tourists. I think he got the joint from someone a lot closer to the situation."

"Who?"

"Somebody who knew him almost as well as he knew himself."

"Randy?"

"Marna."

"Shit! Just because she screwed Romano doesn't make her a player. You think she killed the girl?"

"I think she set up her brother. And I think he tried to protect her, to take the fall for her."

"And if she's the killer, why?"

"Why do you think?"

"Here we go again with the twenty questions. I don't have a fuckin' clue. Maybe because . . . oh! Because she's married to Derrick?"

"I think she's trying to save her marriage. Being with the band, trying to stop his affairs . . ."

"Then why did she sleep with the old man?"

"Maybe that was her little indiscretion. Maybe having an affair with Romano was a way to pay her husband back. I don't know. It just seems like when Derrick is interested in a girl, she dies. And if I'm right about Marna setting up her brother, then we've got our killer."

Vane stared at the wall and said nothing for a good minute. "Heavy stuff. Why did Randy kill his brother?"

"I don't know. Maybe he didn't. But if he did, maybe it was to protect his sister."

"All this protecting stuff. She was protecting her marriage, Randy was protecting his sister, Roland was protecting his sister, Randy is protecting Derrick."

"Okay. Just to lay it out there, let's say that Roland knew his sister was the killer. He got set up by her at the resort. She gave him the ganja so he'd take a break. Maybe she even offered to watch things for him. He comes back and the girl is dead and even though he's not the brightest bulb in the pack, he figures Marna is the killer but he doesn't want to admit it. Then, he walks into the bedroom on the boat and sees her changing clothes and the dead girl lying on the bed."

"Changing clothes?"

"Yeah. That's another thing that hit me. She was wearing a different dress in that bedroom than she'd worn on deck. I figured she got a lot of blood on the white one and had to change."

"Wow."

"So now he's got her dead to rights. She breaks down and starts crying and we break into the room. He's like a deer in headlights, doesn't know what to do. He can't turn his sister in, because, after all, she is his sister. So he goes to jail. They probably give him the third degree and tell him that things don't look good for him. Veiled threats and who knows what else. He gets out and talks to his brother. He tells Randy that he loves his little sister and all that, but he's not going to die for her. Randy weighs his two options. One, he's got his brother, Roland, who looks like the perfect fall guy. Two, he's got his sister, Marna, who is married to the prophet. Let his brother take the fall, or let his sister take it. On one hand, his brother is pretty much worthless. He can be replaced. However, the bride of Derrick Lyman is not so easily written off. She plays an important role in this little enterprise. She's married to the lead singer, she carries a certain amount of credibility, and she helps keep things in perspective."

Vane stood up and poured himself a glass of Scotch from the bottle on the desk. He swirled the liquid in his mouth, swallowed it, then laughed out loud. "You should have gone to work for Disney. You've made some good money reporting on rock and roll, but shit, fiction is your forte, Mick. I can't believe what I'm hearing."

Sever nodded. "I'm still working on it, Bobby, but trust me, I'm damned close to the truth."

The phone rang and Vane set the glass down and picked up

the receiver. "Vane here. Yeah, hold on." He handed the receiver to Sever. "Somebody tryin' to get you. The desk put 'em through to my room."

"Hello."

"Mr. Sever? This is Saint Luke's Medical Service. We made the call to the yacht. Our paramedics took Mr. Romano to Broward General and they want to keep him overnight. Seems he may have a severe concussion and the doctors want to keep an eye on him. It's a good thing you called. I have the billing information here and it seems you paid for this with your American Express so we're just informing you."

"Thanks for calling. He's going to be all right?"

"You'll have to check with the hospital. However, they've indicated that he's resting comfortably. They just want to observe him for twenty-four hours."

Sever thanked the lady again and hung up the phone. He looked up at Vane, sitting back in the easy chair, smirking. "Bobby, you believe what the hell you want to, but I think we've got two problems running wild out there. The Jamison brother and sister."

"You're telling me that Marna is the killer? Let's call her right now. Let's get her in here and we'll confront her."

"Do you know where she is?"

"In her room?"

"Call her."

Vane dialed the extension. There was no answer.

"So you tell me, Mick, where do you think she is?"

"I don't know. But I think I know who she's with."

"Who's that?"

"Someone who's had two dinner dates with her husband."

"Well, if we're following your story line, whoever that is will be found stabbed to death tomorrow morning."

"That's what I'm afraid of."

"So, who is it?"

"Ginny."

"Mick, if that's true . . . shit, I'll do whatever I can, man, but we'd better get busy!"

Chapter Fifty-one

The desk clerk had somebody from maintenance open Ginny's room first, then Marna's. Both rooms were empty.

"So where the hell do we start looking?"

"Bobby, they're probably having a drink in some bar. Shit, deep down inside I really don't think anything is going to happen."

"Well, about three minutes ago I was laughin' at your idea, but the more I think about it, the more I worry."

"There's only one place that I can think of. The boat."

"Frank's in the hospital, so there's no one on board, right?"

"It'll be my second trip out there tonight. You want to come along?"

"Yeah."

Chapter Fifty-two

Lights from the harbor bounced off the polished teak deck, sending shimmering silver streaks over the midnight black water. Voices and music from a party down the way drifted lazily on the warm night air as Sever and Vane quietly stepped on board.

"Christ, Mick. It's two in the fuckin' morning. Place here doesn't seem to sleep."

Sever took a hesitant step, his scuffed white Top Siders whispering on the deck. He held his hand up, bringing Vane up short.

"Somebody's in the galley," he whispered.

"Oh, shit." Vane was whispering too. "I should have stayed back at the hotel."

Shadows played on the glass that surrounded the stateroom. The sound from the galley was rhythmic, a soft thud, then a muted clang. Thud, clang. Thud, clang. Sever put his finger to his mouth, motioned to Vane to stand still, and quietly walked to the stairs.

He took a step, hesitated, took another, and quietly descended to the landing. Romano's door was open and he walked in, flipped on the light, and opened the dresser drawer, pushing the underwear aside. The pistol felt cool in his hand. He turned off the light and climbed the stairs with more confidence, keeping the gun low at his side. Vane was frozen to the spot, a frown on his face and his lips pursed together tightly.

"I never thought you were gonna' fuckin' get up here," he whispered.

The yacht moved beneath them, a soft and subtle roll. Sever walked toward the galley, feeling like Wyatt Earp. He nudged the galley door with his toe, pushing it gently open. Swinging his gun arm up, he pressed against the door and spoke, more of a croak than a firm statement. "I've got a gun."

There was no noise. None. The thudding and clanking had stopped.

The harbor lights cast an eerie pall over the wooden floor, the small cooking stove, and the refrigerator and sink. A cabinet door hung open and as the boat slowly rolled, it swung shut, clanking against a pan. It thudded open, then clanged shut, again and again.

Sever stepped out from the doorway and motioned for Vane to follow him. Together they moved slowly to the stateroom. There was no sign of anyone.

"They're not here."

"You were downstairs. Nobody there?"

"No. Oh, shit, the other room. The door was closed. I think it was open when I left the first time."

"You've got the gun, Mick. You lead the fuckin' way."

Sever studied the black pistol. It seemed that when men were stressed out, the swearing increased. Either out of fear or bravado.

Together they walked down the stairs. The door on the right

was closed. Sever turned the handle. It froze in his hand.

"Damned thing is locked from the inside." He spoke in a hushed voice.

"Shit, someone's in there. Now what the hell do you do?"

"Not necessarily. Someone could have pushed the lock, then walked out."

"Then there's someone or something in there we're not supposed to see."

"Bobby, I'm going to kick the door handle. These doors are lightweight, hollow. Shouldn't be any problem."

"You're out of your fucking mind." A coarse whisper. "We call the cops. Right now."

"And if Ginny's in there, the time it takes the police to get here could be life or death." He studied the door handle. The light from outside filtered down the stairs as he stepped back and kicked hard with his good leg. The door held.

"Shit!"

"James Bond! What the fuck are you . . ."

Sever lashed out again and this time the door popped open like a cork exploding from a bottle of champagne. The inky blackness seemed to swirl out and envelop them. He reached inside to find a light switch, flipped it up and there was nothing.

"Bobby, find a flashlight." There was no sound. He spun around. Vane had disappeared. Sever stepped back onto the landing, moving to the side of the opening. He hesitated, ready to bolt up the steps, then saw Vane at the top, flashlight in hand.

"There was one in the bar." He reached down and handed it to Sever.

"Are you coming down?"

"You tell me what's in there, and maybe I'll come down."

Sever swung around and shone the light into the room, swinging it back and forth. The second time he saw the body crumpled on the floor at the foot of the bed. "Shit!"

"What? What is it? There's somebody there, isn't there? Come on, Mick. Who is it?"

He stepped into the room and flashed the light on the face of Randy Jamison.

Chapter Fifty-three

Now can I call the cops?" Vane held the flashlight while Sever checked for signs of life. The body was still warm but there was no breath. No heartbeat. No pulse. Wet blood had spurted from the two stab wounds in the left side of his chest, streaking the tile floor, but now the heart was still. "I'm sorry, man. I really thought—hoped you were wrong about this. Looks like you got it figured out."

"Where the hell are they?"

"They could be anywhere."

Sever heard the sound, steps on the main deck. Rubber soles, softly making their way across the floor. Motioning to Vane with a finger to his lips, he moved to the doorway. He stuck his head out, looking up the stairs. Thin, pale light from the moon filtered down the stairs but there was no sign of anyone. He eased out of the room, climbing the steps, quietly putting one foot in front of the next. Almost to the top, the next-to-last step, his knee buckled. The sharp pain paralyzed him. He hadn't felt it coming, but the leg collapsed and he desperately grabbed the railing.

One hand, two hands and the pistol dropped from his grasp, clattering to the bottom of the stairs.

"Mr. Sever. Why am I not surprised to see you here?" The voice was all too familiar. She reached down to grab his arm, helping him up the last step to the deck. "You seem to be everywhere." She smiled.

"Where's Ginny?"

"Your lovely ex-wife? The former Mrs. Sever? We had a lovely talk this evening. She is truly remarkable. You were perhaps foolish to part company. I would think that a woman like that, one who has her passion for life and for you, would be an asset to a man in your position."

He sat on a lounge chair, rubbing the aching joint. "Where is she?"

"I left her at the hotel."

"Dead or alive?"

His stern tone apparently took her aback. She was silent for a moment, staring out at the harbor lights. Her dark hair glistened and the slight breeze rustled her simple dress, caressing the curves of her hips and breasts. He'd never met a more beautiful killer. A small bag hung from her shoulder, as if she was getting ready to go out on the town.

"She was very much alive. Is there something you wish to tell me? By the tone of your voice, I sense you are accusing me of something."

"Your brother is down below."

"Randy? And where is Frank?"

"Randy is dead. You're telling me you know nothing about that?"

She spun around and glared at him. "Mr. Sever!" Her body seemed to quiver. "What kind of game are you playing?"

"It's no game. You know that."

The tears seemed to spring from her eyes. She grasped his shoulder and sat down. "Tell me true! My brother?"

"Marna, he's dead. He's been stabbed."

"No!" She cried softly, the sobs wracking her small body. Sever sat quietly, questioning his own convictions.

"He's out of control." She looked up at Sever, her eyes red and watery. "That's all he ever wanted, Mr. Sever. Control. Now, it's gone too far!"

"Derrick?"

"Derrick. He killed Roland. And now, because Randy would not kill Frank Romano, he's killed Randy too."

"You're saying Derrick has been responsible for the murders of your brothers?

"Roland lacked strength. Always. He was about to tell the authorities about the other killings."

"And the three girls?"

"Responsible. Yes."

"And you had nothing at all to do with the killings."

"He controls people. He's very very good at it."

"And what about you? Does he control you?" He pressed on.

She reached into her brown leather bag and pulled out a tissue. While dabbing her face, she seemed to regain her composure. "He has. He's a strong man. His passion for his beliefs is overwhelming. I believe he has controlled me."

"But you haven't been involved in any of the killings?"

She seemed to measure him with her look. The height, breadth, width. Finally, in a small childish voice she spoke. "Yes. I have. Derrick believed that . . . that women are weak. He believed that the women who succumbed to him should be punished. I punished them for him."

She stood, suddenly defiant, and reached into her bag, pulling out a knife with a wicked-looking six-inch blade. "I am convinced that he has taken his beliefs too far, Mr. Sever. But I also believe that *you* have pushed us all too far. I hold *you* responsible for the deaths of my brothers." She lunged at him as he ducked.

Sever struggled to stand and tried to move, but the knee wouldn't hold. He collapsed on the chair and she stood above him, her arm cocked, her fist wrapped around the bone handle of the knife.

"I asked you before, do you care for anything so much that you would die for it? Do you? Do you?" She was yelling. "That must be the last thing you think of. I killed for Derrick, Mr. Sever, and I would die for him. What is it, Mr. Sever, that you are dying for right now? For destroying everything we have worked for?" She lunged again.

Sever saw the arm swing down and he leaned to the right, the blade slicing through the sleeve's thin cloth of his knit shirt. He felt the sting of the cut and felt the warm, sticky blood as it flowed from his wound. He saw her raise the blade again, prepared for a second attack, and heard the sharp retort of the gun.

She froze in position with a hard, icy look, then dropped the knife and slowly crumpled on the deck in front of him, the focus in her gaze going blank.

"Holy shit! Holy shit!" Bobby Vane stood at the head of the stairs, the Walther by his side.

"Christ, Bobby, is that all you can say?"

"Holy shit. What have we got ourselves into?"

"You saved my life!"

"Holy shit."

"It's not over."

"What the hell is left?"

"First of all, I want to check and see if Ginny is back at the hotel."

"And second?"

"Derrick wants Frank Romano dead. Probably for screwing his wife. He killed Randy so I would guess Romano is next."

"And what does that have to do with us?"

"I think we need to get to the hospital. As soon as possible." Sever leaned forward and looked into Marna's wide-open eyes. He glanced back at Vane. "She's dead, Bobby."

"Holy shit. I just killed somebody, Mick. I just killed somebody." Vane's face seemed pale in the harbor light as he grasped his stomach and heaved its contents onto the deck.

Chapter Fifty-four

The cops are on their way, but I'm liable to be in for a lot of trouble. Desk sergeant threatened me. Said I'd better be there when they arrived." Vane clutched the cell phone in his hand as Sever raced through the early-morning traffic.

"Those two on the boat aren't going anywhere. But Derrick and Romano, that could be a different story."

"You heard me. I told 'em, Mick. They were a whole lot more concerned about the dead bodies than the possibility of another murder. Bird in the hand and all that shit."

Sever whipped around a slow-moving truck and drove through a yellow light. He flexed his right arm, feeling the restrictions of the binding. They'd taken one of Romano's shirts, torn it into strips, and wrapped his arm to stop the bleeding. It seemed to be only a surface cut, but Sever knew it should be treated. After they took care of the rest of their business. They still had another four to five minutes to reach Broward General. "They'll send someone. They have to. You tell them somebody is about to be murdered, and . . ."

"They didn't sound like they believed any of it."

"Hang on, Bobby!" He spun around a corner, the Chrysler barely tracking as they hit the straightaway.

"And just what the hell are we going to do when we get there? Derrick has probably got an ironclad alibi. You said it yourself, Mick. You think that Marna killed those girls."

"You heard her. He killed Randy and Roland and he wants Romano dead too."

"He's not stupid enough to do it in a public place like a hospital."

"Bobby," he jammed his foot on the brake as the light turned red. There was a slight twinge in the knee, but he seemed to have control of his leg once again. "Derrick is a control freak. He thinks he walks on water and I don't think anything scares him." They were quiet for a minute. "Any other time I'd drive like this I'd pick up two or three cop cars. Now that I need them, I can't get any attention!"

He spun the wheel and turned into the parking lot of Broward General Hospital. Sever asked at the desk for Frank Romano.

"You certainly can't see the man at three A.M. Visiting hours are . . ."

Sever shook his finger an inch from the night receptionist's puffy face. "Ma'am, I don't care what the visiting hours are. Someone may be trying to kill Mr. Romano, and unless you've got a couple of police officers down there already, I'm going to his room right now."

She pushed back her chair, gave him the room number, and picked up the phone. "I am not stupid enough to stop you myself, but security will be visiting you momentarily," she said.

They took the elevator to the third floor, brushing by two white-uniformed nurses who stepped out to stop them. Sever felt certain they'd been warned. Room 386 was just around a corner, out of sight from the main station. He glanced into 384, almost pitch black, but he could make out a uniformed cleaning attendant bent over a mop, swiping it back and forth on the cold tile floor. In the next room the door was open and Romano lay on his back, apparently sleeping, his chest gently rising and falling. Sever let out a sigh of relief.

"Well, he looks okay to me," Vane said softly. "So maybe this thing isn't going to happen."

Conversation in the hall interrupted him as two more members of the cleaning crew walked by. Sever glanced at the man and woman, in maroon shirts, black slacks, and photo IDs. The voices were soft but animated, gentle laughter and what sounded like good-natured kidding. They were silent for a moment, then the footsteps and voices faded as they continued down the corridor.

"Let's go back to the boat, Mick. We're both gonna' be in trouble for leaving the scene. You know that. Shit, what have we got ourselves into?"

Sever stepped into the hall. Someone was pounding down the hall. A uniformed security guard halted, staring at Sever, then walked up to him.

"You'll have to leave. Now."

Sever turned to the room. Vane was nowhere in sight.

The guard grabbed him by the arm and started maneuvering him down the hallway. As they rounded the corner, Sever pulled away. "There's a guy cleaning room three-eighty-four. He's cleaning it, and the light is so dim you can't even see inside. . . ." It sounded ridiculous. A third-rate movie plot.

"What? You can't wander around this hospital at this hour of night like you own the place. Either you leave on your own or we call the cops."

"Then call the cops. That's what I've been waiting for."

The guard pushed him toward the elevator.

"Somebody is going to try and kill the man in three-eighty-six. I think it may be the cleaning guy back there."

The guard pushed the button on the elevator. "Let's get you downstairs, then we'll worry about our cleaning crew. They've got a reason to be here. Believe me, sir, there is no reason at all for you to be here." The door opened and two police officers walked out. The guard backed up, taken aback by the sudden appearance of the men in blue.

"Room three-eighty-six," the bigger of the two men spoke. "Quick."

The guard glanced at Sever, then at the officers. Grabbing Sever by the arm, he did a reverse and started back down the hall. "This way."

The gunshot startled them all. It reverberated down the corridors and Sever saw an orderly hit the floor. For a second he thought the young man had been shot, then realized he was just taking cover. The two officers drew their guns and plastered themselves against the walls. It was difficult to tell where the sound had come from as it bounced around the floor. Sever had a good idea.

They slowly moved along the wall, following it to where it turned. The bigger man eased his head around the corner and followed it with his gun. He motioned to his partner and they turned the corner. The guard seemed hesitant but followed them. Sever knew it wasn't safe, and was somewhat surprised the cops didn't stop them. He stayed close. The police officers had positioned themselves outside the door of 386. There was no sign of any of the cleaning crew and no evidence that Bobby Vane was anywhere around. The nighttime quiet was replaced by an even quieter deathly silence.

The officers nodded to each other, then the smaller one spoke. "We're the police. Kick your weapon out the door, and come out with your hands on top of your head."

A pistol slid into the hallway, and Bobby Vane walked out of the room, his ample stomach preceding him, accented by his arms reaching straight up.

The cop on the right grabbed him, spun him around, pulled his arms down, and cuffed him. They pushed him against the wall and with one hand frisked him. His partner picked up the pistol with a pen through the trigger guard. "You got a license for this?"

Vane looked at Sever. "What the hell have we got ourselves into?"

They turned on the light in the room and saw Derrick, sitting against the wall, holding his left hand over his right bleeding shoulder. His tightly stretched maroon shirt was stained an even deeper red from the bullet wound. Frank Romano lay on his back, eyes closed, his chest gently rising and falling.

"I don't know what the hell they gave him, but we all ought to take a dose of that before we go to bed tonight," Sever said.

Chapter Fifty-five

"The cleaning guy," *Harry Kohls* glanced at a notepad in front of him, "Pasquel Sanchez, he's going to be all right. Maybe a slight concussion. Seems Derrick popped him in the employees' parking lot and got the uniform. The other two from the crew went down to the desk to report this strange guy in three hundred and eighty-four, but by then it was too late."

The early-morning traffic in front of the News Café was busy. Sports cars, luxury sedans, tourists, and locals all mixing in a South Beach jambalaya. Sever watched a curvy blonde walking a large poodle. The dog was bigger than she was. "So is Derrick talking?"

"Rhymes and stuff that don't seem to make any sense. He thinks he's the second coming. He's crazy. Guy is the second coming—of Charles Manson. He wanted the Jamison clan to do everything for him. He had Marna mesmerized and Randy was willing to do just about anything to have Derrick spread his message. Roland . . . Bald Brother Two? Just a dumb pawn. We'll put it together eventually, but he's not going to make it easy. I'll tell you what, Sever. If this self-proclaimed messiah had ever had a real chance to become a superstar, we would have been in a lot more trouble than we are now. He had people wrapped around his finger. God knows what kind of influence he would have been able to exhort once he started selling millions of albums to impressionable teenyboppers."

"What about Flame? Jimmy Washington? He seemed to be very defensive when I brought up his Idaho roots."

"We couldn't find anything. Might have been a girl . . . bad crowd . . ."

Sever took a stab at a slice of bacon, chewed it thoughtfully, then looked Kohls in the eye. "Vane isn't in any real trouble, is he?"

"Nah. I mean, everything he did was in self-defense. You and Romano both owe your lives to the fat guy."

"Yeah. Don't remind him."

"The girl stabbed the three women. Whether she did it because Derrick asked her to, or because she was jealous of them, I don't know. But it all fits." He sipped his black coffee.

"And poor Roland Jamison."

"Yeah. Always in the wrong place at the wrong time. And he didn't want to believe his sister was a killer. You were probably right about her giving him the ganja at the resort. And if she didn't dump her clothes overboard, we'll probably find that dress with the blood all over it on Romano's boat."

"You think Derrick killed Roland?"

"Pretty sure. He set up the meeting by the pool. Then he tried to implicate Randy. This guy is devious as hell. And I think he got Randy all riled up about you. Got him to try to kill you!"

"How often is someone killed for material gain? A robbery, insurance . . . ?"

"Crimes of passion tend to be the norm. Oh, I think there

was a ploy for material wealth. I think that Derrick saw his future clouded with the shadow of Randy Jamison always in the way. He didn't want anyone taking credit for his message and success. And, I think he probably wanted his wife to prove her devotion to him, but I think you're probably right. He believed, with a fervor, that he was the chosen one. And nobody had better get in his way."

"What are you passionate about, Harry? What would you die for?"

Kohls sat pensively, puffing on his cigarette and sipping at his coffee. "Not to sound noble or anything, but I put my life on the fucking line every day. I'm passionate about getting people like Derrick off the street."

"Yeah. I hadn't thought about that."

"What about you, Sever? What would you die for?"

"Nothing. I've still got a lot of life to live. I've got to find some passion somewhere and I'm not sure that's an easy thing to do."

Chapter Fifty-six

How's Chicago?"

"Fine."

"How's the new author?"

"I've got him shaped up. It's the writing, Mick. The writing."

"Yeah."

"So, you're staying in Miami for a while?"

"Clean up some details. Talk to Romano, Vane, Kohls."

"Frankie is all right?"

"Yep. Slept through everything. And Vane still can't believe he shot two people. He's gone from being shocked to bragging about it."

"He's going to have to find a new group."

"Oh, he will. He's got a knack."

"Have you started the book?"

Sever stared at the blank computer screen. "I was just going to start. Had an idea for this one. Rather than write it like the last one, I thought I might do it in the third person."

"Like a novel?"

"Yeah. Maybe. I could write a couple of chapters and see how it flows. A mystery novel that is all fact. What do think?"

"E-mail me the first two chapters and we'll take a look."

"So you want to be a part of it?"

"You couldn't drive me away. You know that."

"Thanks, Ginny. I love you."

"I know." She hung up on the other end.

Sever looked again at the gray screen. He closed his eyes for a moment, picturing the sandy beach in Jamaica and the sexy nude sunbather who had walked down to the shore. He could see in his mind the beginning of the story. He started typing.

"The boatman had come and gone, peddling his drugs to the adventurous tourists in the midday sun. He'd paddled his mud brown canoe up to the sugar-sand beach. . . ."